W9-BSB-520

NO LONGER THE PROPERTY OF
BALDWIN PUBLIC LIBRARY

THE DEVIL IN MONTMARTRE

THE DEVIL IN MONTMARTRE

A MYSTERY IN FIN-DE-SIÈCLE PARIS

GARY INBINDER

PEGASUS CRIME
NEW YORK LONDON

BALDWIN PUBLIC LIBRARY

THE DEVIL IN MONTMARTRE

Pegasus Books LLC
80 Broad Street, 5th Floor
New York, NY 10004

Copyright © 2014 by GARY INBINDER

First Pegasus Books cloth edition December 2014

Interior design by Maria Fernandez

All rights reserved. No part of this book may be reproduced in whole or in part without written permission from the publisher, except by reviewers who may quote brief excerpts in connection with a review in a newspaper, magazine, or electronic publication; nor may any part of this book be reproduced, stored in a retrieval system, or transmitted in any form or by any means electronic, mechanical, photocopying, recording, or other, without written permission from the publisher.

ISBN: 978-1-60598-647-0

10 9 8 7 6 5 4 3 2 1

Printed in the United States of America
Distributed by W. W. Norton & Company, Inc.

In memory of my parents, Eli and Loretta

THE DEVIL IN MONTMARTRE

1

A chattering crowd bustled along the sidewalk on the Boulevard de Clichy; cabs and carriages rumbled up the damp street in a long procession at the foot of Montmartre hill. A steady, chilling, autumn rain had engulfed Paris for most of the day. Now in the evening hours the downpour had turned to drizzle pattering in the gutters and pooling on the pavement.

Pedestrians approaching their destination shook out the droplets and closed their umbrellas. They swarmed toward a beacon of modernity, a man-made radiance beaming from dozens of Edison's electric bulbs glimmering like fireflies in the misty Paris night.

With its electrically illuminated rotating blades, The Red Mill advertised its presence in the Jardin de Paris. Brainchild of a pair of savvy entrepreneurs, Joseph Oller and his manager, Charles Zidler, the sensational new music hall had opened just in time to haul in thousands of well-heeled tourists flocking to Paris during the waning days of the great Universal Exposition. Among them were two elegant women riding in a closed cab. The driver pulled up to the front entrance. An attendant holding an umbrella opened the door and helped the women out of the carriage. The first was tall, fair-skinned and handsome. In her late thirties, she was fashionably dressed in an emerald green Doucet dress. She stepped down to the sidewalk and turned to assist her friend, a gaunt woman of the same age, an inch shorter than her companion and similarly attired in burgundy silk.

As the women entered the dance hall, the reverberating jabber of patrons and the shuffling of their shoes on wooden floors was drowned out by an orchestra playing a quadrille at breakneck speed. Occasionally, a high-stepping dancer would show all of her legs and more, crying, "Hoop-la," to be followed by shouts and applause from an appreciative audience. The Moulin Rouge had quickly gained a reputation—it was a place to ogle the provocative dancers, get roaring drunk, and pick up girls. No one raised an eyebrow at the presence of two women without gentlemen escorts. Such things were frowned upon elsewhere, but after all, this was Montmartre, where the catchphrase was *à chacun son goût*. Most everything was tolerated, as long as you paid up at the end of an evening.

The two women flowed with the crowd through a gallery, its walls lined with posters, paintings, and photographs evocative of modern Paris, including Monsieur Eiffel's controversial tower, then paused on a raised walkway near the long bar, its mirrors reflecting dozens of bottles and sparkling glasses. They found a little corner where they could observe the scene while avoiding collision with bustling waiters bearing refreshment to the multitude of thirsty patrons standing and seated round the mezzanine, main floor, and balcony.

Marcia Brownlow, the frail woman dressed in burgundy silk, took everything in with cool detachment and the keen eye of an artist. She was a noted painter, the founder of a school of West Coast American Impressionists, who had exhibited and won a Silver Medal at the Universal Exposition. Her sparkling green eyes darted round behind a mask of powder and rouge framed by auburn hair swept up in a pompadour. The illness that ate at her lungs had given her a macabre beauty; on first sight she gave the impression of a pretty corpse on display in its silk-lined coffin.

The hall was vast, the ceiling high and vaulted, like a temple devoted to the gods and goddesses of amusement and pleasure. Marcia drank in the colors, the shapes, and inhaled the smells; the greenish-golden glow of hundreds of electric bulbs and gas jets, filtered through smoky haze from countless cigarettes and cigars. Red, white, and blue bunting draped the balconies; dancers kicked and whirled, displaying flashes of white, lace-trimmed linen and black stockings. The odor was a potpourri of tobacco, perfume, rain-dampened clothing, and sweat. She stored each fleeting sense impression, like photographs and sachets in a dresser drawer, wondering: *Can I paint it? Will I have time, or will the memory fade and die with me?*

Betsy Endicott, heiress to a railroad fortune, patroness of the arts, and Marcia's companion for more than a decade, contemplated her friend with worried eyes: *How long can she last in this place? Can I get her back to California before Paris kills her?*

A couple of toffs in evening dress interrupted: "Will you ladies join us for a drink?"

Marcia and Betsy had inadvertently paused in a prime area for pick-ups. Betsy blushed and squeezed Marcia's hand protectively. "I'm sorry," she replied with a hint of annoyance, "we're meeting friends." She then pulled Marcia away into the stream of humanity flowing in the direction of the dance floor.

Gazing after the elegantly dressed pair as they merged with and vanished among the throng, one of the toffs nudged his companion in the ribs and remarked, "I guess we're not their type." His companion grinned and nodded knowingly and the two continued their hunt, setting their sights on more promising quarry.

The two women jostled their way to the end of the bar. Marcia stopped abruptly near a narrow stairway leading down to the dance floor and drew her friend's attention to a man seated at a round table set on the main floor's perimeter. "That's the artist who painted the portrait we admired in Joyant's gallery."

Betsy observed a well-dressed young man with a thick black beard and dark, intense eyes peering through a pince-nez. Despite his impeccably tailored clothes, there was something simian about his physiognomy. She also noticed a short cane, suitable for a dwarf, hanging from the back of his chair. The artist concentrated on the dancers while drawing in a sketchbook, his hand moving swiftly and efficiently in concert with his darting eyes. He occasionally put down his charcoal stick, took a draft of cognac, and then continued sketching furiously where he had left off.

Marcia smiled and tugged at her companion's hand. "Come on, Betsy, I'll introduce you."

Betsy turned to Marcia with a quizzical squint. "You've made that gentleman's acquaintance, dear?"

"Oh yes, in the American Gallery at the Fair. You weren't there that day, I'm afraid. At any rate, he liked my paintings. Come on, you'll find him clever, and we can talk to him about that portrait."

Marcia yanked Betsy onward, and it was as though the consumptive had been wonderfully reinvigorated by the sight of her fellow painter. They arrived presently at his table, blocking the artist's line of sight.

The man put down his charcoal and looked up with an irritated scowl, an expletive forming on his lips. However, upon seeing Marcia Brownlow, his frown turned to a shrewd smile; the expletive remained unuttered. Placing his powerful, hairy hands on the table, he rose a few inches, made a slight bow and greeted the intruders in impeccably accented, aristocratic

English. "My dear Miss Brownlow, what a pleasant surprise. To what do I owe this honor?"

There might have been a hint of sarcasm or condescension in his overly formal greeting, but Marcia chose to shrug it off. "My friend and I saw some of your work at Monsieur Joyant's gallery. We were intrigued by one of your portraits." Marcia caught herself; she had failed to introduce Betsy. "Pardon me, Monsieur, I was so pleased to see you I forgot to introduce my friend. Miss Betsy Endicott, may I present Monsieur de Toulouse-Lautrec, a young artist of considerable promise."

Betsy smiled diffidently and extended her hand. Toulouse-Lautrec grabbed the digits, gave them a friendly American shake, and let go. Then he turned to a passing waiter, snapped his fingers and shouted, "César, two chairs, another bottle, and glasses for the ladies, please." The waiter rushed off to fill the order and the artist grinned at Marcia and Betsy. "You'll do me the honor of being my guests, won't you?"

Betsy hesitated, but Marcia was quick to reply. "Yes, of course we will."

While waiting for the chairs, Marcia realized that they were blocking Lautrec's view. "Pardon us, Monsieur," she said, pulling Betsy back toward a railing separating the low mezzanine from the main floor.

Lautrec smiled appreciatively and continued sketching until the waiter brought the chairs and a fresh bottle of cognac. Once they were seated, the attentive waiter filled their glasses before scurrying off to see to his other thirsty customers. Lautrec produced a gold monogrammed cigarette case and offered the women a smoke. Betsy declined but Marcia took a cigarette, leaning over the table as Lautrec struck a match and gave her a light. Betsy frowned, but remained silent. She could deny her friend nothing, and Marcia seemed so far gone in her illness that insisting upon abstinence would have been cruel, not to mention futile.

The quadrille ended to raucous applause and shouts of "Bravo!" The floor cleared and the orchestra took a break. Lautrec and Marcia maintained a stream of art-related conversation while Betsy mostly listened and observed. At one point, the subject changed to automobiles.

"We saw the Daimler exhibit at the fair, and I sketched the motor car," said Marcia with an enthusiastic gleam in her eye. "The automobile powered by an internal combustion engine has great potential. Of course, it's in its infancy, like the railroad locomotive seventy years ago." She turned to Betsy and sighed wistfully. "I'd so love to ride in an automobile before I die."

Betsy looked down, touched her friend's hand and pursed her lips. She tried to speak, but could only choke back a sob.

Lautrec observed the women closely and guessed at the intimacy of their relationship. He was touched, for an instant, but wished to change the subject to his paintings. Joyant had told him Marcia's companion was a wealthy American collector of new art; Lautrec figured that with a damp, cold winter coming on and Marcia's consumption, the women would not remain too long in Paris.

"My cousin Dr. Tapié admires the automobile. I should not be surprised if some day he turns up driving down the Champs Elysee in one of those things, ha, ha." He drained his glass before addressing Marcia on a subject closer to his heart. "By the way, I recall you mentioning one of my paintings at Joyant's gallery. Could you please tell me to which one you were referring?"

"Of course, Monsieur, it was the portrait of a very beautiful young woman. She was blonde with blue eyes and seemed to gaze at the viewer with the most wistful smile. Please excuse me for making an observation that might seem impertinent; for want of another word, the portrait's *prettiness* and charm distinguishes it from your other work." Marcia smiled enigmatically at Lautrec while awaiting his reply.

Lautrec stared back at Marcia with a bewildered look, as though he did not know how to respond. His English was very good, but perhaps due to a subtle nuance of expression he had misunderstood her? At any rate, he sensed that this prize-winning American woman artist had insulted him. But he regarded this discussion as the beginning of a negotiation, and he was not going to strangle the newborn deal in its cradle with speculations as to her meaning regarding this particular painting's "prettiness." In short, if Marcia's rich patroness wanted to buy his pretty picture to please her dying lover he would be more than happy to oblige, provided of course that the price was right.

"Ah, Miss Brownlow, you have seen my portrait of Virginie Ménard. She is a lovely girl, is she not?"

"Indeed she is, Monsieur. I've sketched her myself at the *Atelier* Cormon."

Marcia's revelation surprised her companions, Betsy more so than Lautrec. "Marcia," she said with a hint of exasperation, "you never said anything to *me* about this young woman."

"Betsy dear, must I tell you *everything*? At any rate, I did tell you that Cormon invited me to his *Atelier*. And it just so happened that the young woman we admired in Monsieur's painting was modeling there that day."

"*Did* we admire the young woman? As I recall, it was the painting that intrigued us, *not* the model."

Lautrec found this incipient lover's quarrel amusing and somewhat arousing as well. So much so that he was tempted to provoke it further. Nevertheless, he prudently tried to steer the conversation back to business. "Mademoiselle Ménard is much sought after—as a model, that is. And she dances divinely. You shall see her tonight, in the Can-Can."

"I can't wait," Betsy muttered peevishly.

Marcia glanced at her friend. "Cheer up, darling. What you need is a drink." Then to Lautrec: "Let's have another bottle, Monsieur. This round's on us."

⌒∞⌒

A blaring cornet fanfare announced the Can-Can. A troop of pretty young women dressed in spotless white shirtwaists and long, flowing skirts of diverse bright colors—blue, green, red, yellow, and pink— trotted onto the dance floor in high-heeled shoes. Forming a line, they raised their skirts and white lace-trimmed petticoats above their waists and began their rhythmic high-kicking dance to the cheers, whistles, and applause of the adoring crowd.

To Lautrec's unerring eye and calculating brain the dancers were a problem in geometry and physics; fluid energy, flashing color, transforming forms and shapes in motion. He worked like a fiend to render them on paper the way the very latest in fast photographic lenses and shutters would capture the moment for posterity. And the focal point of his composition was the lovely, wild-eyed, and uninhibited maenad of Montmartre, the incomparably exquisite Virginie Ménard.

Marcia saw Virginie with her artist's eye, as Lautrec did, and she longed for her sketchbook and pastels. Ill as she was, Marcia could drink almost anyone under the table and she had kept pace with the insatiable Lautrec. Betsy, on the other hand, was fuddled. Her head was swimming and, as her bleary gray eyes tried to focus on Virginie, she saw two ineffably beautiful girls moving in concert like Siamese twins. Betsy rubbed her eyes, blinked, and turned her attention to Marcia. She noticed how her companion fixed upon the dancer as if at that moment nothing else existed. That sobering realization wounded Betsy like a knife stabbing her in the heart.

A pair of angry gray eyes glared at Virginie and those eyes were now clear and cold as ice. *She's been playing around behind my back.* The beautiful dancer rekindled memories of Marcia's past indiscretions.

Betsy's eyes narrowed, her rouged lips tightened and, beneath the table her fists clenched, nails digging into the flesh of her palms until they bled. She turned toward Marcia who, like Lautrec, was unaware of anything except the dance and one particular dancer. Her heart racing and her breath coming fast and shallow, one singular thought repeated itself in Betsy's jealous mind: *You promised to be faithful to me, Marcia. You promised. . . .*

The early morning hours: the orchestra packed their instruments and departed; the dancers were gone; a broadly smiling Zidler counted receipts and locked his safe; the crowd dispersed to home, to bed, or to such further amusement as might be found at that hour in a cheap hotel, brothel, gambling house, or opium den. Toulouse-Lautrec shuffled off into the shadows on his stunted, painfully misshapen legs aided by his button-hook of a cane; Betsy staggered toward a cab supported by her seemingly sober, consumptive companion.

Electric and gaslights winked out; the raucous, riotous Moulin Rouge transformed into a mausoleum haunted by spirits of the evening past. Into this crypt waddled the charwomen, armed with brooms, buckets, and mops to clean up the revelers' rubbish.

Virginie Ménard *nee* Mercier walked alone through dark, narrow streets snaking their way up Montmartre Hill to her rented fourth floor room on the Rue Lepic. Her heels clicked on the cobblestone pavement, footsteps echoing in the shadowy canyon of locked and shuttered shops, houses, and three- and four-story tenements. She lifted her skirts to step around puddles and muck. A yowling black cat chasing a rat rattled a garbage can and darted across her path. She stopped, shuddered, and crossed herself. Her large blue eyes glanced round, searching the murky recesses outside the dim aura of flickering yellow gaslight. She took a deep breath and walked on.

She hated being alone on the streets at this hour, but the money she made from her dancing and contacts at the Moulin Rouge seemed worth the risk. One of her fellow dancers, Delphine, a tough girl raised on the Paris streets, had given her some tips. Virginie carried a straight razor in her purse and Delphine had provided a tactic for self defense. "Slash at the bastard's eyes," she said, "and kick his nuts, then you scream like hell and run in the opposite direction." All right in theory, Virginie supposed, but she dreaded putting it into practice. She preferred to rely on the police and good neighbors in this quarter, who tended to look out for each other.

Virginie relaxed as she spotted the familiar front door at number 62. She had tipped the concierge to wait up for her and longed for the comforting refuge of her room. Walking quickly, she soon reached the entrance and was about to ring when a soft voice startled her. She turned round, wide eyed and trembling, remembering Delphine's warnings and the razor in her purse.

The man, who had emerged silently from the shadows, tipped his hat and smiled reassuringly. "I'm sorry if I surprised you."

Recognizing the intruder, Virginie unwound. "Oh, it's you. You gave me a start."

"I apologize, my dear. Here, this will calm you." He reached into his coat pocket and withdrew a monogrammed gold cigarette case.

Virginie took a cigarette, held the man's hand and leaned over as he gave her a light with a match. She inhaled and then exhaled gray smoke, her tension relieved. "Thank you. I feel much better now."

2

A large rectangular window flooded the operating theater with brilliant white light. Jules Émile Péan stood erect, dressed to perfection and dramatically posed, like an actor in the spotlight about to declaim his soliloquy to a silently anticipating audience. Universally acclaimed as one of the world's greatest surgeons, Péan occupied the Olympian summit of the French medical profession. Before him stood four acolytes, young physicians hand-picked by the master to assist in his most daring and spectacular operations. Among the chosen few was Toulouse-Lautrec's cousin, Tapié de Céleyran, an admirer of the Daimler automobile exhibit at the Exposition.

The acolytes hovered over an operating table supporting a woman in her early thirties, her nakedness covered by a white sheet. A classically educated witness might have compared the young woman to Iphigenia on the sacrificial altar. But unlike the tragic Greek princess of legend, this woman was not there to be slaughtered, but rather to be cured. An anesthetist sat beside the patient to the right of the table, one hand on her pulse, the other holding a chloroform mask.

The audience was a privileged group of physicians and surgeons, but there was an interloper among them: Toulouse-Lautrec. The artist had been attending the surgeries at Péan's invitation, having been introduced by his cousin, Dr. Tapié. Like most, or perhaps all, celebrities, Péan was a savvy self-promoter, and he figured Lautrec's drawings would provide good publicity for his professional services, not to mention a record for posterity.

The acolytes wore clean, white operating coats, but the high priest simply tied a towel around his neck to shelter his immaculate waistcoat from spattered blood. Thus accoutered, the stocky surgeon looked like a gourmand about to crack a lobster. Péan did not follow Pasteur's Germ Theory, nor did he countenance Listerism, but he possessed a practical, commonsense belief in personal hygiene and cleanliness in surgery and the clinic that kept his post-operative infection rate reasonably low.

"Gentlemen," announced Péan, "the diagnosis is Uterine Fibroids; the procedure Vaginal Hysterectomy." With that, the surgeon chose a scalpel from among a sparkling array of instruments set out on a white cloth-draped table.

Toulouse-Lautrec observed and recorded the procedure the way he rendered the dance at the Moulin Rouge. His brilliant mind, curiously active brown eyes, and deft, charcoal-wielding hand operated swiftly and efficiently on the sketching paper, mimicking Péan's audacious precision. As he worked on his sketch, Lautrec marveled at the machine-like functioning of the surgical team as they applied clamps and forceps without a scintilla of time or motion wasted.

Lautrec had barely completed his sketch when the diseased uterus and cervix lay in a pan. Péan removed his bib, washed his hands, and rolled down his sleeves, leaving the clean-up and dressing of the surgical wound to his assistants. Soon, two attendants arrived with a hospital trolley to wheel the patient out of the operating theater.

The drama over, most of the spectators filed out, but a few milled around while discussing the operation. One doctor remarked, "Péan is a virtuoso of the knife *sans pareil*. He operates on his patient the way Sarasate plays his violin." "I agree, doctor," chimed in another. "It's one thing to do a neat job of surgery. But to remove a woman's reproductive organs with such élan, such panache, is a mark of true genius."

Lautrec closed his sketchbook, put away his charcoal sticks, and was about to leave when Dr.Tapié, who was in conversation with Péan near an easel upon which hung an anatomical drawing of the female lower abdomen, gestured for the artist to join them. As Lautrec approached, the great surgeon smiled broadly at the painter.

"Well, Monsieur, did you obtain a good study of our operation?"

"Yes, doctor, I believe I did. Would you care to take a look?"

"Of course, Monsieur; I'd be honored." Péan held out his well-scrubbed hand and received the sketchbook. He examined the drawing with a critical eye, then smiled and returned it. "That's splendid, Monsieur. You know, I was just saying to your cousin Tapié, 'Monsieur de Toulouse-Lautrec has observed and sketched so many of my operations I wouldn't be surprised if he could perform one himself.'"

Lautrec laughed, and the doctors laughed with him.

∞

From Péan's clinic Lautrec took a cab to a popular sidewalk café on the Rue Lepic, not far from his studio. There he joined his friend and fellow artist, Émile Bernard, at a small marble-topped table set up on the sidewalk under a fluttering yellow awning. The day was sunny, warm and pleasant under a clear blue sky. A variety of horse-drawn vehicles clip-clopped and rumbled up and down the cobblestones; a persistent conversational buzz pervaded the café, emanating from its diverse clientele—bohemians, bourgeoisie, working men and women, tourists, and *flâneurs.*

Lautrec and Bernard drank coffee and pastis. As they talked, Lautrec doodled on the tablecloth. His subject was a stocky, balding man with mutton-chop whiskers and a stained bib round his neck. The man was slurping his lunch, an immense bowl of onion soup. The man bore a remarkable likeness to Péan. Lautrec's purplish lips grinned wryly as he drew objects floating in the soup that resembled the woman's extirpated organs.

Bernard, a thin, intense young man in his early twenties with a thick shock of brown hair and slight beard, eyed the tablecloth caricature. "So, you attended another of Péan's surgeries. Frankly, I find the subject morbid and rather distasteful."

Lautrec stopped doodling and confronted his friend with a quizzical squint. "Morbid and distasteful, you say? Leonardo and Rembrandt attended dissections, and Gericault studied guillotined heads and cadavers at the Morgue. I assure you, my dear Émile, we artists can learn something of the human animal by witnessing its evisceration."

Bernard made a face, registering his disgust. He changed the subject. "I've news from Theo; Vincent's making progress at St. Remy. He's working again."

"I'm glad to hear it, though it's his work that put him there. Rather, I should say his work and a host of other things, among them metaphysics, mysticism, hashish, absinthe, whores, the clap, rejection—and Gauguin."

Bernard was accustomed to his friend's cynical observations, and typically let them pass without comment. "Anyway, I'm glad to hear Vincent's doing better. Theo worries too much about his brother and he has his own troubles, with a family to support and his own poor health."

"Life's no joke, Émile. We all have our crosses to bear in this vale of tears."

Bernard used the biblical reference as an opening to a topic much on his mind of late. "Vincent and I corresponded on the subject of religion and the use of symbolism in modern art. In one of his letters he wrote something immensely profound, so much so I've committed it to memory: 'Christ alone, of all the philosophers, magicians, etc., has affirmed eternal life as the most important certainty, the infinity of time, the futility of death, the necessity and purpose of serenity and devotion. He lived serenely, *as an artist greater than all other artists*, scorning marble and clay and paint, working in the living flesh. In other words, this peerless artist, scarcely conceivable with the blunt instrument of our modern, nervous and obtuse brains, made neither statues nor paintings nor books. He maintained in no uncertain terms that he made . . . *living men*, immortals.'

"Until now, I've looked for new styles, techniques, forms of expression suitable to our modern age. But I was wrong. What we really need is a new substance, a new essence in our art, to portray beauty *and* truth and to use our skill to transform souls. I believe that religious symbolism is the way forward. Not the old symbols of the Church, but something different that attempts to see modern life through the eyes of God, or at least as we *conceive* God would see it, and to imitate Him in the transformative, creative process as well."

Lautrec almost snorted, "Rubbish!" but he checked himself. Instead he replied coolly, "That's a fine ambition, and I wish you well. But as you know, I'm not religious and I certainly do not see the world through God's eyes anymore than I see invisible, transcendent beings from the moon. For unlike God, assuming He exists, I'm mortal, changeable, fallible, and ignorant. I see the world with the keen, trained eyes of an artist who just happens to be a misshapen, ugly, dwarf. I make an accurate record of what I observe on the streets, in the dance halls, brothels, café concerts, in the surgery and morgue. What I see might be the work of God *or* the Devil, but that's really of no consequence to me. It simply is what it is."

Bernard knew that an argument with the skeptical Lautrec would prove futile, or worse. Disputes among artists were often vicious and destructive; Gauguin and Van Gogh were a tragic example. Rather than pick a fight, he asked about Virginie Ménard. "Henri, I've begun work on a new project, and I'd very much like to use Mademoiselle Ménard. I know she's modeled for you in the past. I've gone to Cormon and checked with her concierge as well, but she seems to have disappeared. Have you seen her lately?"

"I saw her a few nights ago at the Moulin Rouge, but I've not seen her since," he replied matter-of-factly. "A couple of rich American women were there that evening. As a matter of fact, they told me they liked my portrait of Virginie. I thought I was about to make a sale, but they seem to have disappeared too. Anyway, have you asked Zidler or some of his girls at the Moulin? They may know Virginie's whereabouts."

"Thanks, Henri, I'll try them."

"Well, I wish you luck. These *lorettes* are free, easy, and unpredictable. She could be living it up in Deauville with a rich Marquis, or sleeping it off in some hole with an *apache*."

Émile frowned and shook his head. "Virginie's not like that, Henri. That's why I want her for my painting. I see her as an angel, a saint, or the Blessed Virgin Herself."

Lautrec said nothing. He smiled knowingly, downed his pastis, and called for another round, paying for both.

Bernard thanked his friend. He liked Lautrec and admired his work, morbid and depressing as it was. But he often wondered: *Why must he always be so damned pessimistic?*

3

THE GRAND HOTEL TERMINUS & BOIS DE BOULOGNE

OCTOBER 14

Betsy Endicott and Marcia Brownlow shared a lavish suite at The Grand Hotel Terminus. On this morning, Betsy stood at a window overlooking the broad, tree-shaded avenue. A street-cleaning wagon pulled by a team of horses rumbled by, wetting the pavement with water spraying from its large, cylindrical tank.

She held back the white lace curtain and gazed across the thoroughfare at a great heap of mansard-roofed masonry, the Gare St. Lazare. She recalled how Marcia had admired Monet's painting of the immense, steam- and smoke-filled cast iron and glass train shed. The railway station stirred thoughts of a longed-for journey, her desire to be on board a fast steamer to New York.

She frowned at the leaden skies; the droplets running down the window pane seemed to mirror the tears Betsy had shed over her companion. Marcia lay in bed under the care of Sir Henry Collingwood, an eminent Harley Street physician. Like Betsy, Marcia, and many other affluent foreign tourists attending the Exposition, Sir Henry had chosen The Grand Hotel for its convenient location, luxurious furnishings, first class service, and modern accommodations. The fact that Sir Henry occupied a suite on the same floor as Betsy and Marcia was providential.

Three days earlier, following their evening at the Moulin Rouge, Betsy and Marcia had breakfasted meagerly on a baguette and coffee served in their suite. Neither of them had much of an appetite, and the tension between them smoldered like a smoking match. The tense mood was aggravated by Betsy's hangover and Marcia's chronic illness. Between sips of coffee and mouthfuls of baguette, Betsy rubbed her aching temples and blinked her bloodshot eyes. Her behavior got on Marcia's nerves, and she finally broke the silence:

"You drank too much last night, dear. But then, you almost *always* do."

Betsy looked daggers at her friend. "You needn't remind me of my faults, Marcia. I'm well aware of them, and I feel damned awful. You might show some sympathy."

Marcia smirked. "Darling, I feel damned awful every damn day, but then I don't whine about it."

Betsy always tried to make allowance for Marcia's illness when faced with her sharp tongue. But Betsy had reached the end of her patience; her self-control snapped. Her hands shook; her face reddened and her lips trembled. She dropped a butter knife; it clattered on the china plate. "I might not drink so much," she sputtered, "if you were more careful of your health and showed a little consideration for me too. We've remained in this damp, dreary place because you insisted and I indulged you. But I can't help wondering why we're still here. Staying for the closing ceremonies had seemed an insufficient reason, but perhaps last night you were so good as to have given me a clue."

"You said a *clue*, my dear? Are you playing detective? Or perhaps you've hired a professional to track my comings and goings." Marcia's voice oozed sarcasm, further infuriating her companion.

Betsy rose from the table. Her eyes flashed and she wrung her hands as if restraining them from lashing out at her friend. "All right, Marcia. Let's have it out, here and now. We've stayed in Paris because—because you've formed a relationship with that little blonde bint at the Moulin Rouge!"

Marcia laughed at Betsy's jealous accusation. But her laughter soon turned to violent coughing. Now more worried than angry, Betsy came around the table and began rubbing Marcia's shoulders in an attempt to give her some relief. But the coughing fit persisted and between coughs Marcia wheezed and gasped for air. She shot to her feet, shoved Betsy aside and knocked the chair over in the process. Marcia grabbed a serviette from the table to cover her mouth, and then staggered toward the bathroom. Halfway to her destination she convulsed, hemorrhaged a great clot of blood into the serviette, and keeled over onto the carpet, where she remained unconscious.

Betsy screamed in shock at her friend's sudden collapse, but soon regained her composure. She immediately went to the telephone to call the front desk for medical assistance, but then remembered that Sir Henry Collingwood was staying nearby. Not only was Sir Henry a noted physician, he was also a fine amateur watercolorist and a great admirer of Marcia's work. They had become acquainted at the American Art exhibit and Marcia, Betsy, and Sir Henry had dined together on several occasions.

Betsy ran to Sir Henry's suite and knocked frantically. Fortunately, the physician was in. In the meantime, Marcia had regained consciousness and had crawled across the carpet toward a settee. When Sir Henry and Betsy entered the suite they saw Marcia grasping at an armrest, trying to pull herself up like a helpless infant. Sir Henry knelt beside her, gently placed a hand on her shoulder, and whispered into her ear. Marcia nodded her understanding. Sir Henry lifted her in his arms and carried her to bed.

Later that afternoon, Betsy paced the drawing room carpet, occasionally glancing down at the skillfully woven nymphs and goddesses based on a pattern by Boucher. She stopped at a faint bloodstain that had defied the hotel's attempts at removal. She supposed this memento of Marcia's illness would be charged to their bill.

Her long, slender fingers fussed nervously with the pink ribbon and lace trim of her Doucet dress. Finally, she settled back in an imitation Louis XV armchair and glanced at a small gold and diamond decorated watch pinned to her breast. *It seems like he's been with her forever. What's taking so long?*

The large, ornately decorated bedroom doors swung open and Sir Henry entered the drawing room. Betsy sprang from the chair and almost tripped as she ran to him. "How is she, Sir Henry? I must know—I must know this instant!"

The eminent physician smiled soothingly. "Please calm yourself, Miss Endicott. Let us sit and discuss this over a cup of tea." He took Betsy's hand and led her to a round table in the angle of a bay where tea had been set up in a fine silver service. The hour was too early for a formal tea, but Sir Henry felt the beverage would have a quieting, restorative effect.

Sir Henry Collingwood was as smooth as silk. Tall, aristocratically handsome, and dressed to perfection in a gray Savile Row cutaway and striped trousers, with a fresh pink carnation *boutonniere*, he exuded self-confidence without seeming overbearing. He served Betsy tea, his keen blue eyes studying her facial expressions, gestures, manner, and attitude carefully. He had made a fortune in Harley Street treating high-strung, wealthy society women, and he observed their histrionics with the analytical eye of a critic watching Bernhardt or Modjeska from his box at the theater.

Sir Henry had a perfect sense of timing when in consultation; he knew precisely when to speak, and when to listen. The drawing room was silent except for the ticking of a mantelpiece clock. He stroked his neatly trimmed brown moustache and smiled beneficently before addressing Betsy in his suave, Oxbridge accent:

"I've examined Miss Brownlow thoroughly and had a long, frank talk with her as well. I'm pleased to inform you that she's making good progress towards recovery."

"Oh thank God!" Betsy cried. She wept, as he had anticipated she would. Sir Henry reached into his breast pocket, offered her a perfumed handkerchief, and then waited patiently for her to regain her composure.

"However," he continued once he had ascertained that Betsy was sufficiently collected to comprehend what he had to say, "I have strongly advised her to enter a sanatorium, and she has agreed. I know of an excellent facility near Zurich, and would be honored to recommend Miss Brownlow to the Director, with whom I'm well acquainted. Moreover, should you wish to retain my professional services for the journey, I would be pleased to accompany you and introduce you to the Director and his staff. It's a lovely place in the mountains, with clean, fresh air and beautiful scenery, ideal for sketching and painting."

Betsy said nothing and looked down at her hands cradling the teacup. Sir Henry read her reaction and determined she would need some persuasion. The sanatorium he proposed was world-renowned, its reputation well deserved, and the journey by train relatively short and not taxing. "Miss Endicott, I believe the sanatorium is Miss Brownlow's best hope." If there was another option she preferred, he could be flexible and accommodating. He waited patiently for her response.

After a moment, Betsy looked up with a worried frown. "I was hoping Marcia and I could return to America. We reside in California, where the climate is moderate, sunny and quite healthy. Is there a sanatorium in the American West that you recommend?"

There was an excellent sanatorium in Colorado Springs and Sir Henry knew the Director there as well. The long journey would be harder on Marcia, but he calculated that the benefits to all concerned might outweigh the additional risk. "Ah well, I do know of a fine place in Colorado, quite as good as the Swiss sanatorium. Of course, there's the question of a longer trip. Can you manage first class accommodations on a fast ship and a special train as well?" He was almost certain she could, but he thought it prudent to ask.

Relieved by this alternative, Betsy put down her cup and smiled broadly. "Of course I can. My preference for the Atlantic crossing is the *City of Paris*. She holds the record, and she has excellent accommodations. Of course, we'd have to cross the channel and take the train to Liverpool to catch her. But frankly, British ships are the best. I don't put much trust in the French steamers."

Sir Henry smiled. "Of course; the *City of Paris* would be splendid."

"As for the trip from New York to Colorado," Betsy continued enthusiastically, "I know the President of the railroad quite well. I can wire him and have my private Pullman hooked up to a special train, ready for us upon arrival." She paused a moment. "And of course, I would appreciate your continued medical attendance until we have reached our destination. That is, of course, if you can spare the additional time away from your practice."

Prior to going on holiday, Sir Henry had referred his patients to an old school chum who was quite good when it came to splitting fees. Therefore, he was not worried about his practice, even if he had to leave it in his friend's capable hands for another month or two, or longer. Moreover, the journey would give him time to get better acquainted with the handsome American heiress. He figured that even with the best of care, Marcia could not last much more than a year. Betsy would need consoling, and Sir Henry was quite the willing bachelor. And he was not overly concerned about the true nature of Betsy and Marcia's relationship. He believed he understood women and, in his opinion, Betsy could be quite happy with the *right* man, that is to say a man like Sir Henry Collingwood.

"My dear Miss Endicott, I shall wire one of my colleagues and make appropriate arrangements for my practice. You needn't worry in that regard. If you and Miss Brownlow are agreeable, I shall most certainly accompany you to Colorado."

⚶

Marcia Brownlow appeared doll-like as she sat, her back supported by two plump down pillows, in the midst of an immense Louis XV canopied bed. Betsy reclined on the bedcovers beside her friend. She clutched one cold bony hand between her warm, soft palms as if by that operation Betsy could reinvigorate her dying companion.

When Marcia hemorrhaged and collapsed on the floor, her last thought had been: *This is the end—so be it.* But upon regaining consciousness, a strong will to live had given her strength to crawl to the settee and struggle to get back on her feet. She was thirty-nine, older than her mother had been when she died of typhoid. The last time Marcia looked in the mirror she saw her dead mother staring back at her—gaunt, pale, and exhausted from her battle with death.

Her dry, un-rouged lips smiled wanly, her green eyes gazed searchingly at Betsy. Marcia sighed as she wondered: *Why persist in this farce?* But she would not succumb to despair; as long as she lived and had the use of her eyes and hands, she would draw and paint. And she had discovered a new source of inspiration, Virginie Ménard. She would try to explain her fascination with Virginie to Betsy, but before making the effort she again sighed deeply.

Taking the sigh as a sign of discomfort, Betsy asked with a worried frown, "Are you all right, dear? Is there anything I can do?"

"No, I'm quite well, I assure you. Frankly, I'm getting cabin fever lying in this catafalque of a bed day and night. This afternoon, I'm going to insist that Sir Henry let me get up and walk about."

This was what Betsy wanted to hear. "I shall insist upon it too! If the weather permits, I'll hire an open carriage and take you for a ride through the Bois de Boulogne."

Marcia smiled and nodded in agreement. "Yes, that would be splendid." She paused a moment to collect her thoughts before pursuing a touchy subject. "I've been doing a great deal of thinking, these last couple of days. There's something I must explain to you; I want you to understand—"

Betsy apprehended her meaning, and interrupted: "Let's not discuss anything unpleasant, dear. It's unnecessary; I understand perfectly."

Betsy understood nothing, and her moods shifted unpredictably between passivity and aggression. At times, she would confront danger or adversity with an almost inhuman composure. At others, she used wealth to avoid unpleasantness, purchasing a first class cabin ticket on the next luxury steamer bound for somewhere else.

Marcia thought she knew all Betsy's moods; she would plead for comprehension and hope for the best. "Please dear, what I have to say is important. It's the truth, and it's not what you think. I'm going to tell you everything about Virginie Ménard."

Betsy dropped Marcia's hand. "No, no, no! I don't want to hear it!" She put her hands over her ears like a petulant child.

Marcia put her arms around Betsy and held her until the tension subsided. "Darling," she whispered, "believe me, I don't want any more lies on my conscience. Not now; it's too late for lies."

Betsy retrieved a lace handkerchief, wiped her tears and blew her nose gently. "All right, Marcia, I'll listen. I apologize; I've promised the doctor not to do anything to upset you."

Satisfied that Betsy had pulled herself together, Marcia began her "confession" with the past as prelude. Years earlier, Marcia had impersonated a man to achieve success in the male-dominated art world. Calculating and opportunistic, she had entered into the deception on the theory that it was a small price to pay for recognition, patronage, and lucrative commissions. Betsy was one of the wealthy women she had deceived.

Betsy listened patiently, but she could not help interrupting: "Please Marcia, why dredge up the past? It's too painful."

"Life *is* painful, dear. You've been kind, generous, and forgiving but those lies I told you still weigh on my conscience. I'm now confronted with the horrible realization that my art, my life's work, has been a lie. Since childhood, I've tried to see beauty in nature, to capture beauty's essence and transform it into art. And my paintings have been popular and sold well because I painted the world as people wanted to see it, not as it really was. But can beauty exist without truth? I've asked myself that question over the years, without having reached a conclusion.

"When I first saw Virginie, her beauty ignited the flame of my artistic passion, a flame, I might add, that had been guttering of late. I wanted to paint more than the beauty I saw; I needed to get under her skin, to penetrate her very essence. I desired the most intimate knowledge of her, to discover her secret so that truth and beauty could be merged into one ineffable image on canvas. That's why, after sketching Virginie at the *Atelier* I invited her to a nearby *boîte* for drinks and conversation. Despite our different life experiences, we seemed like kindred spirits, sharing our innermost secrets. She opened up to me, revealing a world I could have hardly imagined. She had suffered a cruel childhood and was haunted by a memory of her aunt and uncle slaughtering Virginie's pet pig, Buttercup."

Betsy listened sympathetically to a story of physical and mental abuse, until she interrupted: "Please dear, that story is too awful to relate. And what in heaven's name has it to do with art?"

"That story has inspired me. But there's more. Virginie told me about a revenge fantasy. It gave her strength to endure her aunt's beatings. The fantasy took place in the slaughterhouse where the Mercier's had slaughtered Virginie's pet. Madame Mercier came out of the chute, naked, covered with filth, crawling on all fours and grunting like a swine. Buttercup followed, walking upright with a prod in her human-like hand. Prodding Madame's rump, the anthropomorphized pig growled in Virginie's voice, 'Move your arse you ugly sow, before I flay it raw!'

"Virginie waited by the gate, mallet in hand. When Madame entered the shed she glanced up in terror as the girl gleefully poleaxed her squealing aunt. Then, assisted by Buttercup, Virginie hoisted, stuck, boiled, singed, scraped, butchered, and dressed Madame Mercier, grinding what was left into feed for her porcine friends. Pretty little Buttercup always got the most generous portion."

Betsy made a face as though she'd smelled something offensive. "How disgusting. But then, you were always drawn to the macabre. Thank goodness it hasn't affected your painting."

Marcia smiled. "Virginie's tale of cruelty and imagined revenge gave me an idea. I would paint her experiences as an indictment of child abuse. It would be something entirely new, at least in my art; a plea for tormented children, the victims of indifference and intolerance.

"Until now, I've avoided social comment like the plague. I've spent my life earning good fees and prizes painting pretty pictures for the well-heeled bourgeoisie, so I suppose my deathbed conversion will strike many as insincere. Do you think I'm a hypocrite?"

Betsy took Marcia in her arms and held her close. She pitied her longtime companion, but could not forget Marcia's past transgressions. Even in her present condition, Marcia might be lying to cover-up an affair. Betsy closed her eyes, her jealous mind conjuring a vision of the beautiful dancer. "No, dear," she whispered, "I'd never think that of you."

⚬∞⚬

Marcia, Betsy, and Sir Henry rode in an open barouche down a shady avenue of the Bois de Boulogne, past the race course and round the serpentine lake. The weather had changed for the better. The afternoon was unseasonably balmy with a few wispy clouds in a bright blue sky. Sir Henry considered it a good opportunity for Marcia to get some fresh air and sunshine. She sat across from Betsy and Sir Henry, half-lulled to sleep by their monotonous chatter, the clip-clop of horses' hooves, and the rumble of carriage wheels.

Marcia looked tiny sitting by herself on the broad leather seat; she seemed to be fading away by the hour. Her wasted body was wrapped in a pure white, furbelow-frilled dress, her gaunt skull half hidden under a black ribbon-trimmed and flower-bedecked straw hat and small, fringed parasol. A crocheted shawl draped her bony shoulders.

Marcia's bright green eyes fixed on Betsy, who giggled like a schoolgirl while flirting with the handsome English doctor. *She's far away from me now. So much the better.* Marcia did not want her friend to be shackled to a corpse. Life is for the living; the dying dwell in a twilight world of their own, a sort of limbo between the quick and the dead. A wry smile crossed her rouged lips. *Où sont les neiges d'antan?* Villon's poem had taken on a new meaning for her. She would soon join those beauties of yesteryear.

Marcia turned her attention to the trees and their dying leaves. Bright red, orange, and old gold, they fell from branches, drifted in the mild breeze, floated for an instant before landing on the surface of the mirror-like lake. *How beautiful.* She had devoted her life to beauty, her art. But her art was dying, too. Why had she committed herself to something so ephemeral? Beauty was fragile and transitory, like the floating leaves. Truth endured, though it could be ugly. She predicted the new art would be ugly in its uncompromising honesty, reflecting a changing world, a fin de siècle ethos oriented toward darkness and despair.

She had changed her mind; she would not return to America to die in a sanatorium. She had not yet told Betsy or Sir Henry, but she intended to remain in Paris. Marcia wanted to finish one last great testament, her painting of Virginie's suffering, but her will had been dissipated by disease, oozing out of her like gummy sap from a dying tree. She closed her eyes and sought inspiration in a vision. The image of Virginie Ménard appeared shining through Marcia's closed eyelids like a celestial being floating in a golden nimbus. A single tear formed a rivulet running slowly down her powdered cheek, but no one noticed.

4

L e Chat Noir occupied a three-story half-timbered building on the Boulevard de Clichy, not far from the Moulin Rouge. Originally located on the Boulevard de Rochechouart, the popular cabaret had opened to promotional hoopla; a torch-bearing parade of *Hydro-pathes* costumed like Swiss Guards, led by a flamboyant mountebank, Rodolphe Salis.

Prior to opening his cabaret, Salis, an artist of modest talent, and three of his painter friends, had eked out a living by painting cheap religious paintings. Each friend contributed to the product, the Stations of the Cross, according to his specialty, drawing and painting faces, bodies, draperies, or background. But in a marketplace glutted with shoddy art-work the scheme could never prove lucrative. On the other hand, Salis's idea for a new cabaret was, like Oller and Zidler's Moulin Rouge, a stroke of entrepreneurial genius, meeting a demand for bawdy, avant-garde entertainment in exactly the right place at the right time.

Salis based his interior design for the cabaret on a fanciful seventeenth-century tavern that might have been frequented by Cyrano de Bergerac or Dumas père's Musketeers. Customers sat at long wooden tables in a hall lit by cast iron chandeliers. Paintings and posters decorated the walls, and Salis added iron, glass, and stone *objets d'art*, the genesis of Art Nouveau.

In addition to serving cheap wine and absinthe to his thirsty crowd, Salis provided an innovative form of amusement—the stage was open to anyone who had the daring to take it and the fortitude to hold it. On a given night a genius like Verlaine might recite one of his poems, but for the most part the performers were amateurs. And Salis encouraged these naïve hopefuls with free absinthe.

Fortified with cheap liquor, the trembling tyro would brave his audi-ence like the condemned at the guillotine, showing his grit to the blood-thirsty mob. He would begin his quavering declamation in relative silence, which he might mistake for rapt interest. But the performer would soon be disabused by the rowdy audience, consisting of all classes, almost all of whom were pissing drunk.

The merry crowd would pelt the poor performer with sarcastic invec-tive the way their forbears showered a pilloried criminal with rotten veg-etables, dung, piss, and offal. This was jolly good fun, especially when the scorned and rejected artist fled the premises and wandered off into the darkness crying tears of despair and harboring suicidal thoughts. This theater of the cruel and absurd appealed to Toulouse-Lautrec.

Salis guarded the entrance, where he greeted his customers sarcasti-cally, saving his most singular insults for celebrities and regulars. "Hey Lautrec, what have you done with our sweet, little Virginie? I hear the cops are dragging the Seine for her body."

Lautrec laughed while noting, with some concern, that this was the second time someone had alluded to Virginie Ménard's disappearance. Inured to the impresario's caustic wit, Lautrec hobbled over to his favorite spot at the foot of a table, where he ordered absinthe and began recording the scene in pastels on brown paper. He was soon joined by Émile Bernard. The young man seemed agitated.

"Where have you been hiding, Émile? I haven't seen you," Lautrec checked his watch, "for at least *six whole hours*. Pull up a chair, old man, and have a drink."

Bernard sat and stared wildly at Lautrec. "I've been running round looking for Mademoiselle Ménard. I talked to her concierge, to Cormon, to Zidler, and to her best friend, Delphine; nobody's seen her for days."

Lautrec took a deep breath and smiled. "You worry too much. They all turn up, sooner or later."

"This isn't funny, Henri. People are worried, and you're taking it awfully cool. After all, she was your model and your—"

Lautrec put up his hand and shook his head. "If you were about to say 'lover' that was true once, but no longer. Mademoiselle has since moved on to greener pastures. That is to say, she has abandoned me for those who can better afford her charms and talents. But if you and others are concerned as to her whereabouts, why not go to the police?"

"If she doesn't turn up soon, I believe that's what I'll do."

Lautrec shrugged. "Do as you please," he muttered, and then returned to his sketch.

⌒∞⌒

Shortly thereafter, they were interrupted: "Hello Lautrec, Bernard. Do you mind if I join you?"

"Not at all, Sir Henry," Lautrec replied. Lautrec and Bernard had become acquainted with Sir Henry Collingwood at Cormon's *Atelier*.

Lautrec and Sir Henry had formed a special bond, a consequence of the doctor's interest in art and the artist's interest in surgery.

Sir Henry settled in and ordered a drink. He glanced round the room to see if he could recognize anyone, and then lit a cigar. Relaxed, he leaned back, tucked a thumb in his waistcoat pocket and blew a few smoke rings. After a moment he remarked, "I say, Lautrec, I saw you at Péan's clinic today. A neat little hysterectomy, eh what?"

Lautrec raised his eyebrows in surprise. "I don't recall seeing you there?"

Sir Henry smiled. "Oh, I can be a furtive fellow, at times. Besides, you were concentrating on the operation and your sketch. I doubt you would have noticed if Gabriel had blown the last trumpet." Sir Henry and Lautrec laughed. Then the doctor turned his attention to Émile, who seemed pensive and detached. "Why so gloomy, Bernard?"

Émile remained silent. Lautrec answered for him. "He's worried about a girl gone missing."

"Oh, that's too bad," Sir Henry said. He placed a hand on Bernard's shoulder sympathetically and asked, "Do I know her, Émile?"

Bernard turned his sad eyes toward the doctor. "I believe you do, Sir Henry. She's the pretty little blonde we sketched at the *Atelier*."

The doctor stared blankly for a moment and then his eyes brightened. "Yes, of course, that was Mademoiselle uh—Mademoiselle Ménard. I saw Lautrec's portrait of her at Joyant's gallery. Well, let's hope she turns up soon. By the way, here's an odd coincidence. I'm treating another admirer of Mademoiselle Ménard and the portrait, an American artist, Marcia Brownlow. Do either of you know her?"

"I do," said Lautrec. "She and her rich companion were at the Moulin Rouge a few evenings ago. I thought they were going to make an offer for my painting, but I've heard nothing since."

"Oh, I see. I'm afraid Miss Brownlow is quite ill. Her friend, Miss Endicott, is making arrangements to return to America as soon as Miss Brownlow can travel, and I will accompany them to a sanatorium."

"I'm sorry, gentlemen, I don't see what this has to do with Virginie. If you'll excuse me." With that curt declaration, Bernard got up and left the cabaret.

Sir Henry watched Émile go out the door, then turned to Lautrec. "Poor fellow. I diagnose a case of Virginie on the brain. I suppose he's sweet on her."

Lautrec muttered, "Perhaps." He turned his attention to a slender man walking toward the piano. "You see the man who's about to play?"

Sir Henry screwed a monocle into his eye and gazed across the smoke-filled hall. "Yes; who is he?"

"His name's Satie; not bad, really. The crowd listens when he plays."

⌯∞⌯

Lautrec abandoned Le Chat Noir in the early morning hours. He ventured into the rabbit's warren of dark, narrow streets snaking up the hill. His button-hook tapping the cobblestones, the artist limped painfully up a murky, echoing brick cavern roofed over by a cloudy, moonless sky. Cats crouching in cubbyholes hissed and yowled as he passed. Gaslamps glowed, their feeble yellow flames lighting his way toward his favorite whorehouse. There the artist would drink, sketch, and joke with the girls, afterward engaging in a game of rumpy-pumpy until the sun rose, shining its light on the alabaster dome of Sacré-Cœur.

Puffing with fatigue from the steep walk, Lautrec rested under a lamp and reached into his coat pocket for his cigarette case. Unable to locate the case, he muttered, "Damn," then patted and rummaged round in his other pockets until he found a packet of cigarettes and a box of matches.

Continuing up a flight of steps, the always perceptive artist failed to notice someone tailing him, a silent observer lurking in the shadows. As Lautrec approached the brothel, a powerful stench assaulted his nostrils. Staring ahead he noticed a familiar form, the oval iron tank of a sewage wagon parked beside a cesspit. The night soil collectors were pumping human waste, some of which had slopped over onto the pavement where it commingled with piles of horse dung and unswept rubbish. Lautrec cautiously skirted the work area and proceeded to the *maison*, where he rang for the madam.

The proprietress, a feather-bedecked trull with flaming red hair, recognized the little gentleman and greeted him with a grin. But her smile soon turned to a comical grimace as she got a whiff of the street. Lifting a perfumed handkerchief to her nose, she urged, "Quickly, Monsieur, come in before my house fills with miasma." Lautrec crossed the threshold, chuckling at the madam's unscientific objection to the stench.

The stalker watched from an unlit passageway between two houses across the street. As Lautrec entered the brothel, the stealthy observer made a mental note of the time and address.

∽∾∾

Nine years earlier, during the hot months of August and September, Paris experienced the Great Stink, a foul, putrid odor that pervaded the entire city. Many Parisians feared the "miasma," which they believed was the source of typhoid and cholera. The bacteriologists, led by Pasteur, pointed to the microscopic source of the stench as the cause of epidemic diseases. There was a fuss in the press and the harried government formed a commission to study the matter, raising a debate about the sewer system and the methods of waste disposal. In the end, with cooler weather the stink disappeared, the feared epidemic never materialized, and the city's methods of dealing with human excreta remained, for the most part, unchanged. In the early morning hours, hundreds of foul-smelling sewer wagons rumbled through the streets of Paris, cleaning out cesspools and cesspits and emptying waste receptacles in thousands of cellars.

This night, the two night soil collectors finished pumping, closed the pipe, mounted their wagon and moved on. Dressed in their typical workers' blouse and cap, incessantly puffing on clay pipes to mask the stench of their trade, the collectors bantered and cracked jokes to break the monotony. The older man managed the reins and the brake; their powerful gray horse strained against its leather traces, pulling the heavy load uphill. The young man connected the hose and worked the pneumatic pump at each stop.

They were nearing the end of their run on the Rue Tourlaque. Soon, they would journey through the city to a central collection point on the Seine embankment, where the waste would be emptied into tanker barges for transport to a suburban sewage farm. The senior man, Papa Lebœuf, a burly fellow of fifty with a grizzled beard flowing halfway down his chest, halted the wagon. "All right Jacques, last call for this morning."

"Thank God," the younger man said as he sprang from his perch onto the pavement. A wiry fellow with thick, brawny arms and powerful hands, Jacques un-reeled the rubber hose, connected the nozzle to a pipe, and returned to the wagon to work the pump. After a moment he growled, "Damn! It's stuck; something must be clogging the pipe."

"Bloody hell!" cried Lebœuf. "That's just our luck; trouble on the last damned job on our route. Well, I guess you better pull up the manhole cover and we'll take a look." He grabbed a long pole with a hook and held a lantern while Jacques tied a handkerchief over his face and opened the cesspool.

As Lebœuf approached the open hole with his lantern, Jacques warned:

"Hey, Papa, stand back with that lantern. There might be a gas leak."

"I know, dammit. I've been cleaning out shit-holes since before you were born." He handed the pole to Jacques and stood back, shining the light into the cesspool.

Jacques grabbed the implement and poked round the masonry-lined receptacle. "God, what a stink," he muttered. Then: "Hey, Papa, I've got something. It looks like some bastard dumped a hunk of meat wrapped in a cloth."

Lebœuf snorted in disgust. "I'd like to make the damned fool clean out every shit-hole on this hill. Well, no use bitching about it. Go ahead and fish it out."

Jacques hauled up the smelly object and flung it onto the pavement where it landed with a thud. Papa turned the light on it. When they saw what it was their eyes widened. The younger man looked away, gagged, and retched.

Papa Lebœuf was proud of his strong stomach, but the bloody thing they fished out of a Montmartre cesspool that morning would haunt his dreams for the remainder of his life.

5

THE INVESTIGATION

D awn crept over Paris. The Île de la Cité emerged from the shadows; the sun, an orange disc in a slate sky, shone its pale rays through a cloud bar onto the grimy gothic towers of Notre Dame. Nearby, on the south bank of the Seine, in an office building on the Quai des Orfèvres, Paul Féraud, Chief Inspector of the Sûreté, began his day with coffee, bread, and a mysterious police report.

Mote-sprinkled light streamed through half-opened blinds; an oil lamp burned feebly on Féraud's cluttered mahogany desk. The streets below were quiet; a good time for the chief to work and to think through a problem. He took advantage of this early hour to review new reports of unusual suspected homicides, his specialty. A thirty-year veteran, Féraud had risen through the ranks, learning his profession in the hard school of experience.

The office was a study in organized confusion: files, dossiers, reference books, photographs, strewn about in an order known only to the chief. Among the papers littering his desktop stood a gleaming brass telephone, the aforementioned green-shaded lamp, a photograph of Féraud's late wife in a black-crepe-decorated silver frame, and photographs of the Chief's four adult children: three married daughters and a son in the military. In addition, there was a cigar box, a copper ashtray with an engraving of the Eiffel Tower, and a curiosity, a guillotine cigar cutter, a gift from the "old boys" on the force in recognition of their chief's thirty years of public service.

The drab gray-green painted walls were lined with dusty bookshelves and cabinets overflowing with paperwork, curios, and memorabilia. On the wall opposite the chief's desk hung the Rogue's Gallery, a grouping of photographic portraits of criminals brought to justice by Féraud, many mounted side by side with photographs of their guillotined heads posed on slabs in the Morgue.

One particular file had just arrived and it occupied the chief that morning. It had, pursuant to his instructions, been marked "Urgent" and rushed to him by special courier. The file contained a police report concerning a female torso discovered in a Montmartre cesspit by a pair of night soil collectors. The sergeant on duty had immediately notified Féraud; that was at five A.M. (the time the chief arrived at his office each morning) and this too was according to instructions. Moreover, the police had erected a rope-line barricade and assigned a gendarme to guard the area, preventing the curious from contaminating the scene with their footprints, cigar and cigarette butts, and so forth.

Paris was full of tourists, the closing ceremony of the Universal Exposition was only two weeks away, and the Whitechapel Murders of 1888 were fresh on everyone's mind. Scotland Yard's widely publicized failure in that case had placed all detectives and their methods under a dark cloud of popular mistrust. Any hint in the press that Jack the Ripper had crossed the channel could cause panic, not to mention embarrassment to the police and the government. Therefore, as a precautionary measure, a preliminary report of any suspected homicide resembling the Ripper's *modus operandi* went directly to the Chief Inspector as a matter of the highest priority.

The detailed description of the body disgusted Féraud and, as always, filled him with a sense of outrage. Though he had seen many horrific things in his years on the force, he always wondered what drove people to commit such crimes. Gruesome photographs would be taken at the scene and at the Morgue later that morning, before and after the autopsy. He scratched his short, graying beard. *It could be a prank.* He hoped that was the case, that some medical students or drunken riffraff had gotten hold of a cadaver and dumped it into the cesspit as a hoax. Paris was a world-renowned medical center, after all, and cadavers quite easy to come by. *Stupid bastards*, he muttered. But then, what if it wasn't a hoax? He could not afford to take chances, to make a mistake that might cost other women their lives. A knock on the door interrupted the chief's train of thought. *It must be Achille.* "Enter," he growled.

A tall, slender man of thirty entered the office and stood at attention before his chief. Inspector Achille Lefebvre was a new breed of detective, a graduate of the prestigious École Polytechnique, a fervent advocate for scientific methods of detection. Achille's pale, clean-shaven face, near-sighted blue eyes aided by a gold-rimmed pince-nez, and stiff, soft-spoken manner made him seem an "odd fish" to the veterans. The old boys had nicknamed him the professor, but after five years on the force Achille had gained their grudging respect, not to mention what mattered most—the confidence of their chief.

The chief smiled at the young man's soldierly stiffness. "Relax, Achille; take a load off your feet. You've got plenty of legwork ahead of you, my boy." Achille sat in a small armchair on the other side of the desk; Féraud handed over the file. After giving him a minute to scan the report, the chief continued: "You're going up to Montmartre on the Morgue meat wagon. Take Rousseau and a good photographer. Do you know the neighborhood?"

"Yes, sir, it's a quiet area near the summit of the hill."

Féraud nodded. "Yes, it *was* quiet and I want to keep it that way. I've already given a release to the newspapers: Body of unknown female discovered in Montmartre. And that's all they'll get until we make a positive identification. Give them any more and the reporters and morbid curiosity-seekers will be swarming Montmartre hill like flies on a turd. Anyway, let's hope this is all a stupid prank, but for now we'll proceed as though it's a homicide. To begin, we know from the report that the night soil collectors had last pumped the cesspool the morning of the 13th. So the body must have been dumped between then and this morning's collection.

"Start gathering evidence and question the residents at that address. We're a long way from going to the *juge d'instruction* for a warrant. There's a gendarme guarding the scene and they've set up a barricade. You've worked with Rousseau before; he's a good man and you both know the drill. When you've got what you want, you and the photographer can take the body to the Morgue on the meat wagon. Rousseau will stay in Montmartre to interview the neighbors.

"I'll contact Bertillon. He owes me a favor or two, and I'm going to ask him to supervise the autopsy and work directly with you. Telephone the Morgue from the Montmartre station to confirm the appointment. When you've finished at the Morgue you may go home, but I want you and Rousseau in my office with a written report first thing tomorrow morning. Any questions?"

Achille had no questions; as his chief had said, he knew the drill. And he was well aware of the urgency of the situation with the Universal Exposition ongoing and the fear whipped up by lurid newspaper accounts of Jack the Ripper. His wife and mother-in-law would ask, "Will Féraud permit you to eat and sleep?" But of course, the question was rhetorical. As the old boys said, your hours at the Sûreté were from midnight to midnight.

⌒∞⌒

When he arrived at the police barricade Achille was relieved to find things quiet and orderly. He was greeted by Sergeant Rodin, a beefy man with a long, drooping red moustache, a gruff voice, and a gimlet eye. "There it is, Inspector." Rodin pointed to a large lump on the pavement, covered by a white cloth splotched with ochre-colored stains, next to the cesspit. According to the report, the torso was found wrapped in the cloth. "No fuss, so far, but the landlady is upset."

Achille made a quick mental note of the stains on the cloth: *Could be paint—or blood.* Then: "Does she know the cause of the stoppage?"

Rodin grinned and shook his head. "No, she doesn't. The only ones who know about the stiff are me, my men, the night soil collectors, and the person, or persons, who dumped it."

"That gives us a little time, I suppose, but sooner or later the press will get nosy, especially after we start questioning people. And there's a damned dirty job ahead. Where are the sewer cleaners? We need them to pump and rake out the sludge. Then the muck must be searched for evidence."

Rodin grimaced and checked his watch. "They should be here soon, Inspector."

Achille glanced up. The gray clouds looked threatening; he and his crew would need to work fast. Rain could wash away clues. It had rained intermittently the past few days. God only knew what had already been lost. He continued with urgency. "Who lives here besides the landlady?"

"She's the only one on the premises. The upper story is rented by a painter, Monsieur de Toulouse-Lautrec. He uses it as his studio."

Achille raised his eyebrows. "Toulouse-Lautrec. Is he related to the Count?"

Rodin chuckled. "He's the son and heir, Inspector. An odd fellow; if you saw him once you'd never forget him. He's a sawed-off cripple, no more than 150 centimeters in his shoes, and he hobbles along with the aid of a tiny cane. Monsieur's legs are stunted, but he has the body, arms, and hands of a normal man with better than average strength. He looks like a circus ape dressed in swell's clothing. Black hair, thick black beard, dark brown eyes, and he peers through a pince-nez sort of like yours, Monsieur. Speaks like a toff, which is to say like the son of a count. Oh, and he's got big ears, a bulbous nose, and thick, purplish lips. No mistaking him in a crowd."

Achille commended the Sergeant for his *portrait parlé*. Then: "Does the gentleman live hereabouts?"

The Sergeant rubbed his chin. "Not *too* far, Monsieur. He rents an apartment on the Rue Pierre-Fontaine in the 9th *arrondissement*, near one of his hangouts, the Moulin Rouge. He goes there to drink and draw pictures, and you can find him doing the same in the cabarets, *bal musettes*, *maisons close*, and *boîtes*. He's a well-known figure in Montmartre and Pigalle. And there's more. Like most of these fellows, he likes to have a little sport with his models. No doubt, he pays well. And there're rumors about shouting matches and violence between Monsieur and his *lorettes*."

"Thank you, sergeant." Achille asked Rodin to give Lautrec's name and address to Rousseau for his list; he was definitely a person of interest.

"I hope we don't have the Ripper on our hands. It would be awful if the butchering bastard turned out to be a stunted French aristocrat," Rodin quipped with a sly wink.

Achille winced in response to his friend's gallows humor. Then he left the sergeant and walked toward the cesspit and the corpse, where Gilles, the photographer, had set up his camera. Gilles was a dapper young man, blue-eyed and fair-haired with a neat little waxed moustache. Dressed unseasonably in a white suit with a straw boater set at a jaunty angle on his handsome head, he looked more like a *flâneur* at Le Touquet than a crime scene photographer, but that appearance was deceiving. Gilles was one of the best in his profession.

"Hey Inspector, I've already got several photographs of the scene. Is there anything else you want before I pack up my equipment?"

"Yes, there is." Achille pulled a magnifying glass out of his jacket pocket and crouched beside the stained cloth covering the torso. He focused on the ochre stains; as he suspected, they were handprints. What's more, the fingerprints were distinguishable, especially the thumb and forefinger of a right hand.

The prints intrigued Achille. Bertillon had not incorporated finger-prints in his identification method and neither Scotland Yard nor any other eminent criminal investigation division had a system for using them. Moreover, he was unaware of fingerprints having ever been admitted into evidence in a criminal case. But he had read a recently published paper by the English anthropologist Sir Francis Galton which made a persuasive argument for the unique individuality of prints and set forth a method for categorizing them that could prove useful in criminal cases. Achille lowered his glass, turned and looked up at Gilles. "Can you get a sharp image of the fingerprints?"

Gilles shook his head. "That'd be awfully tricky out here. I might do better back at headquarters with a change of lenses, faster plates, filters, and flash powder."

"Very well, please do that." Achille got up and circled the manhole cover. Something half-hidden by the cover caught his eye. Crouching, he spotted a cigarette butt smoked almost out of existence. "Gilles," he cried, "Have you been smoking?"

"Of course not, Inspector; I know better than that."

Achille lifted the butt with tweezers. He sniffed and eyed it carefully. "No, this was smoked some time ago. If it was the gendarme there'll be hell to pay. Where's Rodin?"

"Over there, by the meat wagon, talking to Rousseau and the Morgue attendant."

Achille whistled to get the sergeant's attention and then gestured for him to come over. "Hey Rodin, look at this cigarette butt. Have any of your men smoked around the barricade?"

"No Inspector, they're under strict orders not to."

"Do you think one of the night soil collectors could have dropped it?"

Rodin shook his head. "No, that's a gentleman's smoke. The ladies like them too."

Achille smiled at the sergeant. "That's very perceptive, Rodin. Have you ever thought of coming to work for us?"

The sergeant smiled broadly. "That's kind of you Monsieur, but I'm quite happy where I am."

"Well, that's our loss, I guess." Achille had learned that it paid to be friendly with the gendarmerie. They did their duty, but they would go the extra mile for an Inspector they liked. "Could you please ask Inspector Rousseau to come over here?" Rodin went to fetch Achille's partner.

Achille dropped the cigarette butt in an evidence bag. He made a final inspection of the area. As he walked the perimeter of the barricade, he noticed a small pile of dung near the curb. It was not fresh and he had noticed it before, but now he suddenly realized he had missed something. One of the droppings had been flattened, or squashed. He knelt down, and almost stuck his nose in it.

"What's the matter, professor, aren't they feeding you enough at home?"

Achille turned and looked up at Rousseau's grinning moon face. "Don't you see it, Rousseau?"

"Yes, professor, I see it. It's a pile of horseshit. Lots of them just like it on the streets of Paris."

Achille sighed in exasperation. "It's a shoeprint! My God, how could we have missed it?"

Rousseau lowered his bulk to a squat. "Damn it, you're right." Then he sprang up and pointed to a few prints on the pavement. "Look here and here, and then they stop; but all in the direction of the cesspit."

"We have something, Rousseau. Our man left the sidewalk here, carrying the body. He stepped in the dung, stopped to scrape off the sole, and then continued on to the cesspit. Look, I can draw a line from here to where I picked up the cigarette butt."

Thoughts whirled round Achille's brain: *Did he carry the body from one of these houses or did he use a vehicle of some sort? He couldn't have carried it far; someone would have noticed. But there are no more footprints, and if he used a cart or wagon there are no marks, nothing discernible on the pavement.*

Achille pulled out a ruler and measured the shoeprint and the length of the stride. They belonged to a very small individual. But the handprints were large, and he would have been strong enough to carry the torso, lift the manhole cover, and stuff the remains into the cesspit. Achille remembered the sergeant's description of Toulouse-Lautrec: *Monsieur's legs are stunted, but he has the body, arms, and hands of a normal man with better than average strength.*

"Gilles," he cried, "I want you to photograph something up here." Then to Rousseau: "I'm going to try to make a plaster cast of the shoeprint."

"You're the boss, professor, but have you ever made a cast of a turd?"

"There's a first time for everything, Rousseau."

◦∞◦

The Morgue was a modern building erected on the Île de la Cité following the demolition of the medieval slums vividly described in Hugo's *Notre Dame de Paris*. Upon entering, a visitor could look up and read the noble sentiments of The Republic: "Liberty! Equality! Fraternity!" Some might ponder a grim truth implicit in the revolutionary motto, for in this place the dead barons, bourgeoisie, and beggars were liberated from class distinctions and thus equal in fact rather than theory.

The Morgue was open to the public from morning to closing at six P.M. The morbidly curious with time on their hands came to gawk. They milled round the gas-lit corridors, gathering before immense plate glass windows, shivering in the cold air and inhaling the sharp odor of chlorine disinfectant, rubbernecking at the frozen *macchabées*—Parisian slang for corpses—whose naked bodies were propped up for display on steel slabs. Refrigeration was a recent improvement over the older preservation method: cold running water that gave the corpses a bloated, discolored appearance and chemicals that exuded an eerie, grayish-green mist round the bodies.

Many of the corpses on display were suicides fished out of the nearby river; some were murder victims whose bodies had been dumped by their killers. Regardless, all remained unidentified; the authorities hoped that viewers might recognize a loved one, friend, acquaintance, or co-worker. Indeed, some came to the Morgue searching for a lost relative, viewing the cadavers in the hope that identification might provide certainty and some closure to their personal tragedy. But, as with public executions, most just came for the show.

The Morgue attendant parked the meat wagon in a dark, narrow, cobblestoned passageway and unloaded the torso onto a trolley. He wheeled the corpse through a guarded back entrance closed to the public; Achille displayed his credentials and followed along with Gilles toting his camera and tripod. They passed through a murky corridor until they made a sharp right turn and entered a small, low-ceilinged dissection room.

The place reeked of carbolic disinfectant and formaldehyde. A blood-stained dissecting table stood in the middle of the room under a blazing gaslamp. Next to the table was a tray covered with neatly arranged scalpels, probes, forceps, clamps, and sutures. A mahogany and glass instrument cabinet occupied a corner of the drab, green-painted wall behind the dissection table. Two vividly colored folding anatomical charts with cutaway views—one male, one female—hung from the wall.

The gray-haired pathologist greeted them with a cold, bored stare. He had cut up too many corpses, a slave to routine like a factory worker who, over the years, had turned innumerable bolts on countless widgets. In contrast, Alphonse Bertillon was animated and enthusiastic.

Bertillon was an up-and-comer in his mid-thirties with a neatly trimmed beard, curious eyes, and a brisk manner. His brilliant career had begun ten years earlier, as a records clerk. Immediately recognizing the need for a better system of filing and organization, he pushed his new ideas on his superiors until they gave way from sheer exhaustion.

Young Bertillon was a force of nature, like a youthful Bonaparte telling old generals how to do their jobs. Having cleaned up the records system, he turned his attention to a better method of identification. Before long, the police had adopted his anthropometric system, incorporating multiple photographs, careful attention to features, and numerous, precise measurements. Now chief of the department of identification for the prefecture of the Seine, Bertillon was at the top of his profession, but he had not yet recognized the significance of fingerprints, a fact of which Achille was keenly aware.

His sleeves rolled up and ready to proceed, Bertillon smiled and extended his hand. "Pleased to meet you, Inspector Lefebvre. I'm Bertillon. I've heard good things about you from your chief. You've brought me an interesting case—a very interesting case indeed." Bertillon spoke rapidly, leaping from sentence to sentence and thought to thought with the agility of an intellectual acrobat.

Achille admired Bertillon; he shook his hand warmly. "I'm honored, Monsieur. As you say, it's an interesting case, and a tough one to crack."

"Well, perhaps we can simplify things. Let's take a closer look at the corpse. We have a moment while your photographer sets up his equipment, and there are some observations I can make before the doctor opens her up." Achille followed Bertillon to the dissecting table, where the chief began his remarks with a theatrical flourish. Pointing a finger at the torso, he declared, "Keen observation and clear thinking can solve any mystery. We don't chase our tails, we don't waste time. For example, certain things are obvious to the trained eye. Your chief questioned whether this might have been a prank; some tipsy medical students stuffing a cadaver in the cesspit. But cadavers are embalmed prior to dissection, and the embalming fluid causes a grayish discoloration. That is not present here. On the other hand, if you look closely, you'll notice a slight greenish spot on the lower abdomen. That is the first sign of decomposition. By that spot alone, I can place the time of death from forty-eight to seventy-two hours ago, and further examination can confirm my hypothesis and perhaps narrow it down. Do you know how long she was in the pit?"

"About forty-eight hours at most, Monsieur; the time between collections."

"Ah then, whomever left the corpse would have known the schedule. And we can estimate the interval between the time of death and deposit in the cesspit. Then we'll posit as to how the corpse was transported and from whence it came."

Achille took out a pencil and pad and began scribbling notes.

Bertillon smiled at his attentive pupil and continued: "There are no visible signs of exposure to the elements, animals, or insects. Her skin is smooth and quite lovely, even with the pallor of death. We must look for scars, moles, birthmarks, tattoos or other identifying marks. Hmmm, nothing on the front. Let's turn her over, doctor." Bertillon and the pathologist rolled the torso onto its stomach, and then examined the neck, shoulders, back, buttocks, and thighs. "One small mole on lower right buttock; one smaller mole inner lower left thigh. We'll measure them, and you'll note them in the photographs. All right, doctor, let's turn her right side up."

Bertillon continued: "She was very fair, Inspector, and beautifully proportioned. A little, blonde Venus de Milo. I'll make careful measurements and extrapolate her height and weight. Considering her skin color and fine, fair vestigial hair she most probably had light blue eyes. Now here's something of significance. Either she, or someone else, has shaved her armpits and pubic hair; there's nothing but fair stubble. Generally speaking, women of the lower classes don't shave their body hair, and few women of any class, with the exception of artists' models, shave the *mons pubis*. Considering these facts, her symmetrical proportions and beautiful skin, one might conclude that this woman had been a model." Bertillon paused a moment, as if for dramatic effect. Gazing intently at Achille, he added ominously: "But there's another explanation for the shaved pubic hair, although it doesn't necessarily negate my proposition that she was an artist's model. The woman may have had an operation, and quite recently."

That last remark got the blasé pathologist's attention. He lowered his wire-rimmed spectacles, which until then had been pushed up onto his forehead, as if he anticipated viewing something of consequence.

Bertillon turned to the pathologist. "Doctor, will you please examine the vagina?"

The doctor put on a head mirror and spread the vulva; Bertillon and Achille leaned over for a closer look. The pathologist spoke first: "You see that, gentleman? A fresh surgical wound; a neat incision cleanly sutured." He inserted a speculum and performed a pelvic examination.

"Doctor," asked Bertillon, "do you know what sort of operation this was?"

The pathologist backed away from the corpse and wiped his hands with a towel. He eyed Bertillon and Achille with a worried frown. "I'd say it was a vaginal hysterectomy. I'll confirm that for the record when I open her up. But—" The pathologist stopped speaking, and stared as if suddenly struck dumb.

Bertillon's impatience was palpable. "But what, doctor? Please continue."

The pathologist breathed deeply and exhaled slowly before continuing: "The uterus is usually removed through a large incision made in the lower abdomen just above the pubic bone. This operation through the vagina is rare. As far as I know, only one surgeon in Paris has performed it successfully—Péan." The doctor lowered his eyes and stared at his hands.

Achille turned to Bertillon. "Péan? Is that possible, Monsieur? Could he be a—a suspect?"

"Péan—the great Péan? That's unthinkable!" sputtered the pathologist.

"Please, gentleman," Bertillon said calmly, "we must not jump to conclusions. Anything is *possible*, but to suspect Péan is, as the doctor puts it, unthinkable. Still, this is certainly a lead we must follow. I know Péan; he's given lectures at the Morgue. He may provide us with information that is useful in solving the case. Now, Inspector, before we proceed is there anything else you want me to consider?"

"A couple of things, Monsieur. We're going to search the contents of the cesspit. If I find anything of interest, I'll bring it to you immediately."

"Very well, Inspector. Anything else?"

"Yes, Monsieur. The torso was wrapped in a sheet smeared with what appear to be bloodstains. There are perceptible handprints and fingerprints; I want them photographed to see if they can be enhanced. They might prove useful."

Bertillon's eyes narrowed. "Fingerprints, eh? Of course you know we don't use them in our system?"

Achille replied firmly, "I understand, but I believe in a matter like this we shouldn't overlook anything that might help solve the case."

Bertillon's stare turned to a smile. He placed a hand on Achille's shoulder. "I can see why your chief values you so highly. Very well. Have the cloth sent to my laboratory. I'll examine the fabric and the prints as well. Your photographer can take before and after images for the file."

Relieved, Achille smiled warmly. "Thank you, Monsieur. I look forward to working with you."

⌾

Following the autopsy, Achille stopped at a café, purchased a bottle of beer and a sandwich, and returned to his office. He sent a message to his wife, Adele, and told her not to wait supper for him. He then typed his report for Féraud. The old boys hated the typewriter; they refused to use it, and the chief did not insist. But Achille had mastered the new machine, and he preferred its neatness and uniformity to the typical detective's scrawl.

As he worked he could not shake the image of the torso on the dissection table. What sort of monster could have committed such a crime? It's as though the Devil had come to Montmartre. Might the Devil have been a deformed, aristocratic painter, or France's greatest surgeon? Could it be Jack the Ripper, as Rodin implied in his morbid joke? *Don't jump to conclusions*. They knew so little, but hopefully in the coming days they would learn more. Could the murderer strike again? Scotland Yard's failure in the Ripper murders loomed large.

Shortly after ten P.M., Achille finished typing his report, closed his file, rubbed his weary eyes, turned out the lights, and headed for home.

☙

Achille, his wife Adele, their four-year-old daughter Jeanne, and Adele's mother, Madame Berthier, lived in a spacious second-floor apartment in the 1st *arrondissement*, not far from Sûreté headquarters. The building was one of Baron Haussmann's elegant modern creations, located on a quiet, tree-shaded avenue. The apartment belonged to Madame Berthier, widow of a much decorated cavalry colonel, a fervent Bonapartist and friend of General Boulanger.

Achille paid rent to Madame and she retained a commodious boudoir and an adjoining study. This arrangement allowed the family to live a very comfortable bourgeois life, much better than that of a typical civil servant of Achille's rank. They could even afford a maid, a cook, and a nanny for the little girl.

Achille got along reasonably well with his mother-in-law, despite the fact that she disliked his chosen profession. She had formed an image of detectives from the first Sûreté chief, Vidocq, who employed reformed criminals like himself, on the theory that it takes a thief to catch a thief. She also railed against the government for its treatment of General Boulanger, looked forward to a war of revenge against Germany, and blamed the Germans, their Jewish bankers, Protestants, and Freemasons for all the evils of mankind. Achille found Madame's politics and prejudices illogical and distasteful. But as a good husband and son-in-law he tried to maintain peace at home. Therefore, whenever in conversation with Madame Berthier, Achille avoided discussing his job, politics, or anything controversial; if she raised these matters he simply nodded sympathetically, tried to switch the subject, or if possible, politely excused himself.

When he arrived home that evening, his mother-in-law had already retired to her boudoir. Adele greeted him in the front hall, with a petulant frown:

"Cook made your favorite cassoulet for supper, and Jeanne wanted you to read her a story before she went to sleep. She cried when I told her you weren't coming. Why can't Féraud be more considerate? He works you like a slave."

Achille's eyes were sad and tired; the last thing he wanted was an argument. He smiled and stroked Adele's soft cheek. *Such bright green eyes; such warm red lips. How pretty she is*, he thought. He noticed a change in her expression from mild vexation to deep concern. "Please my dear," he whispered, "I'm dog-tired. Féraud's assigned me to a case of the utmost importance and I must report to him at five A.M."

She held his hand and kissed it softly. "I'm sorry, darling; how thoughtless of me. Go relax in the sitting-room, and I'll join you. Would you like a cognac, or sherry?"

Achille smiled. "A cognac would be heaven." Adele went to fetch the brandy. He wandered into the sitting room and collapsed in his favorite, well-stuffed armchair. Placing his aching feet on a footstool, he rubbed his eyes and yawned. Achille wanted to forget the case and get a good night's sleep, but he knew he wouldn't; it would occupy his thoughts, day and night, until the murderer was brought to justice.

Adele returned with a decanter and two glasses on a silver tray. Her husband did not seem to notice her; he was staring into the darkness like someone sleeping with his eyes open. She set down the tray on a small round table and then turned up the lamp. "It's too dark in here."

Achille murmured, "Huh," as if coming out of a trance. Adele was about to sit next to him on a settee. He reached out, took her hand and pulled her onto his lap. She giggled as he nibbled her tiny earlobe and nuzzled her fragrant neck. Achille wanted her; he needed to forget his job, to erase the horror of it from his mind. His hands cupped the soft material over her breasts. She sighed, and his mouth covered hers, his tongue making a gentle entrance into her sweet mouth. He closed his eyes and started lifting her dress until the naked torso on the dissection table broke into his mind like a thief in the night. Achille shuddered, and then pulled away from her gently. Smiling nervously, he muttered, "You see how much I've missed you? Anyway, I'm ready for that brandy."

Adele frowned with disappointment, but she poured the drinks without complaint.

6

The regulator clock on the wall facing Féraud's desk registered five A.M. On the walls and ceiling, gas jets hissed and glowed greenish yellow. The chief sprang the guillotine; the blade clipped the tip of his cigar neatly. Féraud plucked the severed "head" from a little basket and dumped it into the ashtray. He struck a match, lit up, and took a few deep, satisfying puffs.

Fat Rousseau mopped sweat from his low forehead. The chief had an old-fashioned aversion to night vapors and kept the windows shut tightly until dawn. Achille sat next to his partner across from the chief, nervously anticipating Féraud's response to his report. Rousseau turned to Achille and gave him a furtive wink, as if to say: *Don't worry professor, we've got it covered*.

Féraud closed the file, rested his cigar in the ashtray, and leaned back in his chair. He closed his eyes as if in deep concentration and fiddled with a charm on his watch chain, a golden skull with glowing ruby eyes. After a tense moment, he leaned forward, stared at his subordinates, and cracked a smile. "Good work, men."

Achille and Rousseau breathed sighs of relief.

Féraud continued: "Achille, you're going directly to La Villette to sift through the muck?"

"Yes, sir. The cesspit contents are being held in a shed near the quay. When I'm finished, I'm returning to the Morgue to meet with Chief Bertillon and Dr. Péan."

Rousseau laughed. "I pity you, professor. From the slaughterhouse and shit barges of La Villette to the putrefying stiffs. You'll need to bathe in perfume before you go home."

Achille tried to smile in response to his partner's crude humor, but it came off looking like a wince of pain. He continued with his itinerary. "Following the meeting, I'll go to Bertillon's laboratory to pick up a copy of the pathologist's report, a chemical analysis, and some information concerning the cloth, the footprints, and the cigarette butt. All we've got so far is a headless torso. Bertillon will provide an estimate of the woman's height, weight, and physical appearance, including the distinguishing marks. From there, I'll go to records to check the missing persons' reports." Achille paused a moment; then: "I assume you don't want to put the cadaver on display?"

"Hell no!" Féraud growled. "No need to stir up a hornet's nest, at least not yet." Then to Rousseau: "What's your plan for today?"

"Follow up on my leads, chief. I've interviewed several people on the Rue Tourlaque and Rue Caulaincourt; no eyewitnesses, so far. I heard some gossip about Toulouse-Lautrec and his *lorettes*. Drunken brawls and late night shouting matches; that sort of thing. Evidence of jealous rage—one of the oldest homicide motives in the book. But you wonder why any girl would take up with a monkey like that; money and title, I suppose. Anyway, I've got my snoops in Montmartre and Pigalle keeping their ears open for chatter about missing girls, especially models. Do you want me to interview Lautrec?"

Féraud frowned and shook his head. "No, not yet. He's the son of a count, not an *apache*. But I want him tailed. Pick your two best men, and put them on twelve-hour shifts. Include their findings in your daily reports."

"Right, chief. And I'd sure like to get a look at that studio. Wouldn't you, professor?" Rousseau grinned at Achille, a gleam in his piggish eyes.

"I would indeed, but we don't have enough evidence for a warrant."

Féraud leaned further over his desk and lowered his voice. "Listen, boys, what the *juge d'instruction* doesn't know won't hurt him. This is strictly between us. Within the next day or two, I want you to have a look at Lautrec's studio—without a warrant. Rousseau, you know who to use on that job."

"Right chief; just leave it to me." He turned to Achille: "You O.K. with that, professor?"

Achille did not like the old extrajudicial methods, but he figured in a case like this the ends justified the means. And he was not about to harm his career by crossing Féraud. "As long as the chief approves, it's fine with me."

⚬∞⚬

The stench of La Villette on an unseasonably warm autumn morning struck Achille like a punch to the gut. Home to the stockyards and great abattoirs that provided meat for the tables of two million Parisians, La Villette was also a hodgepodge of factories, warehouses, working class dwellings, *boîtes*, cafes, administrative buildings, and markets. Located in the northeastern corner of Paris, a district annexed during the reign of Napoleon III, the modern industrial site and docklands were built around a large basin and main canal that flowed into the Seine through a system of locks.

The main canal was itself fed by a network of smaller canals polluted with industrial waste and slaughterhouse effluent criss-crossed by iron footbridges and railway bridges. The emissions from hundreds of loco-motives and factory chimneys enveloped the area in a yellowish-brown haze. A steel spiders-web overspread the vast acreage, traversed day and night by smoke-belching engines pulling long trains of cars loaded with lowing cattle, bleating sheep, grunting and squealing pigs, brought by the thousands to be offloaded into the slaughterhouse pens. Trains with ice-cooled boxcars conveyed the butchered product to the Paris markets.

La Villette was also a collection point for sewage pumped from the Paris cesspools. In the early morning hours, hundreds of wagons filled with human waste lined up on the quayside, waiting to pour out their cargo into tanker-barges bound for the suburban sewage farms. Achille supervised two workers in a dark shed near the quay as they raked and sifted through excrement removed from the cess-pit where the torso was found, looking for clues. The foul sludge had been pumped into a galva-nized iron vat and sprayed with disinfectant, but the odor in the stuffy shed was still overwhelming.

Does filth breed crime? Achille pondered this question as he anxiously awaited a discovery that might shed light on his case. He had read Zola and was familiar with the author's literary theory of naturalism, according to which character was formed by a combination of social conditions, heredity, and environment. That might hold true for the common criminal, but would it apply to a monster that could murder and horribly mutilate a woman? Try as he might, Achille could not picture the individual who committed the crime.

Lombroso, the celebrated Italian criminologist, believed the criminal was a definite anthropological type bearing physical and mental stigmata, the product of heredity, atavism, and degeneracy. Could you read evil in a face, a body, mannerisms, and gestures? Would the man Achille was looking for be simian and grotesque like Lautrec? Perhaps alienation from decent society had motivated him to destroy beauty in revenge for the rejection brought on by his deformity. Achille pondered another literary association, Hugo's hideously deformed Quasimodo. According to Lombroso's theory of criminal physiognomy, Quasimodo would have been a prime suspect in a Ripper-type murder investigation. Nevertheless, Hugo had portrayed the hunchback as a noble, self-sacrificing character who loved the beautiful Esmeralda. But then, Hugo was a great Romantic of the previous generation, not a modern scientist.

He recalled something from his religious instruction that had troubled him since his youth: *Intra feces et urinas nominem natus est*—Man is born between feces and urine. Achille thought that a singularly offensive way of saying we were born in sin and must be ritually cleansed by baptism. But he would not have dared express his opinion to the brother who had taught him the religious adage. At any rate, the odious quote brought to mind another literary association, again with Zola. Achille recalled a satirical cartoon reference to Nana, in which the author presented his protagonist as Venus rising from a chamber pot. The infamous courtesan had, like The Great Stink, arisen from the sewers of Paris. She was disease carrying excrement behind a façade of female beauty, polluting society and ultimately leading to the humiliating defeat of 1871. Achille remembered Zola's metaphor, Nana's horrible death from smallpox; corruption oozed from her countless festering sores while beneath her window jubilant soldiers on their way to the debacle marched past crowds cheering, "On to Berlin!"

"Monsieur, we've found something!"

Achille stopped pondering and ran to the vat. One of the workers had fished out a shiny object and set it on a table; Achille put on a pair of rubber gloves and examined it. It was a gold cigarette case, monogrammed with an ancient coat of arms. He opened the case, and found three cigarettes.

Toulouse-Lautrec? But this is too obvious. He might as well have left his carte-de-visite. Achille took out a magnifying glass and examined the surface of the cigarette case. There were barely visible fingerprints on both the front and back, and no one had touched the case since it had been dropped in the pit—at least not with their bare hands.

"The Devil!" he exclaimed. A common expression, but under the circumstances he might have meant it literally.

∞

Dr. Péan completed his examination. He walked from the dissection table without uttering a word, and went straight to a washstand where he scrubbed his hands and forearms in chlorinated lime solution. Bertillon and Achille watched silently as the surgeon completed his ablutions with a vigorous application of the nail brush.

After inspecting his hands and fingernails carefully, Péan rolled down his sleeves, fastened his cuffs, and retrieved his frock coat from a peg on the wall. Then he turned to Bertillon and stated matter-of-factly: "Based on the pathologist's report and my examination of the corpse, I conclude that a vaginal hysterectomy has been performed on this individual, and that the operation was done recently, perhaps within the past few days. Moreover, I concur with the pathologist's conclusion that the head and limbs were surgically removed. However, I have no way of determining whether or not the hysterectomy contributed to the cause of death. For all we know, the operation might have been performed on a corpse." Péan stood silently without a gesture, a twitch, or the slightest change in his stony expression.

Achille questioned: "Doctor, do you know of any other surgeon in Paris who performs the vaginal hysterectomy?"

"No, Inspector, to my knowledge I'm the first surgeon in Europe to have used this technique successfully. I have only done this once, and very recently at that. But I assure you, my patient is alive and recovering splendidly." Péan paused. Then: "Am I under suspicion?"

The tension in the dissecting room was electric. Bertillon, as the senior man, answered immediately: "Of course not, Doctor Péan. However, we must ask questions, and we greatly appreciate your cooperation."

Bertillon's response eased the tension—somewhat. "I understand gentlemen, and I shall do what I can to assist in your investigation."

"That is most kind of you, doctor," Achille said respectfully. "You've indicated you performed this operation just once. Can you tell us when?"

"Yes, Inspector, I operated Wednesday afternoon, the 14th. It's documented in the medical record."

Achille did a quick mental calculation. According to the night soil collection schedule, the body must have been dumped in the pit between the early morning hours of the 13th and the 15th. That timeframe was consistent with Bertillon and the pathologist's estimate of the time of death. Could the murderer have witnessed the operation on the afternoon of the 14th and then committed the crime sometime between that afternoon and the early morning hours of the following day? Based on the state of decomposition, death must have occurred on the early end of the scale, either shortly before or immediately after the operation. Then the body could have been disposed of several hours later, under the cover of darkness and at a time when the act was least likely to have been observed.

After a brief pause, Achille continued: "And I assume you also have a record of those attending the operation?"

"Of course, my assistants were in attendance, but I assure you they are young gentlemen of spotless reputation."

Achille smiled in an attempt to put the surgeon at ease. "I have no reason to doubt that, doctor, but you do understand that I may want to ask them some routine questions?"

"Of course, Inspector, I shall provide you with their names and addresses, as well as the hours when they may be reached at the clinic."

"Thank you, doctor. I believe there was also a small group of visitors who witnessed the operation?"

"Yes, a few of my trusted colleagues were present, and an artist, Monsieur de Toulouse-Lautrec. He made a sketch of the operation. The gentleman's cousin is one of my assistants."

"Do you have a list of the attendees?"

"Yes, Inspector; attendance is by invitation only. My clerk at the clinic keeps a journal containing the names and signatures of those present, the time they arrived as well as the time they signed out."

"I would very much appreciate having a look at that journal."

"Very well, you may contact my clerk," Péan said with a hint of annoyance in his voice. "I'll leave you a card with his name. Now, if you gentlemen are finished, I must go to the hospital. I have a very busy day ahead of me."

"Thank you, doctor. I apologize for the inconvenience. I have one more question. In your professional opinion, do you think a layman who witnessed the operation could have performed the surgery?"

Péan's face reddened; his hands shook visibly, as if the question were a gross insult. "Absolutely not! The amputation of the head and limbs was skilful enough, but the hysterectomy is a procedure of the utmost delicacy. Only the most proficient and experienced surgeons would attempt it."

Achille was put off by the doctor's reaction to a perfectly reasonable question. Nevertheless, he smiled and spoke very respectfully in an attempt to placate Péan. "Thank you so much, doctor. You have been most helpful." He turned to Bertillon. "Do you have any questions for the doctor, Monsieur Bertillon?"

Bertillon frowned and shook his head. "No, that will be all for today." Smiling sheepishly he turned to the fuming Péan: "Thank you, doctor, for your cooperation. This is a difficult case, and we very much appreciate your assistance. I would ask that you do not discuss this matter with anyone. If your colleagues or employees have questions, you may refer them to Inspector Lefebvre or to me. We will be discreet in our questioning, and would like to keep this matter out of the newspapers for as long as possible."

"That goes without saying, Monsieur Bertillon. Nobody wants the press poking round in his business. At any rate, I knew your father well; a fine physician. Now I must be off." Péan turned abruptly to Achille. He pulled out a card and a pencil, scribbled his clerk's name, and handed it to Achille. "Good-day, Inspector." Then he grabbed his hat from a rack and left before Achille could reply.

⚭

Bertillon's laboratory was located at the top of a dark, secluded stairway in the Palais de Justice, a grand white marble Second Empire edifice not far from the Morgue. Pale light flooded in through large, grimy rectangular windows; natural light was supplemented by several large, overhead brass gas jets. Long wooden tables in the center of the room were covered in paraphernalia: microscopes, test tubes, alembics, and retorts. Achille and Bertillon conferred in a corner, where they stood next to a cluttered desk and a row of dusty filing cabinets. For the moment, they were alone. Gilles was to meet them shortly to present his photographs of the prints on the cloth.

"I'm afraid Dr. Péan didn't like my question about a layman per-forming the surgery. Nevertheless, it's a question that had to be asked." Achille frowned.

"Don't worry about it, Inspector. Péan's a proud man and rightly so. Naturally, it troubles him to think that a member of his profession might have committed such a heinous crime, especially since our suspect might be a trusted colleague or friend. What's more, he's a man of spotless repu-tation. Imagine how it would look in the newspapers if our murderer turns out to be a well-regarded doctor of Péan's acquaintance."

Achille was well aware of the situation; he also knew that Bertillon's late father had been a physician. This case could cast a shadow over the entire French medical profession. "That's understandable, but the doctor's professional opinion has put another twist to this convoluted case. So far, most of the evidence has pointed to Lautrec; now Péan seems to have exculpated him. Of course, we can't go much further until we identify the woman."

Bertillon scratched his beard. This matter was bewildering indeed. "Here's another twist. We tested for alkaloids using the Stas-Otto method. I just received the results. There was a large amount of morphine in her system."

Achille raised an eyebrow. "Enough morphine to have killed her?"

"I believe so. She appears to have been heavily drugged when the killer cut her up. She may have died under the knife, or from the overdose. That appears to rule out Jack the Ripper. Morphine was not part of his *modus operandi*. And to complicate matters, in addition to morphine, she may have been given chloroform or a chloroform derivative such as chloral hydrate. Unfortunately, we have no test to confirm that or rule it out. At any rate, I suggest you start checking with chemist's shops in Montmartre and Pigalle to see who's been buying the stuff. Your partner Rousseau probably has a list of known addicts, at least those who've had a run-in with the police. And you'll need to check the hospitals and clinics to see if any drugs have been walking out the back door. We'll look at records for reports of stolen opiates."

Achille's eyes widened. He stared at Bertillon for a moment, making a mental note. *Could the morphine have been taken from Péan's clinic?* Then: "Do you think this could have been an experimental surgery gone wrong? And that—that the surgeon cut off her head and limbs and dumped the body to cover up his malpractice?"

Bertillon shook his head; the thought of surgical malpractice and criminal concealment was particularly disturbing to the son of a famous physician. "To my knowledge hysterectomies are performed for three reasons: to remove cancerous tumors, uterine fibroids, or in the treatment of female hysteria. Considering the general appearance of health in this individual we might consider the latter. It's certainly possible, based on current practice. But Dr. Charcot at the Salpêtrière, our foremost authority, believes hysteria has nothing to do with the uterus; he treats it as a neurological disorder and does not approve of the operation." Bertillon paused a moment, his frown an expression of concern as to where he feared this investigation might lead. Then he muttered, "But at this point I don't know what to think." He pulled out his watch and added impatiently: "Where *is* that photographer?"

At that very moment, like a genie conjured from a magic lamp, Gilles burst into the laboratory through the swinging double doors: "Good morning, gentlemen! Sorry I'm a bit late."

As he approached, Gilles was greeted by two frowning faces. "Why so gloomy, my friends? Anyway, I've got something in this satchel that will cheer you up." Gilles dropped a heavy leather satchel onto the desktop, stirring the pile of papers and raising a little dust cloud. He opened the flap and pulled out a brown paper envelope containing several photographs. "Take a look; I believe I've achieved excellent results."

Achille immediately went to the photographs of the thumb and fore-finger prints. Holding them up to the light, he pointed out the pattern to Bertillon. "You see the distinct whorl, Monsieur. I can now categorize these prints according to Galton's method and present them as evidence. How did you enhance them, Gilles?"

"Oh, just a little photographic wizardry—the right lighting, shutter speed, lenses, filters, *et voilà*!"

Bertillon studied the prints for a moment. "This is very well done, Inspector. Now all you need are the suspects' prints for comparison, and you might have something. But obtaining those prints could prove difficult without an arrest."

Achille detected a hint of skepticism in Bertillon's comments. Nevertheless he replied confidently: "Monsieur, I'll cross that bridge when I come to it." To Gilles: "I want you to take a look at a gold cigarette case. Let's see if you can work your wizardry on that."

Achille and Gilles followed Bertillon to the evidence room where the cigarette case had been tagged, catalogued, and deposited. The guard retrieved the numbered evidence bag and then escorted the trio to a well-lit table where they could examine the case. "Of course," Achille said to Gilles, "we'll need identifying photographs highlighting the mono-grammed coat of arms and the hallmarks. And I'll need photographs of the cigarettes as well. But I want you to see something else." Achille put on rubber gloves, held the case up to the light, and took out his magni-fying glass. "These are latent prints. We're damned lucky they're still visible after lying in all that muck; you can barely make them out under magnification in a bright light. Is there any way you can enhance them photographically?"

Gilles shook his head. "That's impossible, Inspector. Unless you can bring out the lines on the case to at least the definition we have on the cloth, I can do nothing with them."

Bertillon smiled wryly. "Seems to be another bridge for you to cross, eh Inspector?"

"Difficult, but not impossible," Achille replied.

Bertillon and Achille checked out the evidence bag and took it to the laboratory; Gilles went to his van for his camera and equipment. While they waited for the photographer, Bertillon provided his estimate of the woman's appearance: early twenties; fair skinned Caucasian; straight light-yellow hair; pale blue eyes; height 163 cm; weight 54 kg; well-proportioned; firm musculature; two small moles in intimate places not visible to the public. "She appears to have been well fed and in good health. Unless her face was disfigured by accident or inflicted injury, I'd deduce she was quite pretty. She was also very fit. She might have been an artists' model, a dancer, actress, or circus performer. Without the head or the limbs, that's the best I can do. I assume you're searching for the rest of her?"

"Yes, Monsieur, my partner Rousseau's handling that end of the inves-tigation, along with his search for witnesses."

"Very well, Inspector; I wish you luck. Now, a few things before we go to records. We tested the cloth fibers; it's a high quality canvas, the sort a well-heeled artist would use. You can find out where Lautrec buys his supplies, see if they carry this particular canvas, and determine if he's made a recent purchase. As for the cigarettes, they're an expensive Turkish blend, rolled in high quality paper—a gentleman's smoke no doubt. And we did find a small amount of opium, which might be of interest in light of the morphine in the body. On the other hand, most of these bohemian types indulge in drugs. You might trace them to Lautrec's tobacconist, and I'll bet the cigarettes in the case match the butt. Finally, I took a look at your cast of the shoeprint and the measurements you made of the stride. They appear to belong to a small individual, about 147 cm in height and proportionate weight. By the way, my congratulations for spotting the print and getting an excellent cast from a horse dropping. "

Achille smiled grimly. "More evidence pointing to Lautrec—or perhaps a well-planned frame-up?"

Bertillon rubbed his chin and squinted. Turning from the light, he muttered, "Well then, you may look for someone who had a motive to murder this as yet-unidentified young woman, mutilate her body, and pin it on Lautrec." He pulled out his watch. "I'm running late, Inspector. Let's go to records; then I must bid you good-day."

7

OCTOBER 16, AFTERNOON & EVENING
REUNION

Marcia rested on a drawing room settee in the hotel suite, her back propped up on a velvet bolster. Sir Henry and Betsy had gone on a shopping excursion to the Rue de la Paix. The doctor had recommended she remain in the suite and rest. Marcia acquiesced, but in her mind she questioned Sir Henry's motives. She wondered if his advice was based less on his professional concern for her health and more on his desire to have Betsy all to himself. What difference did it make? Love had long since departed their relationship; what remained was loyalty and memories of better times. And Betsy seemed infatuated with the handsome, gentlemanly physician, so much so that she might be eager to see the back of her consumptive companion.

Marcia sighed and reached for her sketchbook, which she had set down on a nearby coffee table. She opened the book to a pastel drawing of Virginie Ménard. She had drawn the portrait from memory based upon her vision during the ride in the Bois, but the work did not completely satisfy her. *It looks too much like Lautrec's portrait. I must go to Cormon's Atelier to draw her from life. What's more, I must talk to her, get to know her better.* She put down the book and gazed at the ceiling.

Marcia had a practical side. She had not yet told Betsy of her desire to remain in Paris for an obvious reason—money. She had a few thousand dollars in a San Francisco bank, the proceeds from the sale of her artwork. And Theo Van Gogh of Goupil & Co. had made her an offer; his clients were very interested in her Silver Medal landscape. He said he could get her a handsome price for the painting and for any new work as well. Of course, she had serious doubts she'd live long enough to finish anything new—the projected venture into social realism was perhaps nothing more than a valetudinarian dream—but she did not say that to Theo.

She probably had enough to last the brief remainder of her life, but she feared dying alone in a foreign city, and she especially dreaded the time when she could no longer care for herself.

A ringing telephone interrupted. Marcia swung her thin legs over the edge of the settee, took hold of an armrest and raised herself with a grunt. She walked slowly to the telephone table, paused to catch her breath, then lifted the earpiece and raised the transmitter to her mouth. The voice on the other end surprised her. "Arthur, is that really you?"

"Yes, my dear, it is I in the flesh! I've crossed the channel to see some old friends, visit the Fair, and witness the closing ceremonies. Imagine my delight when I discovered that you and Betsy were staying at this very hotel."

"This is a pleasant surprise. I would very much like to see you, talk of old times, and catch up on things. I've read your latest writings with great admiration."

"Splendid! How about we pop over to the Café Riche? If Betsy's around, she may certainly join us."

"There's nothing I'd like better, but I fear I'm a bit fragile right now."

There was a pause—then: "Oh, I'm sorry to hear that. Are you well enough to receive?"

"Of course, my dear; they haven't buried me yet."

"All right, then, how about this afternoon? Let's say in one hour?"

"Bless you Arthur; that would be lovely!"

It wasn't until she had left the telephone that Marcia realized the extent of her loneliness.

⌒∞⌒

Arthur Wolcott, the famous American expatriate author, sat across the tea table from Marcia, fine china cup in hand. Arthur had changed since their last meeting. Gray whiskers streaked his dark brown beard, his hair had thinned to a fringe, and his waist had expanded to prosperous bourgeois proportions that could not be completely concealed by his expert Savile Row tailors. Now fully acculturated to the style and manner of an English gentleman, he affected a monocle that would have been mocked in Boston and New York; his rough Yankee twang had been polished smooth and coated with a thick upper-class Anglophone varnish.

"I say Marcia," he remarked with his characteristically affable smile, "I'm awfully pleased to find you looking so well. You seem to have exaggerated your illness." This was a polite, well-intentioned lie.

Marcia smiled wanly. "That's kind of you, Arthur, but no need for pretense between old friends. Fact is, I look frightful, and for the most part I feel worse than I look. But your appearance has had a tonic effect. And I'm very glad to see you've harbored no grudge against me for my deception all those years ago." Her green eyes sparkled as she sipped her tea and nibbled at a brioche.

"Oh, that's all water under the bridge; long since forgotten. 'Mark' Brownlow was a great artist and a friend, and that artistic greatness and cherished friendship continues in you, his female alter-ego." Arthur put down his cup and wiped his hands on the serviette. He reached into his breast pocket and withdrew a cigarette case. "Do you mind if I smoke?"

"Please do."

Arthur took out a cigarette, tamped it on the case, and then offered one to Marcia.

"Sorry, Arthur, I'd like to join you, but my new doctor forbids it."

He lit his cigarette, took a puff and blew a smoke ring. Then he leaned back and hooked a thumb in his waistcoat pocket. "Sorry to hear that. I suppose longevity requires giving up life's pleasures, one by one, until there's nothing left. By the way, who is your physician?"

"Sir Henry Collingwood. Do you know him? I hear he has a very successful practice in Harley Street."

Arthur rested his cigarette in an ashtray and leaned forward as though he were about to reveal a confidence. "Indeed I do know of him, and I've met him socially on more than one occasion. He's good looking with an excellent manner, a clever fellow, and a fine amateur water-colorist. He's also quite successful, welcomed in the best society, and he limits his practice to ladies of quality."

"Oh, really? I find that fascinating. Please do tell me more."

Arthur's sunny expression darkened to a worried frown, as though he already had said too much and did not want to proceed. "It's really a delicate subject, or rather *indelicate*, if you follow my meaning."

"Arthur," she said with impatience, "the man's my doctor. What's more, he's been playing up to Betsy; I think she's sweet on him. If you know something about him, please tell me. I promise I won't be shocked. Just pretend you're speaking man to man with your old chum Mark."

"All right, since you put it that way, here's what I know. Sir Henry specializes in treating female problems, most particularly cases of hysteria. His treatments are—of a very intimate nature."

"Treatments of a very intimate nature, you say? For a famous author, your description lacks information."

"Very well, Marcia, since you require me to spell it out, I'll tell you what I've heard on good authority. Sir Henry treats hysteria by massaging and manipulating the—uh, female parts. He also provides the ladies with vibrating—uh, implements that they may use in the privacy of their homes. Finally, he prescribes strong sedatives to help them through their, uh, uh. . . ."

Marcia interrupted to spare him further embarrassment. "That's enough, thank you, Arthur. I get the picture. No wonder he's so popular. Anyway, I'm a woman and familiar with what you call female problems. And I assure you Sir Henry has used none of these techniques on me. It would surely be a stretch to think them helpful to a consumptive, though Lord knows but some desperate woman in my condition might submit to such treatment if she were convinced it would do her good. I just hope Betsy doesn't—" Marcia stopped short. She coughed lightly into her serviette, and took a sip of tea.

Arthur tried to reassure her. "Betsy's always been sensible; I doubt she'd—but you did say she's sweet on him?"

Marcia nodded. "I've lived with Betsy for almost eleven years; she's not always so sensible, especially when she drinks, as you well know. I'm worried, Arthur."

Arthur reached over the table and held her thin, cold hand. "Don't worry, dear, you must think of your health. Betsy can take care of herself." He gazed at her fondly before proceeding: "I've purchased a fine Georgian manor near Rye in East Sussex. It's a lovely place, not far from the sea. There's a perfect English garden; you should see it when the roses are in bloom. I could have a studio fixed up for you, just like in the old days. There's plenty of room. I entertain frequently, and you'd like the society: English, Americans, Europeans, writers, artists, theater people, intellectuals, and a sprinkling of swells, a jolly crew on all occasions. And our old friend Sargent's in London. He's doing quite well since he left Paris following the *Madame X* portrait scandal. What do you say?"

Marcia looked down at their intertwined hands. "It sounds lovely, Arthur, but—" She paused for a moment, eyeing him sadly. "Would you want to burden yourself with a sick woman?"

"Stuff and nonsense! We'll have you up and about in no time. What you need is work, my girl; a new project, a painting for the ages, something to equal or surpass the best of the Mark Brownlow *oeuvre*."

She stared at him with tear-moistened eyes. "I do have an idea, Arthur. Let me show you." She got up and walked to the coffee table with more vigor than she had shown in days. After fetching her sketchbook, she returned to the tea table. Marcia opened the book to her drawing of Virginie and handed it to Arthur. "Tell me what you think."

Arthur examined the pastel sketch. "It's beautiful, Marcia. But then, you always had a knack for portraiture. Who is she?"

"A model I met at Cormon's *Atelier*. I want to use her for a painting with strong social commentary, something along the lines of Luke Fildes."

Arthur had his doubts about the project, but he did not let that dampen his enthusiasm. "I think that's a splendid concept, and you can bring it to fruition in Rye as well as anywhere else. You might also receive Fildes's blessing; we're still on quite good terms and he might be flattered by your emulation."

"Oh Arthur, I think it might work. But how would I break it to Betsy?"

Ever the pragmatist, he asked, "How are you fixed financially?"

"I have a few thousand in a San Francisco bank, and Van Gogh thinks I can get another thousand—that's dollars, not francs—for my Silver Medal landscape. And Goupil will represent my new work in their gallery, too."

Arthur smiled. "That's more than enough, and of course you'll be staying with me rent free and meals *gratis*. And I'm good friends with an excellent doctor who lives nearby." He approached Marcia, took her hand, and gave sensible advice as gently as possible. "If what you say about Betsy and Sir Henry is true, perhaps a break is best for all concerned."

Marcia stared at him for a moment. Then: "I'm inclined to agree, Arthur; but it's much easier said than done."

∞

"Papa's home! Papa's home!" The little girl broke free from her nanny and scampered in a flurry of curls, ribbons, and lace through the front hall to Achille. He swept her into his arms, kissed her rosebud mouth, and hugged and squeezed her until she giggled. "I miss you, Papa. Why are you never here?"

Achille stroked her silky golden hair. "I'm sorry, little one. Papa's very busy keeping Paris safe from wicked people."

"Wicked people? Do you mean the Germans, the Jews, and the Freemasons?"

Achille stared over the child's shoulder at Adele; she looked away and fussed with some frills on her dress. Jeanne had obviously been listening to her grandmother. He looked back at his daughter and smiled. "No, my angel, I mean the wicked people who break the laws of the Republic."

Confused, Jeanne pouted and stuck her thumb in her mouth. Achille put her down and handed her back to the nanny. He waited until they were out of earshot before speaking to Adele:

"I wish your mother wouldn't fill the child's head with reactionary rubbish."

Adele pouted like her little girl. "I'm sorry, Achille. I can't correct Mama."

His patience wearing thin, he replied harshly: "Well, perhaps it's time someone did. I won't have my four-year-old daughter's mind polluted with extremist propaganda."

Adele's face reddened; she was on the verge of tears. "You *finally* come home at a decent hour, and the first thing you do is criticize mother and pick a quarrel over nothing. You didn't even notice my new dress. It's your favorite color; or at least you used to *say* it was your favorite."

Achille calmed himself. He took a moment to admire the green silk gown trimmed with lace ruches. His voice softened. "It's very pretty; the fabric matches your emerald eyes, it brings out their luster." He walked to her, put his hands on her shoulders and smiled. "I'm sorry, dear. I'm tired. I just wish your mother would be more careful about expressing such controversial views around Jeanne."

Adele had the pleased look of a wife who had won yet another minor skirmish with her husband. "Well, since you liked my dress and apologized nicely I'll permit you to kiss me."

He kissed her lips and held her tightly until he heard a familiar rustle of silk, creaking of stays, and smelled the sharp odor of camphor transfused with sweet overtones of attar of roses. Madame Berthier entered the hallway. A dumpy woman in her fifties with a vestige of prettiness around her hazel eyes and full red lips, Madame looked like a Gallic Queen Victoria dressed in old-fashioned black bombazine crinoline and white widow's cap. "Good evening, Achille. It was most kind of Chief Inspector Féraud to permit you an evening with your family."

"Good evening, Madame." Achille walked to his mother-in-law, bent down, and kissed her proffered cheek. "I have the pleasure of dining *en famille* this evening, but I'm afraid I must retire to my study immediately after dinner. I must finish my report for tomorrow morning."

Madame smiled, displaying crooked yellowish teeth and spreading dozens of wrinkles through a layer of white powder round her eyes and rouged mouth. "I'm honored to have a son-in-law so devoted to his duty. It's a shame you can't turn your singular talents toward rooting out France's *real* enemies rather than chasing common criminals through the gutters of Montmartre."

Achille glanced at Adele with a wry smile before inquiring: "Oh, and who might these *real enemies* be, Madame?"

"Read Monsieur Drumont's *La France Juive* and you will be enlightened, my boy."

Adele interrupted judiciously: "We're having veal chops with sorrel and an excellent Chateau Haut-Brion. I think you'll prefer it to your usual sandwich and bottle of beer."

Madame grimaced at the mention of her son-in-law's common, workday supper. "Beer," she muttered, "how disgusting."

Achille laughed. "To what do we owe this feast? Is it some special occasion of which I'm unaware?"

"Yes, my dear," Adele answered with a smile. "It's to celebrate your dining at home."

⚬∞⚬

The dinner was superb, but after two hours of listening to Madame's conspiracy theories, Achille was relieved to return to work. He sat at his desk bent over a typewriter, straining his eyes in the yellow glow of an oil lamp. Constantly referring to his notes and considering a number of leads developed from new evidence, he completed his report to Féraud.

In addition to the evidence he had discussed with Bertillon at the laboratory, he made two intriguing discoveries in records. First, a concierge on the Rue Lepic had reported a missing young woman, Virginie Ménard, and the police had questioned an artist named Émile Bernard who had been roaming Montmartre and Pigalle searching for the girl. The time of her disappearance and physical description matched what they knew from the corpse.

Second, he found a file on a dwarf, Joseph Rossini, aka Jojo the clown. Jojo was an ex-convict with a record of violence against women, a circus performer who rented a room on the Rue Lepic, not far from Virginie Ménard. His photographs looked like Lautrec's twin, and his measurements matched the footprint cast and stride measured at the crime scene. Achille wondered what Rousseau's investigation had turned up; at any rate, he'd know first thing in the morning. Achille finished typing, and turned his attention to the latent prints on the gold cigarette case.

In 1863, Paul-Jean Coulier, a chemistry professor, published his discovery that latent fingerprints could be developed on paper by iodine fuming. He also explained how to preserve the developed impression and mentioned the potential for identifying fingerprints by use of a magnifying glass. Achille had read Coulier's paper. But without a credible classification system and a sound argument for the individuality of fingerprints that could be accepted as evidence in a court of law, there was no practical use for them in criminal identification. Galton had provided the supporting argument for individuality and the classification system, what was needed was a means of capturing the prints at the crime scene so they might be compared to the suspect's fingerprints and presented to the court.

Achille knew that the prints on the cigarette case were impressions made by the oily residue and perspiration on the fingertips. What he needed was a reagent, the equivalent of Coulier's iodine fumes that could sufficiently enhance the prints so they could be classified accurately, photographed, and compared to the prints on the canvas.

He yawned, removed his pince-nez, rubbed his bleary eyes, and then focused on the loudly ticking desk clock. Eleven P.M.; time for bed. Achille rose from his desk, stretched his weary arms and legs, and walked to the doorway that entered into a short corridor leading to the master bedroom. He had already removed his shoes and changed into slippers to keep the carpets clean and not make too much noise. The gas was off; he groped through the shadows, careful not to trip over toys Jeanne often left on the runner. When he reached the bedroom door, he knocked gently. Adele bid him enter.

He saw her seated at her dresser. She had changed into a nightdress. Her hair was down, and she slowly brushed the long, brown strands while gazing at her reflection in a lamp-lit mirror. Achille came up behind her, leaned down, brushed away some stray hairs and caressed her bare shoulder. She put down the hairbrush and accidentally knocked some face powder onto a silver box. "Oh," she muttered. Then she bent over and blew away the powder.

The accident caught Achille's attention. "Wait a minute!" he exclaimed. "Don't move; don't touch anything."

"What's the matter, dear?" Adele turned around with a worried frown. But Achille was already out the door, sprinting up the corridor toward his study. She heard a crash and a cry of "*Merde!*" Achille had tripped over Jeanne's toy duck, Oscar.

Presently he returned, limping and rubbing his knee with one hand and carrying his magnifying glass in the other. Scowling, he muttered, "Nanny must teach Jeanne not to leave her toys in the hallways, or at least pick up after her."

"Yes, dear, I'll speak to them. But what's all the fuss? What are you doing with that glass?"

Achille forgot his throbbing knee. He bent over the dressing table and examined the silver box. "My dear, we're conducting an important experiment in forensic science."

He handed the glass to Adele. "Here, see for yourself."

"Oh, very well," she grumbled. "What am I looking at?"

"Your fingerprints enhanced with face powder."

"How disgusting!" She handed back the magnifying glass with a peevish glare. "Why is it so important?"

Achille explained patiently. "Fingerprints might be significant to the solution of the mystery surrounding my case. They can provide the missing pieces to a puzzle that, when completed, could catch a dangerous criminal. But I'm breaking new ground, practically writing the book as I proceed." He lowered his voice, smiled, and stroked her hair. "I'm sorry if my behavior seems peculiar at times, but I'm under pressure and it's a matter of the utmost urgency. Your little accident put me on the right track, and I'm grateful. Now, I just need to find something, a fine dark powder that will increase the definition of the lines so they can be clearly identifiable and photographable as well."

Adele grasped his hand and rose from her chair. She smiled, looked into Achille's eyes and spoke softly: "I think I understand a little now.

Perhaps it might help if you shared your work with me, from time to time. Not the grisly things, but your theories, your methods, your problems. I'll help, if I can."

He kissed her. "Thank you, I'd like that very much."

"All right, it's a bargain. And now, Inspector, I'm going to test your powers of observation further. Have you noticed anything different about me?"

He rubbed his chin thoughtfully. "Let's see now. Does is it go with your new dress?"

"Good question; you're warm."

He sniffed her neck and bosom. "Ah, I detect a new fragrance."

"Bravo! And you approve?"

Achille opened her night dress and caressed her breasts. "Yes," he whispered. "It's perfection."

"Inspector Lefebvre, for your unerring skill as a detective, excellent taste in perfume, and unwavering devotion to duty, I award you the highest honor I can bestow." She lifted his hand, smiled mischievously, and nibbled his fingers.

Achille laughed, swept Adele into his arms, and carried her off to bed.

⊗

Just before midnight a brilliant lightning flash lit the sky over Sacré-Cœur. Thunder rumbled, stirring memories of the Prussian Krupp guns that pounded Paris day and night during the siege of 1870-71. Wind-whipped rain battered shutters, poured through drainpipes into overflowing gutters, washed over twisting streets and alleyways down to the boulevard at the foot of the hill. Lautrec and a few others sought shelter in a small *boîte* in Pigalle. The artist sat alone at a small table, drinking absinthe while sketching a young woman seated at the other end of the bar. She appeared through a grayish haze of tobacco smoke tinged yellow by flickering candles and gaslights. The place reeked of fumes emanating from clay pipes and cheap cigarettes re-rolled from discarded butts, interfused with the odor of damp clothing clinging to infrequently washed bodies.

The young woman sang in a husky mezzo-soprano about her life on the streets to the accompaniment of an old man fingering a wheezing, out-of-tune concertina. The working-class patrons paid little or no attention to her; a couple of men played draughts while another watched, one in a dark corner behind Lautrec laid his head on his arms and snored, another plied his woman with liquor while groping her under the table, the few remaining men and women smoked, drank, stared into space, and grumbled about the weather, work, politics, and life in general.

Lautrec recognized his subject; she was Delphine, a dancer at the Moulin Rouge. Too hard-boiled and streetwise to be called pretty, there was still something attractive about her; dark hair and eyes, dusky skin, flat nose, thick sensual lips, large, even white teeth, perhaps all evidence of her mixed blood. He rendered her honestly with a facial expression reflecting the worldly resignation of her lyrics.

Delphine finished her song, turned toward Lautrec, and stared defiantly. He responded with a casual smile and a tip of his black bowler. She sauntered to his table, placed her hands on her hips, and said, "I know you, Monsieur. You're the artist who hangs round the Moulin. Buy me a drink?" The ultimate phrase of her greeting might have been a command rather than a request, had it not been for a questioning upturn to her inflection and a curious aspect in her large brown eyes.

Lautrec had already made a quick study of her gestures, mannerisms, shabby dress, poor but proud demeanor. He immediately replied, "But of course, Mademoiselle. Name your poison," and beckoned the bartender.

Delphine ordered absinthe. The bartender brought her drink; she took a swig, then for a while said nothing while Lautrec finished his drawing. Then: "I'm a good friend of Virginie Ménard; did you know that?"

Lautrec put down his charcoal and looked up at Delphine. "Yes Mademoiselle, I recall her mentioning you on occasion."

"Oh, really? And I suppose you know that she's gone missing. No one's seen or heard from her for almost a week."

"Yes, Mademoiselle, I have already been informed of that fact." Lautrec exaggerated his toffee-nosed accent and continued smiling as though he were baiting her. He enjoyed picking fights; it broke the monotony and this woman looked tough enough to make it interesting.

Delphine drank some absinthe; her hand trembled and there was a noticeable quaver in her voice. She put down her glass and glared at Lautrec. "Have you also been *informed of the fact* that a woman's body was found stuffed in a shit-hole on the street in front of your studio?"

"Yes, my landlady has told me as much." He glanced at her empty glass. "Would you care for another absinthe?"

Delphine leaned over the table; her hand gripped a bag containing a razor. Her husky voice deepened and hardened into a *sotto voce* snarl: "If I thought—if I believed you had done anything to harm Virginie, I'd slit your ugly throat, here and now."

Without a flinch or the slightest change of expression, he replied, "You might *try* to slit my throat, Delphine, but I'm quite capable of stopping you. I fear you'd be seriously injured in the process. So for both our sakes, please don't think of trying. Nevertheless, I assure you I've not harmed Virginie, nor do I know her whereabouts. As for the unfortunate young woman in the cesspool, I know nothing about her either, and I wouldn't jump to conclusions by assuming she's Virginie. At any rate, this is a matter for the police. Have you gone to them with your concerns?"

Delphine backed off; she sighed and shook her head. "Monsieur Lautrec, people like me don't go to the police; they come to us." She paused a moment to calm down; then: "May I have another drink?"

He signaled for the bartender. The woman's passionate concern for her friend had an effect on Lautrec. He dropped the sarcasm and tried to put her at ease. "Maybe she suddenly took off from Paris for some good reason. Perhaps she went to Rouen? I believe she has relatives there."

Delphine shook her head. "She'd never go back there; she hates it. I know you were close to her, Monsieur. Didn't she tell you about her aunt?"

Lautrec looked down at his sketch; for a moment he was at a loss for words. Virginie had tried to tell him about her life, the abuse, her fears, her nightmares, but he would not listen. As usual, he had cut her off with sarcasm; it was his defense mechanism. He had enough trouble struggling with his own monsters. Finally, he looked up with sad eyes: "I'm sorry, Delphine. I hope she's all right but there's nothing—nothing I can do."

"I understand, Monsieur." She turned her attention to the sketch. "May I see it?"

"Of course you may." He handed her the drawing.

She studied it for a while before pronouncing: "It's really good. Is it—is it worth something?"

Lautrec smiled. "If I may?" She returned the sketch and he signed it. "There, Mademoiselle, you may have it as a memento of our meeting on this stormy midnight in a dingy *boîte*. As for its value, depending on the laws of supply and demand, in a few years it might indeed be worth something. On the other hand, if you're not inclined to wait for an upswing in the market for my work you may take it to Salis, the proprietor of Le Chat Noir. Tell him Henri said it was worth free drinks for a week, no less."

"Thank you Monsieur." She crooked a finger as if to return the favor by taking him into her confidence. He leaned forward, and she whispered: "Watch out for Rousseau."

"Who is Rousseau?"

"A fat pig, Monsieur. One of the inspectors running the investigation. His paid snoops and snitches are crawling all over Montmartre and Pigalle. He's already questioned me, and your friend Bernard. His partner, Lefebvre is all right, but Rousseau's a bastard. If he thinks you're guilty, he'll stop at nothing. He planted evidence on a friend of mine and got him twenty years transportation to Guiana."

"Thank you, Delphine. I'll be on my guard."

They sat together for a while, smoked, made small talk, and finished their drinks. The rain let up and the *boîte* emptied. Delphine and Lautrec were among the last to leave. The sleeping man in the corner watched them go, making a mental note of the hour. With a half-opened eye and keen ear, he had been watching and listening all along.

8

OCTOBER 17

A THEORY OF THE CASE

S o Achille, you think Virginie Ménard's our victim?"

"Given what we've got, she's our best likelihood," Achille replied. "I base my conclusion on the post-mortem examination, Chief Bertillon's identification analysis, the missing persons' report, and Inspector Rousseau's inquiries.

"Mlle Ménard's from Rouen; she's an orphan, born Virginie Mercier, raised by her uncle and aunt. Ménard's a stage name, taken from her former employer and benefactor, now deceased. Assuming we've identified the victim, I've developed a plan for proceeding with the investigation. Do you want to wait for Rousseau? He'll be here shortly."

"No, I have his report. Let's start without him."

They held their early meeting in Féraud's office. Achille had prepared a chart with a map of Montmartre indicating Virginie's route from the Moulin Rouge to her flat, including a timeline. He'd set the chart on an easel, and referred to it with a pointer.

"To my knowledge, no one has seen or heard from Mlle Ménard since Sunday the 11th at approximately two A.M. The last person to speak to her was a friend, a dancer at the Moulin Rouge, Delphine Lacroix. According to Rousseau's interview with Lacroix, Ménard did not feel threatened by anyone, nor did she express any specific concern about her safety at the time. But she had in the past expressed her fear of walking the streets unescorted at that hour, which of course is understandable. Following Lacroix's advice, she carried a razor in her purse for self-defense.

"Under normal conditions, it would take Ménard about thirty minutes to walk to her flat. She tipped the concierge to wait up for her, and the woman was concerned when Ménard didn't arrive on time. The concierge waited about one half-hour before checking the front door. She found a note in the girl's handwriting indicating she would be out of town for three days, but there was no indication of where she had gone or for what purpose.

"After three days had passed the concierge became suspicious and reported the missing girl to the police. The report was considered routine until the body was discovered in the cesspit. Sergeant Rodin notified us immediately and Rousseau questioned the concierge. She told him that Ménard was a 'good girl' with regular habits; she also provided information about Mlle Ménard's relatives in Rouen.

"I contacted the Rouen police to see if they could locate Mlle Ménard. They made inquiries, but turned up nothing. However, they did provide some interesting information about her relationship with her aunt and uncle. According to the locals, the Merciers abused the girl and treated her like a servant. Moreover, there's a neighborhood rumor that the aunt and uncle cheated their niece out of a small inheritance, and that she discovered their malfeasance and threatened legal action."

"Ah, they had a motive!" Féraud broke in.

Achille shrugged. "Perhaps, but further inquiry traced the rumor to a former employee of the Merciers who bore them a grudge."

The Chief nodded knowingly and said, "I see; please continue."

"The Merciers are butchers, so initially I thought they might have had the skill to cut her up. And they were out of town around the time the victim died."

The Chief's eyes widened. "Now you may be on to something!"

Achille frowned and shook his head. "They have an alibi. They went to Louviers to visit relatives. There are plenty of witnesses to confirm that. Further, considering the results of the post-mortem, I believe the victim's wounds are more likely the work of a surgeon rather than mere butchery."

The Chief sighed and leaned back in his chair. "All right, Achille. So it looks like the aunt and uncle are in the clear. What else have you got?"

"After her benefactor M. Ménard died, there was only one man in her life, Toulouse-Lautrec—"

There was a loud knock; Rousseau entered. "Good morning, Chief, professor. Sorry I'm late. That was one hell of a storm last night. Water and fallen branches all over the place. A bloody mess."

"Yes," Féraud replied. "The sewers in my neighborhood backed up; my damned cellar's flooded. Anyway, Achille's been briefing me about Virginie Ménard. We're concentrating our attention on her as the probable victim."

Rousseau walked round the easel and stood next to Achille. "That's right, Chief. If you ask me, it's Ménard for sure."

Achille addressed his partner. "We need to question everyone on her route. Even at two A.M. it's likely someone saw, or at least heard something."

"Right, professor. I'm on it."

Turning back to Féraud: "We believe she died during the afternoon or evening of the 14th and the body was dumped in the cesspit during the early morning hours of the following day. That means she lived at least three days after the disappearance. We know she was heavily drugged when she died. But we don't know where the death occurred, and we're still searching for her head and limbs.

"I'm going to check the records at Doctor Péan's' clinic, most particularly those relating to a vaginal hysterectomy performed the afternoon of the 14th. Lautrec was there, but I'm looking for a doctor who was present and might have a connection with Virginie Menard. I'm also going to check to see if there are any drugs missing from the dispensary. Which brings me to the subject of Péan's opinion regarding the mutilation: he thinks only a surgeon would have had the skill to cut her up that way."

"So, you think we're looking for a runty sawbones?" Rousseau interjected.

"I thought of that, but no. I believe we're looking for two individuals; a doctor and his stunted accomplice. What's more, despite the location of the body, the cigarette case, and Mlle Ménard's relationship with Lautrec, I think the accomplice is a short individual who a witness could *mistake* for Lautrec. In other words, I think the case was stolen and planted in the cesspit with the body by someone with a strong motive to pin the crime on the artist."

"What makes you think that?" the Chief asked.

"Although he lives like a bohemian, Lautrec's an aristocratic intellectual with a fine sense of honor. He doesn't seem the type to cut up a girl, dump the remains in the nearest hole, and leave a calling card."

Rousseau smirked. "Aristocratic intellectual, eh? Sounds like the Marquis de Sade."

Achille glared at his partner. "I wouldn't compare M. Lautrec to Sade."

"Have it your way, professor," Rousseau grunted.

Féraud narrowed his eyes skeptically before asking, "You're not completely ruling out Lautrec, are you?"

"No Chief, not completely," Achille replied. "However, as I've already indicated, I believe only a surgeon would have had the skill to perform the hysterectomy and amputations so neatly. On the other hand, Lautrec knows anatomy, he's observed operations, and by all accounts he's highly intelligent with strength and manual dexterity much like that of the most skilled surgeons. So, for the time being I can't rule him out as a suspect."

Féraud leaned back in his chair, closed his eyes, and fiddled with his watch fob; a habit when confronted with a thorny issue. Rousseau turned to Achille, shrugged, and made a face as though he'd smelled a fart. After a moment, Féraud opened his eyes and said, "The accomplice makes sense if we accept Dr. Péan's opinion. Do you have an individual in mind?"

"Searching the records I found a file on a circus performer, a dwarf named Joseph Rossini who lives near the victim."

"Jojo the Clown?" Rousseau broke in. "I put him inside for pimping, awhile back. A mean little bastard; the girls hated him. He had a method for dealing with whores if he thought they weren't handing over all their earnings. First offense, he'd strip the girl, tie her to a bed, and whip her ass with his belt. Second offense, he'd cut her with a stiletto. And if the bitch was stupid enough to cheat him a third time, well then he got *really* rough. Anyway, he's got a job in a circus and a clean record since he was released from prison." Rousseau turned to Achille with a grin. "And he's proved to be a good snitch, on occasion."

"Well," Achille replied, "I think we list him as a possible suspect. We might want to shadow him, see if he can lead us to the killer. Which brings me back to Lautrec; I want to question him myself, but I don't want to bring him in on a warrant. Despite the evidence, I'm not convinced he's our man. So I want to lay my cards on the table. Instead of doing a warrantless search behind his back, I want to get his permission to search the studio and his apartment. I also—"

"Wait a minute," Rousseau interrupted. "You want to tip him off?"

Achille turned to Féraud. "Chief, if he's innocent, he'll want to help us; he'll have nothing to hide. And I was about to say that I'd also ask him to let me take his fingerprints to compare them with the prints on the cloth and the cigarette case. If he refuses my requests I'd take that as evidence of guilt, in which case we can get a warrant and turn him over to the magistrate for questioning."

"Well, I don't know," Féraud muttered. "Rousseau, have you picked up anything from tailing Lautrec?"

"Not much, chief, except to confirm that our aristocratic painter's a degenerate little monkey. He spends more time scribbling and daubing in the brothels, cabarets, dance halls, and *boîtes* than he does in his studio. Oh, last night he met up with an old acquaintance of mine, the victim's girlfriend, Delphine Lacroix."

Féraud's brow knitted: "Oh really? And just how long have you known Lacroix?"

"A few years ago I put the screws on her for street-walking; I sent her man up for a nice, long vacation in *Le Bagne*."

Féraud smiled at Rousseau's reference to the infamous penal colony. "I suppose the young lady wouldn't hold a warm and friendly opinion of you. Anyway, I see the logic of Achille's approach. If Lautrec's got nothing to hide, he ought to cooperate, and his knowledge of the victim could be useful in helping us catch the criminal—or criminals." To Achille: "Have you anything else to tell me before I let you go?"

"Yes, chief. We're going to track down the shop that sold the canvas the body was wrapped in. And I've located Lautrec's tobacconist. I'm going to question him about the cigarettes found at the scene; they contain opium. If they're Lautrec's and they were stolen along with the cigarette case, that doesn't tell us much one way or the other, except that he's got a bad habit. On the other hand, if they aren't his, and I can track down the real opium smoker, well then, we'll have something."

Féraud nodded and began fumbling with his paperwork. "Very well, boys, carry on."

Betsy and Sir Henry had arrived early at the Javanese Village on the Esplanade des Invalides. Notwithstanding their timeliness, they were obliged to wait in line to enter the Pendopo, a columned, thatch-roofed, open-walled hall, where they would experience one of the Exhibitions' most popular shows, the four lovely Javanese dancers accompanied by a gamelan orchestra.

They had an almost perfect day for attending the Fair—bright, clear, and pleasantly cool following the storm. However, the tempest had left its calling card in the form of fallen leaves, branches, and muddy puddles that threatened the dragging hemlines of the female fair-goers' skirts.

Even in such conditions, Betsy was happy and content to wait. Sir Henry amused her with anecdotes and society gossip; when her mind wandered, she could breathe fresh, botanically perfumed air and drift off to faraway places conjured by the exotic surroundings. She consciously avoided a burgeoning subliminal desire to be freed from her invalid friend. But despite Betsy's mental evasion, her repressed fear of death's proximity emerged like drifting clouds, casting a guilty shadow over her sunniest moments.

Sir Henry pointed his stick at a tiny creature slowly wending its way up the muddy trail. "I wonder which will reach its destination first, this queue or that snail. Will you give me odds if I take the snail?"

Betsy laughed. "Oh Sir Henry, I think I should have the odds if I take the queue!"

Sir Henry smiled and stroked his moustache. "At any rate, I hear the show's worth it. The exotic, Oriental music and dance have had their impact on our young musicians. It may be a subtle form of colonial retribution. We've taken their lands by force of arms, imposed our religion, laws, and social values. Now they're paying us back with attractive novelties that insinuate themselves into our culture. Thus, the conquerors shall be ingeniously subverted and transformed by the conquered. You mark my words, Miss Endicott, within a generation instead of waltzing to the melodious strains of Strauss we shall gyrate to heathen yammering and the banging of pots and pans."

Betsy smiled in response to Sir Henry's fanciful prognostication. "You forget that we Americans are former colonials. Do you think our rough frontier ways will undermine the foundations of Western Civilization?"

"You Americans are transplanted English who have strayed from the fold. Nevertheless, we forgive you. After all, our differences are political but our culture remains the same."

"Don't be so sure of that, Sir Henry. You haven't experienced our Wild West."

Sir Henry screwed in his monocle, as if to get a better look at her. "Cowboys, Indians, and buffalo herds; should be jolly fun. I look forward to it."

Betsy laughed, but her expression changed suddenly. "I'm afraid you may not see it. When I last spoke to her about a sanatorium, Marcia seemed to have changed her mind."

He dropped his flippant manner, altering his demeanor with the alacrity of a chameleon to match her changed mood. "It appears we're moving, at last. We'll speak of this matter later, over luncheon."

⬿

After the dance, they lunched at the Anglo-American Bar on the first level of the Eiffel Tower. From their vantage point they could look out through plate glass windows and admire the panoramic view of the fairgrounds on the Champ de Mars. Many of the structures were ephemeral, but the great iron tower was there to stay. To some it was an eyesore, an ugly, brutal symbol of industrialization, but to most it was emblematic of French ingenuity and progress. Love it or hate it, the tower asserted itself magnificently as a prime attraction, a landmark and nascent cultural icon implanting the idea of Paris in the popular imagination.

Sir Henry studied Betsy's fine features as she sipped a light, white wine and stared into space. A large, garishly decorated red, white and blue balloon floated across her field of vision; Betsy's eyes focused on it and followed its progress. Her consciousness seemed to imitate the soaring object, drifting away from her troubles, at least for the moment.

"The dance was lovely, wasn't it?" he remarked quietly, as if to bring her imagination back to earth with a gentle tug on the tether. "Much better than I'd expected."

She turned her attention to Sir Henry. "Yes, I was thinking how much Marcia would have loved it. She would have sketched—" Betsy lifted a handkerchief to her eyes; she sobbed softly for a moment, and then controlled herself. "Forgive me, Sir Henry, I'm making a spectacle of myself."

He reached across the table and touched her gloved hand gently. "Think nothing of it. I understand your feelings, but you have no reason to reproach yourself. Marcia Brownlow's a great painter; she's devoted her life to art. If she wants to complete her work outside a sanatorium, there's nothing either of us can do. You must stop worrying about her, and start thinking more of yourself."

"I—I know you're right, but the past eleven years have meant a great deal to me. I'll see to it that's she's properly cared for. She's been discussing plans with an old mutual friend, Arthur Wolcott. She told me Arthur invited her to stay with him at his country home in England. If she doesn't return to America, I'll do what I can for her whether she remains in Paris, or goes to live with Arthur."

Sir Henry seized an opportunity. "Ah, you think she might go with Arthur? All things considered, it might be best for her."

Betsy's eyes widened. "Do you really think so? I know she and Arthur get along, and she'd love the countryside and the society."

"Yes, and since she doesn't want to go to a sanatorium, I think it's a splendid alternative. And here's another idea. You might consider taking up residence in London, for a while, that is. You could visit her regularly; it's not far by train." He paused a moment and smiled. "Of course, I can't claim to be disinterested. After all, if you *were* in London, I should have the hope of enjoying more of your company."

Betsy blushed and said nothing; but she did nod her head agreeably. She continued gazing fondly at the handsome physician, as though he were the answer to her prayers.

∽∞∽

Péan's clerk was a well-dressed, well-groomed, middle-aged, officious little man with a high-pitched voice and meticulously waxed *impériale*, making him appear like an actor impersonating the late Emperor. He opened a leather-bound journal on a lectern near the entrance to the operating theater and flipped the pages to October 14, 1889. "Here we are Inspector, a list of the gentlemen who witnessed the vaginal hysterectomy."

Achille went through the list, six witnesses in all. Four were well-known physicians and surgeons with practices in Paris. The fifth was Toulouse-Lautrec, and the sixth appeared to be an Englishman. "Who is Sir Henry Collingwood?"

The clerk smiled as he proudly extolled the clinic's operations and its widespread reputation. "Sir Henry Collingwood is an eminent English physician and surgeon, a very affable gentleman. He's on holiday in Paris, enjoying the Fair and the many attractions of our city. He takes a particular interest in gynecological surgery and therefore has come to our clinic to observe Dr. Péan's world-renowned operations."

"I see, so naturally I assume he would want to be present when Dr. Péan demonstrated a new and very important technique in his specialty?"

"Of course, Inspector. As I recall, Sir Henry was most keen to observe the vaginal hysterectomy.

Achille smiled amiably. "I assume you can provide me with a detailed description of the English gentleman?"

"Yes, of course."

"Can you show me how many operations Sir Henry attended?"

"They're all logged in the book. I believe the first was a few weeks ago."

Achille examined the journal. It confirmed that Sir Henry had witnessed four gynecological surgeries: two abdominal hysterectomies (one with ovariotomy) and two mastectomies (one single, one double). Lautrec had also been present at these operations.

"I'm afraid I must take this journal to headquarters so the relevant pages can be copied. I apologize for the inconvenience. I'll issue you a receipt and have the book returned by courier as soon as possible."

"Oh very well, Inspector," the clerk replied with an air of annoyance.

This peevishness irritated Achille; the clerk had a civic duty to cooperate. But he maintained his composure and congenial smile. He needed the clerk's cooperation, and he understood how an investigation interfered with the ordinary citizen's routine; unlike the "old boys" (Rousseau being a prime example), he rarely resorted to intimidation. "Now Monsieur, I have a question about the dispensary. Have you had any report of missing supplies, most particularly narcotics, sedatives, or anesthetics such as morphine, chloroform, or chloral hydrate?"

"No, Inspector; the apothecary keeps those items in a locked cabinet and maintains an inventory. Any suspected theft would have been reported to the police."

"I see; does your apothecary replenish those items on a regular basis?"

"Of course; he orders them from a chemist. I can give you his name and address."

Achille was pleased to note the clerk's reversion to a more accommodating manner; his little snit appeared to have been temporary. "Thank you, Monsieur; you've been most helpful. Now, before I leave, I'll need to interview all the doctors who assisted in the vaginal hysterectomy. If they're unavailable today, I'll require their addresses. I'll also need contact information for the gentlemen who are listed in the journal, including Sir Henry."

The clerk nodded. "I'll do what I can to assist in your investigation."

Achille trusted the offer of assistance was sincere. "Thank you, Monsieur. If anything turns up that you believe might be helpful, or you have any questions regarding this case, please don't hesitate to contact me. You have my card."

∞

Arthur escorted Marcia to the Luxembourg gardens, where he hired a bath-chair and gallantly pushed her up and down, skirting puddles, fallen branches, and dead leaves scattered over the winding lanes. After a while, his increase in girth and years caught up with him. Puffing from unaccustomed exertion, he pulled to one side of a wide promenade, stopped, lifted his hat, and mopped his brow.

Marcia turned her head and looked up at him with a wistful smile. "Do you recognize this place?"

He gazed up the lane that forked round a fountain, with benches to the left, shrubbery and flowerbeds bordering the right. Beyond the fountain was a pair of statues in the Greco-Roman style, more benches, and an antique urn filled with bright red flowers. Further on, a staircase led to a white balustraded walkway fronting a stand of broad shade trees.

"By Jove, you painted this scene, didn't you? As I recall, Betsy posed next to the fountain. She wore a bright yellow dress."

"Your memory is sharp as a tack. That was eleven years ago when I was masquerading as Mark and Betsy fell in love with a man who never was."

"Ah, yes," Arthur sighed and said no more.

"Betsy and I lunched at a nice outdoor restaurant not far from here. A band was playing *Je suis Titania*. I wonder if it's still there. The restaurant I mean."

Arthur needed rest and refreshment and replied enthusiastically. "I know the place well. Shall we go there?"

"Oh yes, that would be lovely."

They found a table under a breeze-ruffled awning where several floating leaves had settled. The band wasn't playing; the only sounds were the distant shouts and laughter of children playing with hoops and balls, the trickle of a nearby fountain, chattering birds perched in tall, denuded branches, and the polite murmuring of their fellow lunchers.

Marcia picked at her roast chicken, but she enjoyed her wine. They made pleasant small talk, until she turned to the subject of Betsy. "This place brings back memories, Arthur. Now, I feel like a pentimento in her portrait; a ghostly, over-painted figure watching from a balcony while Betsy and Sir Henry make love in the garden below."

For a moment, Arthur was at a loss for words. Then: "I realize this is difficult for you, but you've already indicated your intentions. A clean, amicable break seems best. And, by all accounts Sir Henry is a decent fellow."

Marcia smiled wryly. "As an independent, freethinking woman I fear I must question his 'decency.' In my humble opinion, the diagnosis and treatment of 'female hysteria' is a medical dodge, a pseudo-scientific means of keeping us in our place. When one of our sex asserts herself, demands her right to vote and full equality under the law, and then reacts to all the abuse, ridicule, and scorn directed at her, it's all too easy to say she's 'hysterical' or suffering from 'female troubles' and prescribe treatments that range from the demeaning and humiliating to the brutal and cruel."

Arthur found the subject awkward and embarrassing, but he had written about the inequality of women and was not unsympathetic to their plight. Nevertheless, he tried to divert the unwelcome drift with a question: "Have you found Sir Henry's treatment unsatisfactory?"

Marcia thought a moment and took a sip of wine before answering. "No, I'd say he's quite professional and he does have an excellent bedside manner. But then, my illness does not fall within his peculiar specialty. On the other hand, he might see Betsy as a subject ripe for his nostrums. She's moody and unpredictable, especially when she drinks. What's more, she's past thirty and hasn't been under the influence or domination of a man since she came of age. And of course, there's her considerable fortune."

Arthur sighed. "You paint a bleak picture. However, if Sir Henry were a bounder I doubt he'd be able to maintain such a sterling reputation and lucrative practice. People talk in London society, as you well know, and you can't keep objectionable behavior covert for too long. People won't know you; they'll cut you dead in public."

"I suppose you're right." Marcia sighed and turned to gaze at a stand of gently rustling beech trees.

Arthur hesitated; he wondered if Marcia's worries were more the consequence of jealous envy than concern for her friend. Considering the hopelessness of her condition, he opted for the latter. "You might speak to Aggie Fitzroy. She was one of Sir Henry's patients."

Aggie Fitzroy, formerly Lady Agatha Clifford, was one of the great society beauties of the previous decade. As Mark Brownlow, Marcia had painted a portrait of Lady Agatha that caused a sensation and, for a brief time, they had been lovers. Marcia's ears pricked up and her eyes widened at the mention of the name. "How is Aggie? I haven't seen her in ages."

Arthur already regretted mentioning Agatha, but he answered forthrightly. "She's seen better days, I'm afraid. When she married Colonel Fitzroy she had quite a fortune from her first marriage, and she believed the Colonel was flush as well. After all, he had Brodemeade, a fine manor and lands. Everything looked beautiful on the surface, but was mortgaged to the hilt; Aggie didn't learn the worst of it until four years ago when the colonel died. The whole kit and caboodle had to be sold to satisfy creditors; Aggie was lucky to keep some of her separate property. But that wasn't the worst of it. Her health and looks declined along with her fortune. That's why she consulted with Sir Henry. Now, she's no longer welcomed in the best society, and from all accounts lives a sad and lonely life."

"Poor Aggie," Marcia murmured. "*Où sont la neiges d'antan?* She was once my ideal of the sublime and the beautiful. I'm afraid I've misspent my brief career chasing aesthetic butterflies." She paused a moment; then: "If you don't mind, I'd like to go to the *Atelier* Cormon to ask about a model, Virginie Ménard. She may have inspired me to use what time I have left to do something important."

Arthur raised an eyebrow. "Could she be another of your 'aesthetic butterflies'?"

Marcia laughed. "You'll never change. Always ready with a caustic observation. But I know your secret, my old friend. Beneath that sardonic exterior beats a kind and generous heart. You're just ashamed to show it."

9

OCTOBER 17, MORNING, AFTERNOON AND EVENING

AN INTERVIEW

Your graphite powder has done the trick, Inspector. The lines on the fingerprints are as sharp and clear as can be."

Gilles displayed his photographs with pride. He and Achille studied the results of their experiment aided by the bright morning light streaming through the windows in Bertillon's laboratory. The photographs of the cigarette case with enhanced latent fingerprints had been set next to the photos of the stained cloth for comparison. After a minute of careful examination, Achille smiled.

Pointing first to the cigarette case and then to the cloth, Achille said, "You see the difference, Gilles? It's most obvious in the thumbs. One has what's called an ulnar loop; the other doesn't. I'm certain these are the fingerprints of two different individuals."

Gilles looked carefully and nodded. "I see, Inspector, but how does this aid your investigation?"

He replied cautiously. The new method of identification might be viewed as a radical challenge to Bertillon's established system, though that was not what Achille intended. Rather, he conceived of fingerprinting as a supplement to the *portrait parlé* and anthropometrical method. But means of enhancing the prints and "lifting" images at the crime scene needed to be developed before the widespread fingerprinting of suspects became practical. Premature advocacy for the new system might subject Achille to ridicule, not to mention Chief Bertillon's ire for poaching on his preserve. At this point, fingerprints might be useful, but only on a case-by-case basis. "If I can fingerprint a suspect and compare his prints to these photographs, I'll either have evidence of criminal activity to support an accusation or exculpatory evidence to rule out that suspect. Either way, it's a step forward in the investigative process."

"I see, so all you need to do is haul in a suspect or two and fingerprint them."

Achille smiled wryly. "Yes my friend, it's as *simple* as that."

He returned to his small corner office on the same floor as Féraud's. Achille's cubbyhole was in stark contrast to the chief's cluttered workspace: neat, spotless, and well-organized, with little personalization and nothing whimsical or macabre. The only items that proclaimed his "ownership" were a nameplate and desk photographs of Adele and Jeanne. Otherwise, the place could have been exchanged with any other inspector assigned to the case.

Achille sipped lukewarm, black coffee and nibbled a stale brioche while reviewing his file and planning the rest of his day. Féraud had assigned him more detectives; he was pushing for results. He most particularly feared a surge of "Ripper mania" in the newspapers. Reporters were snooping round Montmartre, searching out every gossip and crackpot with a theory of the case. If the penny-a-liners couldn't find anything sensational enough to satisfy their editors, they would surely make it up.

As for the leads, none of the hospitals had recently reported thefts of narcotics or anesthetics; the chemists and apothecaries provided lists of hundreds of Parisian doctors who routinely used the drugs in their practice, but so far they hadn't turned up anyone connected to Virginie Ménard.

Lautrec's tobacconist examined the cigarettes; he recognized the paper and the Turkish tobacco, but he swore he didn't use opium in his blends. However, he did refer to tobacconists who included the drug for special customers, but further investigation hadn't yet uncovered anything of interest.

The search through the art supply shops had also proved fruitless. There were more painters in Paris that used the particular type of canvas in which the torso was wrapped than doctors who administered narcotics and anesthetics. The old cliché applied; it was like looking for a needle in a haystack.

Tomorrow was Sunday, a day off, and Féraud was impatient. He wanted an arrest before another body turned up and made more of a stink in the newspapers. Rousseau was itching to arrest Lautrec. But the chief backed Achille, partly because he hesitated to accuse a descendant of Raymond, the great crusader. Not that Féraud gave a damn about nobility, but he was very sensitive when it came to the nation's history and the honor of France.

Achille doubted they were dealing with Jack the Ripper, or another criminal in that vein. And he also believed that the fingerprints, along with a search of his studio and apartment, would exculpate Lautrec. Much of Achille's thinking along these lines was intuitive; Lautrec seemed too obvious a suspect, as was often the case with a frame-up. As for the Ripper, the surgery in this case was too neat and clinical, whereas the Ripper's victims had been savagely butchered. Yet he feared that some failure on his part, a missed clue or inadequately investigated lead, might result in another woman's death.

Achille finished his coffee and dumped the unappetizing remains of the brioche in the wastebasket. He would have worked all day Sunday if he thought it would help the case. But he'd promised Adele a day in the country at a quiet *auberge* only twenty minutes from central Paris by train. They'd leave Jeanne with Madame Berthier and nanny. *Madame will enjoy that. More time to infect my child with her grandmamma's prejudices.* There was no telephone at the inn, but the station was nearby; if a telegram came from headquarters Achille would return immediately.

He lit a cigar, packed his briefcase, pocketed his credentials and service revolver, and prepared to leave. He was about to confront Toulouse-Lautrec. There was a risk in asking the artist to cooperate voluntarily without a warrant, but Achille thought it was worth it. If possible, he wanted to know the man, to gain his confidence and assistance in cracking the case. He checked his watch; two detectives would meet him outside Lautrec's apartment. Two others were detailed to the studio; they waited at the local station with Sergeant Rodin. They would begin the search as soon as Achille issued the order by telephone. It was time to go.

∞

Established in Montmartre near the foot of the hill, the *Atelier* Cormon was located in a spacious workroom with large exposed wooden beams, unpainted walls, and immense glass windows, lamps, and reflectors suspended from rafters to provide the desired lighting. High shelves stacked with white plaster casts of nymphs, Caesars, gods, and goddesses lined the unpainted walls, and there was a centrally situated dais for models. A sharply distinctive, but not unpleasant odor of linseed oil and turpentine permeated the atmosphere; several students seated themselves at easels surrounding the dais, concentrating their attention on a dark, young woman posing nude, in a semi-reclining position. Marcia immediately recognized her as Virginie's friend, Delphine Lacroix.

Arthur held Marcia's arm as she scanned the premises, searching for the *maître*. But Cormon was not there; he only attended once a week to provide friendly critiques, suggestions for improvement, and encouragement where it was due. She saw Émile Bernard and waved to catch his eye. A young man working next to Bernard spotted her first. Recognizing the noted American artist, he leaned over and nudged his friend.

"Hey, Émile, you see that woman standing near the entrance, next to the gentleman? I believe she's waving at you. That's Mademoiselle Brownlow, isn't it? Her landscape won a Silver Medal at the Fair."

Bernard put down his brush and looked up. Surprised, he replied to Marcia's friendly greeting with a curt nod. Then he got up from his chair and picked his way gingerly around the sketching and painting students.

Marcia greeted Émile with a handshake and introduced him to Arthur. "Good-day, Monsieur Bernard; I don't believe you know my friend, Arthur Wolcott?"

Bernard shook Arthur's hand and greeted him: "I'm honored, Monsieur Wolcott. I've read and enjoyed many of your novels and stories."

Arthur smiled warmly. "Thank you, Monsieur. That's very kind of you. And Miss Brownlow has recommended your work to me on several occasions." That was a courteous deception. Marcia had said little to Arthur about Bernard, and what she had said was indifferent at best. But the polite deceit ran both ways; Émile had read little of Arthur's writing.

Bernard turned to Marcia with a curious look in his eye: "What brings you to the *Atelier*, Mademoiselle?"

"I was looking for Virginie Ménard, but I see she's not here. I'd like her to model for me, privately. Do you know how I might get in touch with her?"

Bernard's mildly questioning expression transformed into a bewildered stare. "You haven't heard, Mademoiselle? No one's seen Virginie for days. Now the police are going round asking questions of everyone who knew her. They suspect foul play. But perhaps you haven't read the newspapers about the unidentified woman's body found on the Rue Tourlaque?"

Marcia said nothing. Her eyes registered shock; she fixed her gaze on Émile, but did not see him. Instead, she had a vision of Virginie's corpse laid out on a slab in the Morgue. Arthur immediately sensed something was wrong. He put his arms around Marcia to prevent her from collapsing, and spoke to Bernard in a hoarse, urgent whisper: "Please Monsieur, would you kindly fetch a chair for Mademoiselle?"

Bernard ran to the nearest empty seat and returned shortly. Arthur thanked him, and helped Marcia into the chair. By now, almost all the students had abandoned their work to observe the drama; Delphine broke her pose, twisting her head round to see what the fuss was about.

"May I get you a restorative, Mademoiselle? I'm sure someone has a flask of brandy."

Marcia shook her head. "Please don't trouble yourself, Émile. I'm all right; I apologize for disrupting the class. Your news came as quite a shock. You see, Virginie had inspired me to conceive something new, something different in my art. I was hoping—" She caught herself mid-sentence and paused a moment before continuing: "But of course, my art means nothing now. It's Virginie I'm worried about."

Bernard took her frail hand and smiled sympathetically. "Please don't reproach yourself. She has affected us that way. I too had a glimmer of hope for something new, but now. . . ." He sighed and shook his head. "But now, I'm at a loss. There's nothing we can do for her. It's in God's hands—God and the Sûreté."

⌦

Marcia stared out the window as the cab rolled along the boulevard. Her painter's eye acquired an impression of a city under a grayish-blue sky; cloud-diffused light glanced off slate roofs, gray stone walls, and shaded windows; russet leaves rustled gently in a mild breeze, purple shadows danced on the pavement. As she took in the scene visually she listened to an accompaniment, the steady, rhythmic clip-clop of horses' hooves, the rumbling wheels. She swayed with the incessant rocking of the carriage, which had a calming, almost hypnotic effect.

Arthur sat across from her, worried that the day's events and revelations had been too much of a strain; they'd taken a toll. He would normally attempt an amusing quip, but he doubted whether anything he could say would cheer her up. Finally, he ventured a hopeful comment if only to break the uneasy silence:

"It's sad news about the girl. But perhaps she'll show up."

Marcia turned away from the window and regarded him wistfully. "Do you remember our early days in Florence when we used to discuss problems of perception, the difference between appearances and reality?"

Arthur smiled. "Yes, I recall some of our metaphysical chit-chat. I was playing the Socratic schoolmaster; I could be awfully pretentious in those days."

"No Arthur, it wasn't pretense. You've always been perceptive, well-read, and worldly-wise; I've benefitted from all you've taught me. We live in a world of illusions; little or nothing is certain. We presume probable truths are certainties, until someone clearly rebuts our presumption. As for our will and freedom to choose, in most cases it seems our choice is limited to those falsehoods we wish to believe. I've always preferred beautiful lies to ugly ones. Perhaps I also prefer a beautiful lie to an ugly truth.

"Lately, I've been thinking a lot about my life and career. At some point I made a crucial decision. Putting up all my talent and skill as collateral, I borrowed beauty from nature and invested her precious treasure in my art. For a time, I reaped a rich reward. But the market for beauty—at least *my* stock of beauty—has dropped of late. Now all my capital's spent; my credit's blown. Virginie Ménard appeared like a rich new resource to draw upon, a life-saving bank of beauty. But she's gone, most likely the victim of a brutal crime. The damnable thing for me is that, deep down, I mourn my own loss from her absence more than I care for her suffering and death. I'm guilty in a moral sense; I'm little better than her murderer."

Arthur stared at her for a moment. Then, his voice choked with emotion, he replied, "No, my dear. You're tired and you've had a shock. I believe you loved the girl, as you loved Betsy and Aggie Fitzroy. I think I know you as well as anyone. You've given far more to the world through your art, than you ever took in return."

Arthur crossed over to the opposite seat and put his arm around her. Marcia laid her head on his shoulder and wept.

⌘

Achille puffed nervously on a small cigar as he waited in a cab outside Toulouse-Lautrec's apartment. The two detectives were stationed on either side of the street, ready in case he tried to make a run for it. Not that Achille expected a son of the Count of Toulouse to bolt like a common criminal; it was simply a routine precaution.

He glanced at his watch, leaned out the window, and pitched his half-smoked, half-chewed cigar into the gutter. Lautrec was coming up the sidewalk. Achille signaled his men and exited the cab. He approached the artist, flashed his credentials, and introduced himself: "Monsieur de Toulouse-Lautrec, I am Inspector Achille Lefebvre of the Sûreté. If you please, I'd like you to accompany me to headquarters where you may be of assistance in an important investigation. I apologize for the inconvenience, and I promise not to detain you any longer than is necessary."

Lautrec looked up at Achille's slate-colored chin and black nostrils; the bright sunshine made him squint and he shaded his eyes with a hand. "Inconvenience, you say? It's a damned liberty, accosting me this way. Have you a warrant for my arrest? If so, please state the charge."

Achille smiled and spoke calmly. "No charge and no warrant, at present, Monsieur. However, if you insist, I can obtain one. But I do have some property that belongs to you, a gold cigarette case."

Lautrec raised his eyebrows in surprise. "Oh, you've found my cigarette case? It's quite valuable. I've been searching for it for days. But why couldn't the police notify me rather than approach me in such melodramatic fashion?"

Achille noticed Lautrec's response; his attitude and tone of voice in expressing his primary concern for lost property reinforced Achille's belief in the artist's innocence. "The cigarette case was discovered at a crime scene, and is being held in evidence. If you'll kindly accompany me, I'll explain the matter on the way to headquarters. My cab is waiting up the street."

"All right, Inspector, if you insist. Lead on, and I'll follow."

∽∾

Lautrec accepted Achille's "invitation" to wait at headquarters while the detectives searched his studio and apartment. Achille detailed a promising young man, Inspector Legros, to head up the search. Legros was one of the "new men," a recent polytechnic graduate skilled in Bertillon's methods. Achille left Rousseau to his specialty, working the dragnet with the aid of his network of snoops and snitches. But there was something else to Achille's thinking besides assigning the man best suited to a specific job; in his opinion Rousseau seemed much too eager to have access to the artist's premises where he might make a brilliant "discovery" that established Lautrec's guilt, QED. It wasn't that Achille didn't trust his partner; he just preferred not to lead him into temptation.

To gain Lautrec's confidence and kill time, Achille took the artist on a Cook's tour of the Palais de Justice before returning to his office for questioning. Achille and Lautrec sat facing one another across the desk. He offered the artist a cigarette, which he declined, preferring to smoke his own brand.

Lautrec struck a match, took a few puffs, leaned back and observed Achille with a shrewd smile. "Thank you, Inspector, for that delightful excursion through the bowels of our justice system. I found it most edifying, like the popular tour of our sewers and catacombs, or a charming day at the Morgue. Now I am in your debt and completely at your mercy. You may commence with the thumb-screw and rack."

Achille laughed. "You are a wit, Monsieur, but a poor public servant is hardly a worthy target for your rapier thrusts. At any rate, my men are very efficient." He glanced at the wall clock. "They should finish their work presently, so you needn't be bored much longer." He opened a drawer, retrieved an evidence bag and a pair of gloves, and carefully displayed the cigarette case on his desk. "Can you identify this object? But please be so good as not to touch it."

Lautrec leaned forward and examined the cigarette case. "That's mine all right. But why do you handle it so gingerly, and with gloves?"

Achille returned the case to the bag, put it back in the drawer, and removed his gloves. "I'm preserving the fingerprints. It's a new technique, an experiment in forensic science."

"Oh, that interests me, Inspector. It appears you're very progressive and well-educated—for a policeman. Now I just happen to be a good Cartesian."

Achille smiled broadly; he saw an opening. "A good Cartesian, you say? Is that why you enjoy observing surgical operations?"

"That's a clever comment, Inspector. I thought you were going to refer to Cartesian rationalism, his a priori reasoning, and forget the empirical side, such as his dissection of animals to discover how they work. Break things down to their simplest components. After all, we must use some induction to set up our hypotheses before we proceed to our deductions.

"Yes, I do enjoy watching people being cut up. Surgery is like my art. I probe for the truth; I apply scientific method, dicing things down and then reassembling them on paper and canvas.

"I study facial expressions, gestures, physical attributes, and the underlying anatomical structure, physiology, and psychology to get an impression of character types; I can draw on this bank of knowledge to relate the individual subject of a portrait to a known category."

Achille looked Lautrec directly in the eye before pursuing: "I see, Monsieur. Do you apply your method to your *intimate* relationships?"

Lautrec winced; he clearly found the question offensive. He took a last puff, and then vigorously stubbed out the cigarette in an ashtray. "I'm not sure I follow your meaning, Inspector," he muttered. "Unless you're referring to a syllogism based on the major premise, all whores fuck for money."

Achille remained calm but firm, like a physician sounding his patient. "Tell me about Virginie Ménard. First, I'd like to know when, where, and how you met her."

Lautrec paused a moment to regain his composure before answering. "I met her about one year ago, at the *Atelier* Cormon. She was modeling, and she interested me. I'd already heard of her from a friend, Vincent Van Gogh. At the time, she lived near him and his brother Theo, on the Rue Lepic. He got her to pose a couple of times."

"Excuse me, Monsieur. Do you know where I can find Vincent Van Gogh?"

"Yes Inspector; he's locked up in the asylum at St. Rémy. He hasn't been in Paris for more than a year."

"I see; please continue."

"Well, there isn't much to tell. Our relationship began professionally and developed into something more. But it ended in argument and recrimination. That was about a month ago."

"What was the ultimate cause of the break up?"

Lautrec laughed sardonically. He held out his hands in a mocking gesture. "Clap me in manacles and convey me to the dungeon. I'll admit my guilt, Inspector. I was a jealous lover."

Achille ignored the sarcasm. "Of whom were you jealous, Monsieur? Can you give me a name, or names?"

Lautrec shook his head. "That's the devil of it; she never told me, no matter how hard I tried to pry it out of her. Instead she made up excuses for her long absences, prevarications that wouldn't have fooled a simple child. She insulted my intelligence."

Achille noted that the relationship had left wounds that had not yet healed. "A moment ago, you said she 'interested' you. Could you be specific?"

Lautrec sighed deeply. "You've probably heard that she was a great beauty. Well, I don't require beauty in a model or a lover—or rather a sexual partner. What really interests me is the facial expression, in a model that is. I don't copulate with the face.

"In Virginie's case, she could convey a sense of suffering, sadness, and even madness; at other times she could express joy and unbridled ecstasy. And it all seemed natural; not like what you see on stage or in sentimental art. I'll admit she fascinated me. But living with her was difficult. She was plagued by nightmares, demons from her childhood that drove her to hysterics. I wanted her and hated the idea of sharing her with anyone. On the other hand, living with her could be hell, and I felt relieved when she left me."

"I appreciate your candor, Monsieur. Do you know of any other artists or individuals who took a particular interest in Mlle Ménard?"

Lautrec thought for a moment. "My friend Émile Bernard wanted to use her for a new painting; he saw something spiritual in her. But I understand you've already talked to him. He couldn't hurt a fly. And there is an American woman, Marcia Brownlow, a well-regarded painter. She seemed to like my portrait of Virginie and urged her friend, a wealthy collector, to buy it. But she made an odd comment. It could have been a compliment or an insult; I still don't know quite what to make of it. At any rate, they've yet to make an offer."

"Do you know where I can contact Mlle Brownlow and her friend?"

"Yes, they're staying at the Grand Hotel."

"Can you tell me what was so odd about her comment?"

"She distinguished my portrait of Virginie from my other work by reference to its 'prettiness.' Mlle Brownlow is known and much admired for her vivid landscapes and portraits of beautiful women. She's one of those aesthetic painters who get inspiration from nature's 'beauty.' I'm not such an artist. To call one of my paintings 'pretty' is damning it with faint praise."

Achille nodded without comment. Then: "Can you think of anyone else who might have taken an interest in Mlle Ménard, perhaps a doctor who paints for a hobby?"

Lautrec looked away for a moment, as if searching his memory. "Well, there's Sir Henry Collingwood, an English doctor visiting Paris on holiday. He attended the life drawing classes at the *Atelier*. I know he made sketches of Virginie, but I don't recall him showing any particular interest in her."

Achille had anticipated the answer. He pursued: "Do you recall seeing this English doctor at Péan's clinic?"

"Yes, on a few occasions."

"How about at the vaginal hysterectomy Dr. Péan performed on Wednesday the 14th?"

Lautrec narrowed his eyes. "It's strange you should mention that. I don't recall *seeing* Sir Henry there, but he did turn up at Le Chat Noir that evening. He mentioned attending the operation. Of course, I could have missed him. I was concentrating on the procedure and my sketch."

"Do you recall any details of the conversation?"

"Not much, except that Bernard was there. He'd been looking for Virginie and was concerned that he couldn't find her."

"Did you and Sir Henry share his concern?"

"No, I thought she'd turn up sooner or later. Sir Henry agreed, but then he didn't know her. Or at least, I didn't *think*—" Lautrec stopped and looked down at his hands. For the first time that day he appeared worried. The sarcasm and flippant manner disappeared. He looked back at Achille with a troubled expression: "Inspector, do you think Sir Henry had anything to do with Virginie's disappearance?"

Achille noticed the sudden change in demeanor. "I don't know, Monsieur. You said Mlle Ménard had, on occasion, behaved hysterically. Did you know that Sir Henry specializes in the treatment of female hysteria?"

Lautrec shook his head. "No Inspector, I didn't know that."

The telephone rang. Achille lifted the earpiece and transmitter. It was Inspector Legros. The detectives had completed their search of Lautrec's studio and apartment; they found nothing suspicious, and were returning to headquarters.

For a moment, Achille wondered if he should tell Lautrec the outcome of the search. Under these circumstances, other detectives might have tried to trap a suspect and trick him into a confession. But he decided that dealing forthrightly with this man would achieve the best results. "The search is completed, Monsieur. I'm pleased to inform you the detectives found nothing incriminating."

Lautrec smiled with relief. "Then I'm free to go?"

"I can't legally hold you, Monsieur Lautrec. But I do have a couple of questions and the fingerprinting to complete. If you please, it won't take much time."

"I'll do what I can, Inspector. If anyone's harmed Virginie I—I want to help catch the criminal."

"Thank you. Do you recall the last time you saw Mlle Ménard?"

"After midnight last Sunday morning at the Moulin Rouge; I sketched her dancing, but I didn't speak to her."

"Did you speak or socialize with anyone else?"

"I spoke briefly to a couple of people, Zidler the Moulin's manager and the gallery owner Joyant—just small talk and business. But I did spend some time with the American women, Mlle Brownlow and Mlle uh—Endicott I believe was her name."

"And you discussed Mlle Ménard?"

"Yes, we spoke about my portrait of Virginie."

Achille returned to the subject of the cigarette case. "Did you smoke?"

"Yes, I smoked and offered them cigarettes."

"Did you have your cigarette case at that time?"

Lautrec thought a moment, frowned and shook his head. "I believe so, but I can't be sure. I'm afraid my memory of the occasion is a bit foggy."

"Do you recall noticing anyone suspicious at the time, someone who might have taken the case?"

"Inspector, have you been to the Moulin Rouge on a Saturday evening? The place is packed to the rafters, especially with all the tourists here for the Exposition. Thieves could easily work the Moulin unnoticed."

Achille nodded while making a mental note: *We'll need to question the manager and the staff, and the American women too.* "Thank you, Monsieur; we'll end the questioning here. I trust you don't plan to leave Paris in the near future?"

Lautrec smiled and shook his head. "No Inspector; I shall remain at your disposal."

Achille took ink impressions of Lautrec's fingerprints according to Galton's method. Then he walked the artist to a cab. He thanked him again, adding "You have my card, Monsieur. If you have any further information regarding this case, please contact me immediately."

"Of course, Inspector, and I apologize for my earlier rudeness. I understand your job is difficult and important; you serve the public interest. Good afternoon."

He watched Lautrec enter the cab. Achille had already noticed how difficult it was for the artist to go up and down stairs or to step into or descend from a carriage on his stunted, misshapen legs. *A man with such a disability could not have carried the body very far. As for his motive, jealousy, he made no attempt to conceal it. He did not behave like a guilty man. However, I can't jump to conclusions; it would be a mistake to rule him out completely.*

Achille took the fingerprint card to the evidence room, where he compared Lautrec's prints to those on the cloth and the cigarette case. The difference between Lautrec's prints and the prints on the canvas was obvious. The cigarette case was another matter. The graphite powder dusting had turned up more than one set of prints. He hypothesized that a very faint finger and thumbprint that he had not noticed on initial examination were Lautrec's; he assumed the fresher prints belonged to one of the criminal accomplices.

On the way back to his office, Achille began mentally composing his report for Féraud. He believed he now had enough evidence to rule out Lautrec as a suspect. He would concentrate his attention on his two man theory, focusing on Sir Henry Collingwood and Joseph Rossini, aka Jojo the Clown, while keeping an open mind as to other possibilities.

10

S cattered clouds drifted through a bright cerulean sky. A stand of rustling trees, shrubs, and reeds lined the muddy, sloping banks; forms shaded burnt umber, sienna, ochre, and verdigris cast their reflections in calm, silvery water. The slow-moving river forked round the island of Chatou; in the near distance a Paris-bound train trailing gray smoke rumbled across an iron bridge. A border of rolling hills appeared on the horizon; bright verdure darkened in purplish shadow.

The skiff made steady progress toward the dock; oars splashing rhyth-mically, stirring a mild wake. Adele, dressed in a light blue frock with lace collar, her pretty head adorned with a flower and ribbon-trimmed straw bonnet, sat in the stern and handled the tiller. She smiled at Achille, who sat facing her as he pulled at the oars. Adele admired her husband's powerful bare arms glistening with a thin film of sweat, the muscular power of his broad chest and shoulders, the athletic grace of his stroke. The "professor" seemed like a different man when he took off his jacket, rolled up his sleeves, and got into a boat. He had been rowing since he was a boy, and was an expert in a skiff or a one-man scull.

Achille savored the moment, the rural calm, the peace of the river, the ineffable charms of nature and his young wife. But the sound of a train rushing over a bridge reminded him that his office was only a half-hour away and a message from Féraud summoning him to duty was an unwelcome possibility. The fact of a vicious murderer on the loose was never far from his thoughts. If he pushed the case down for an instant, it always resurfaced, like a gas-bloated corpse breaching the surface of a placid stream.

A persistent chugging, mechanical throbbing, and the piercing cry of a whistle broke the silence. A small steam launch glided by, churning up a white wake that rocked the skiff. Aboard the launch, a party of swells laughed, waved, and lifted their glasses in salute to the boaters, then returned to their champagne and foie gras.

Adele made a funny face and laughed. "What a bunch of loafers. They ought to strip down and get some exercise."

Achille grinned and shook his head. "Oh, I don't know about that. I'd love a steam launch, if we could afford it. We could take longer trips with the little one and your mother along for the excursion."

The thought of her husband stuck in the close confines of a boat with her mother amused Adele. "Would you *really* like that, my dear? Perhaps when Féraud retires and your efforts are recognized with a promotion, then we might indulge in the extravagance of a launch. Mama would be *so* impressed. As for little Jeanne, I fear she might be out of short skirts by then."

Achille regretted the turn in the conversation; on his day off he did not want to discuss his job, household finances, or speculate on his career prospects. Fortunately, they were nearing the wharf and turned their attention to mooring the skiff.

Once they had tied up at the dock, returned the boat, and settled with its proprietor, Achille escorted Adele up the wharf stairway to the restaurant terrace. The bright yellow inn stood amid a garden on a low rise overlooking the Seine. Several tables were set up under an awning surrounded by bushes, flowerbeds, and shade trees. A mild, refreshing breeze blew in from the river. A few lunchers were already enjoying wine and house specialties. The inn was a popular resort for boaters, and the pleasant ambience and picturesque environs attracted many painters, writers, and poets who regularly made the short trip from Paris.

The proprietress, a very attractive and friendly woman, greeted them by name—they were frequent guests—and led them to a favorite table with an excellent view. Achille ordered cheese, fruit, and rabbit pâté served with fresh bread and a house wine. After the proprietress left he commented on the excellence of the cuisine.

"Yes, dear, it's almost as good as at home. But then, you're rarely there. . . ."

Achille broke in with a laugh: "I know, I know, I'm rarely there to appreciate it." He reached across the table and gently took her hands in his. "Darling, let's make a pact for the remainder of the day; no more talk of work, home, or related mundane matters."

"That rather limits our conversation, doesn't it?"

"Not really; we could talk about your adorable bonnet, your sparkling emerald eyes, cute little nose, red lips, rosy cheeks. . . ."

Adele blushed. "Oh Achille, don't be such a fool."

He let go her hands and made a dramatic gesture with a sweep of his arm. "Are poets fools? Only a poet could do justice to your beauty, and some famous poets have been known to lunch here. Shall I compose a sonnet in your honor?"

She knitted her brow in mock severity. "You're behaving more like a silly schoolboy than a senior inspector of the Sûreté."

"Oh please, please, you wound me. For that, you shall pay the ultimate price—a recitation!" Achille began reciting Verlaine:

Je fais souvent ce rêve étrange et pénétrant
D'une femme inconnue, et que j'aime, et qui m'aime,
Et qui n'est, chaque fois, ni tout à fait la même
Ni tout à fait une autre, et m'aime et me comprend.

Adele giggled and slapped his hand playfully. "Stop it. People will think you're drunk."

Achille leaned over, and stroked her cheek. "Let them think what they want," he whispered. "I'm drunk with your beauty."

She smiled seductively. Then: "Will you look at that?" He turned his head and she jerked his hand. "No, no, I didn't mean *literally*." She was referring to a couple who had just entered the restaurant. "You keep looking straight at me and I'll describe them for you. The woman is dressed to perfection, but *much too* perfect for this place. She's wearing the latest Doucet dress, a magnificent hat with egret plumes, and her ears and throat are dripping with diamonds. How vulgar! She *must* be a wealthy American."

He laughed. "I'll bet her companion wears a shiny top hat, loud checked vest with eighteen carat watch chains dangling a rabbit's foot and Masonic insignia, striped trousers and spats. There's an immense diamond and gold nugget pin stuck in his necktie and he's chewing a huge Havana cigar that he lights with dollar bills."

"You're not close to warm. He doesn't look at all like an American. He's elegantly dressed, but tastefully subtle. Savile Row tailoring, I believe. I'll wager he's an Englishman."

Achille's amused expression changed to a sober frown. He gave Adele a good *portrait parlé* of Sir Henry, right down to the monocle.

She raised her eyebrows in surprise. "That's uncanny, darling. You've described him perfectly."

Achille glanced over his shoulder for confirmation. The man matched the description of Sir Henry provided by Péan's clerk. Achille decided to take a closer look. He got up and mumbled, "Excuse me a moment."

The couple were engaged in a lively conversation; they paid no attention to Achille as he casually approached their table while keeping his trained eye fixed on the gentleman. This scrutiny reinforced his first impression; he decided to make an inquiry to satisfy his curiosity. He turned, passed through a gate that separated the outdoor restaurant from the terrace garden, climbed a small brickwork stairway and strode rapidly up the gravel pathway toward the inn. He caught the proprietress's attention near the entrance.

The woman was on her way to the kitchen. She stopped, smiled, and asked "May I help you, Inspector Lefebvre?"

"Yes, if you please Mademoiselle. A very well-dressed lady and gentleman were just seated in the terrace restaurant. Could you please give me their names?"

The woman's friendly smile turned to a worried frown. "Is this an official matter, Inspector?"

Achille smiled to put her at ease. "No, not *exactly*. They're such a distinguished couple. I thought I recognized them, but just couldn't place their names."

Having been relieved of her fear of a scandal, she replied, "I understand, Monsieur. The gentleman is Sir Henry Collingwood, a London physician, and the lady is Mlle Endicott, an American."

Sir Henry and Betsy's presence was fortuitous; Achille smiled and replied nonchalantly so as not to alarm the proprietress. "Ah yes, that's what I thought. Thank you, Mademoiselle." He came closer and lowered his voice to a near whisper: "Perhaps you could do me a little service, for which I'd gladly compensate you. I'd like to have the gentleman's wine glass for my . . . uh . . . collection. But you must handle it carefully, with gloves or a towel. And whatever you do, don't wipe it! Will you please oblige me?"

Her smile reverted to a frightened stare. "What are you saying, Inspector? Does the gentleman carry some loathsome disease? Or perhaps he's a poisoner? God forbid I should harbor such a fiend in my restaurant!"

Achille feared a panic. He laughed reassuringly. "Have no fear, Mademoiselle, it's nothing like that. I'm simply conducting a—an important experiment in forensic science. Should I succeed in this endeavor, my discoveries will most certainly contribute to the glory of France."

Her alarm rapidly transformed to bewilderment followed by patriotic conviction and resolve. "I'll be honored to assist you, Inspector. And please don't worry about payment. After all, it's for the honor of the Republic."

"Bless you, Mademoiselle. And may I add, as always, your rabbit pâté is perfection itself."

Achille returned to the terrace restaurant, glancing furtively at Sir Henry and Betsy as he passed by. In passing, he noticed a detail he had previously missed. *Damn! He's wearing gloves.*

Adele immediately noticed the change in his mood and expression. "What was that all about? Are you all right? Is it something you ate—the rabbit pâté?"

Achille leaned across the table and filled her glass. "It's nothing, dear. Here, your glass is almost empty. Let me pour you some wine."

He filled Adele's glass, and then drained his own and re-filled it. He began thinking of possible connections between the English doctor, the American women, and Virginie Ménard. Then: "Adele, without being conspicuous please have a good look at the English gentleman. Is he still wearing gloves?"

Her eyes lit up with curiosity. "Has this something to do with your case?"

Keeping his voice low, he replied, "Yes it does. Do you remember our experiment with your fingerprints?"

"Of course I do. Is the Englishman a suspect?"

"Not officially, at least not yet. And you mustn't say anything to anyone, *especially* your mother. I need more evidence, and the fingerprints are crucial. Now, what about those gloves?"

"Well what do you know? He's so handsome and distinguished; nothing like a criminal. Appearances are certainly deceiving. At any rate, I've been watching him all along. He hasn't removed the gloves since they sat at the table."

Achille sighed. "It's a problem, my dear. I need to get his fingerprints without bringing him in for questioning. I'll need to figure out something, a ruse perhaps. Or, I must get more evidence without the prints. Anyway, I apologize for spoiling our lunch."

Her eyes sparkled; her face flushed with excitement. Adele spoke while keeping her eyes glued to Sir Henry. "You've spoiled nothing, darling. This is so *fascinating*. No wonder you like your job."

He gazed at her fondly and with renewed interest. Apparently, his wife's lovely surface concealed uncharted depths that enticed his further investigation. Surprised by his discovery, Achille would be an eager and willing explorer.

⚭

Delphine Lacroix passed through a barrier gate that led from the Rue Militaire to the Zone outside the fortified walls that had proved so ineffectual against the Germans in the Franco-Prussian war. This mile-wide strip of wasteland circumscribed by two fortified lines and penetrated by numerous barrier gates providing crossings for railway tracks, canals, and roads, was *terra incognita* to respectable Parisians and foreign visitors. While the berm, glacis, and rubbish-filled dry moat bordering the city's outskirts had outlived its military usefulness, it remained as a dividing line between planned urbanization and refuse dump, a physical, psychological, and socio-economic barrier between the Parisians and the semi-visible outcasts of society.

Delphine had grown up in the Zone among the squatters, *chiffoniers* or ragpickers, junk dealers, street entertainers, Gypsies and mountebanks who had been displaced when Baron Haussmann tore down and cleared the ancient slums of central Paris. She had fled the Zone at the age of fourteen, vowing never to return, but now she had a compelling reason to re-enter the socio-cultural cesspit of her birth—the murder of her only true friend, Virginie Ménard.

Delphine crossed a rickety footbridge spanning a fetid, weed-clogged drainage ditch; on the other side she turned onto a steep, narrow dirt trail that snaked its way up a low ridge. In 1870 the Prussians had cleared the area to make way for their artillery and a field of fire. Nineteen years later, hardy poplars had sprung up amid the weeds and rubbish-strewn wild grasses.

She lifted her skirts, picking her way along the muddy path. Smoke rising from smoldering pits filled with burning trash and leaves made her cough; her eyes watered and her nose itched. Crows circled overhead, swooping down into the trash pits to do battle over the garbage with scurrying rats and cats.

As she neared the crest of the ridge she saw, rising above the scrub and weeds, a familiar compound of unpainted shacks, animal pens, and rubbish dumps. Delphine heard the bleating of goats, the cries of children, the rude shouts of men and women; she inhaled the stink of rotting garbage, human and animal waste. She was about to enter the domain of her putative father, a king among the ragpickers, known as Le Boudin.

The *chiffonier* had gotten his nickname from his service in the Legion; he had seen combat in Mexico and Algeria, where he had lost his left hand. A bear of a man, he had learned to use his government-issued hook to advantage in a brawl. He had spent years picking the streets of Paris, searching for marketable rejects, and had built a successful trade employing several licensed scavengers.

Delphine's long-deceased mother had been one of Le Boudin's many women; he was reputed to have fathered more than twenty children who in turn had born enough grandchildren to populate a village, but he rarely if ever acknowledged parentage.

A girl of about ten and a boy no more than eight-years-old scampered across Delphine's path, stopped, turned round, and stared. They were ragged, dirty, and barefoot; their dark hair, brown eyes, and flat noses bore an uncanny resemblance to Delphine.

"Hey little one," she called out to the girl, who was obviously older, bolder, and more forthcoming, "do you know where I can find Le Boudin?"

The child tugged at her torn sack of a dress, thought a moment and then, without speaking, pointed up the ridge toward a large shanty. Then she laughed, grabbed the boy by the hand and pulled him into the tall grass, where they began a tussle on the ground accompanied by screams, giggles, slaps, and curses.

Delphine continued up the path until she reached the shack. A few low steps led up to a shaded porch where an old, panting yellow dog lay on its side. As Delphine approached, the dog raised itself and confronted her with a low growl.

"Hey, Bazaine, old boy, don't you know me? It's Delphine." She held out her hand toward the dog's muzzle.

Bazaine was half-blind and nearly deaf. He sniffed a couple of times before licking her hand. Delphine smiled, rubbed his muzzle and patted his head. "Good old boy, good Bazaine," she whispered and then walked through the open door.

The interior was dark, stuffy, and filled with the musty, corroded smell of old rags and scrap metal. A faint light streamed through the entrance and an unglazed window cut through the front wall. As Delphine entered she could see a large man seated on a stool behind a low wooden table. He bent over a pile of trinkets and was about to apply the acid test to one, which he had grasped with his hook.

Le Boudin looked up from his work and sang out a familiar greeting in a rough bass: "Hello, Mademoiselle. Are you buying or selling today?"

Delphine smiled and walked toward the table. "Don't you remember me, Papa Le Boudin? It's me, Delphine."

He squinted at her and scratched his grizzled beard. "Delphine, eh? I once knew a girl who went by that name; a skinny, snot-nosed little ragamuffin."

"That's me, Papa. I grew up."

Le Boudin smiled, showing his few remaining brown, tobacco stained teeth. "You call me 'Papa'. Is that in honor of my great age?"

"No, Papa, it's in honor of what my mother told me on her deathbed."

"Folks say lots of things on their deathbeds. Don't necessarily make them true."

Delphine frowned and looked him straight in the eye. "I've no reason to think she was lying."

Le Boudin stared back at her for a moment, and then gave a low, bitter laugh. "I remember your ma; she was Romany. You've got the same dark, wild look about you."

"Considering my trade, it's better for business that I look more like her than you."

Le Boudin broke out in peals of laughter. After a while, he wiped his eyes and coughed. "That's good. After that one, I need a drink. Pull up a chair and join me."

He blew into two dusty glasses and wiped them on his shirt. Then he filled them with cheap red wine and handed one to Delphine. "Let's drink to your ma, God rest her soul."

They drained their glasses, and he poured another round. Then: "So what brings you back to the Zone? I heard you were making out all right, peddling your ass in Montmartre."

Delphine ignored the insult. That was his manner, and it wouldn't improve as he worked his way through the bottle. "Maybe you've heard about Virginie Ménard, the girl who was killed up in Montmartre?"

"Maybe I have. What of it?"

"She was my—best friend. I want you to help me find her killer. I'm not asking this as a favor; I can pay for information."

Le Boudin glanced down for a moment and toyed with his glass. Then he looked back at her with a frown. "Sounds like you're out for revenge."

"Could be, Papa. Will you help me?"

Le Boudin scratched his nose with his hook. "I had a bellyful of killing in Mexico and Algeria. We shot at them, they shot back at us. Look what it got me. There's an old saying: Revenge goes down sweet, but it comes back as bile."

Delphine did not reply. She swung her legs to one side, lifted her skirts, and pulled out a pouch from under a garter. Goggle-eyed, Le Boudin leaned over to get a good look. She smoothed down her dress, turned round, and placed the pouch on the table. "Screw your eyes back into their sockets, old man, and take a look at this." She upended the pouch, emptying a small pile of gold rings, bracelets, earrings, and broaches, all set with semi-precious stones and pearls.

Le Boudin's eyes widened and he whistled. "Where the hell did you get all that?"

"Don't worry Papa, they aren't hot. They're tokens of appreciation from gentlemen, and a few ladies too. My life savings."

Le Boudin stared at the jewelry for a while, then shook his head. "I can't take it from you, my girl. In a few years you'll need it all, believe me. You don't want to end up here, lifting your dress in a stinking alley, selling yourself for a crust of bread, a bottle of cheap wine, and a flop for the night."

"Then you won't help me?" For all her streetwise toughness, there was a plaintive tone in her voice and a wistful sadness in her eyes; she reminded him of a little girl on his knee, begging for favors.

"I didn't say that. I *might* help you for—for your mother's sake, but on one condition. Promise me you won't act outside the law."

For a moment, Delphine stared at him, perplexed by his reference to the law. After all, the cops stayed out of the Zone; it was like a tiny foreign country outside French jurisdiction. But then, she realized that Le Boudin and his *chiffoniers* worked on the streets of Paris; they were licensed and didn't want any trouble with the police. "All right, Papa, I promise."

Le Boudin smiled. He figured he could trust her, or at least he was willing to take a risk. But business was business, and he wanted security. "Here's what I'll do. Tell me what you want. If I think I can help, I'll hang on to your trinkets as a pledge. If you keep your word, I'll return them when the transaction's completed."

"Fair enough. I think Jojo's mixed up in it. I know some of your men scavenge Montmartre. I want—"

"Wait a minute, girl," Le Boudin broke in. "You're going too fast. Do you mean Jojo the Clown?"

Delphine nodded.

Le Boudin laughed and shook his head. "That ugly runt? He's a real *zonard*, a tough little shit. But I thought he went straight after he got outside? Has a job clowning at the Circus Fernando, as I recall."

She frowned. "Jojo's a bastard. Throw him a crooked centime, he'll jump at it. There's an artist in Montmartre named Toulouse-Lautrec who looks like Jojo's twin brother. I think Jojo tried to frame Lautrec, pin Virginie's murder on him. Anyway, the cops are chasing their tails, and that fat pig Rousseau's working on the case; I don't trust him. But his partner Lefebvre's all right, and I think he's been put over Rousseau.

"Your men go picking in Montmartre. It's possible one of them might have seen Jojo dump the body, but so far he's keeping his mouth shut. Maybe he's been bribed or threatened. I want you and your men to help me find out who killed Virginie. It may be Jojo, or he may be working for somebody. Whoever it is, I want revenge, but I'm willing to go to Lefebvre rather than take it on myself."

Le Boudin drank some wine; then he scratched his beard and knitted his brow. "You're asking a lot, my girl. Some of my boys are Rousseau's snitches."

Delphine's eyes flashed and her voice hardened: "Who do they work for, you or Rousseau?"

Le Boudin grunted, drank another glass and wiped his mouth on his sleeve. "A dog works for the man who feeds him."

They were interrupted by the little girl Delphine had seen outside. She walked to the center of the room, stood still, and started chewing on a fingernail.

Le Boudin glared at her. "Hey girl," he snarled, "I told you not to bother me when I'm doing business. Now get out before I tan your ass."

The girl spat a tiny scrap of chewed fingernail on the floor. "I'm hungry, Grandpapa," she whined without looking up.

"Well then, go find your ma and tell her to feed you."

The girl rocked back and forth on her filthy bare feet. "Don't know where Ma is. Ain't seen her all day."

Le Boudin grimaced. "Oh, all right." He reached into a barrel and pulled out an apple. "Here you go, little one." He lobbed the apple; the girl caught it deftly in one hand, took a bite, chewed and grinned. Then she turned her curious gaze on Delphine. Her mouth half-full, she mumbled, "Who's she?"

Le Boudin gave the girl a mock frown and waved his hook menacingly. "She's your Aunt Delphine. Show some manners, you little demon, and then scram."

The child giggled, turned her back on Delphine and ran out the door.

"A wild one," Le Boudin muttered, "just like you. Anyway, I'll talk to the boys and see what they can find out. I'll put up some trinket as a reward—at *my* expense, not yours. You mind what I said about your savings. And remember, if the dirt we dig up leads to Jojo or anyone else you take it to that inspector—what's his name?"

"Lefebvre."

"Yeah, you take it to him and don't mess with it yourself. You ain't as tough as you think. Now, it's been nice seeing you after all these years, but I've got a business to run."

Delphine laughed. "I know, Papa. Guess I better scram too."

Le Boudin raised his bulk from the stool and lumbered round the table. He lifted Delphine out of her chair 'til her feet dangled a foot above the floor, and gave her a bear hug. "You take care of yourself, my girl," he whispered huskily.

"You too, Papa," she replied.

⁂

Arthur Wolcott occupied a marble-topped table on the sidewalk fronting a popular café on the fashionable Boulevard des Italiens. He experienced the clear, fresh autumn afternoon, his coffee and cigarette, his desultory reading of a newspaper article reporting President Carnot's latest remarks on the Exposition's success, the rumbling of cabs and omnibuses, the bustle and chatter of well-dressed boulevardiers, the sparrows flitting among the shedding branches, russet leaves floating in a mild breeze, a large, high-soaring red, white, and blue balloon advertising the Fair, the countless congenial impressions summing up a pleasant afternoon in the city. But whenever his mind tried to anchor itself in a sheltering harbor, a place of agreeable repose, it soon broke from its mooring and drifted back into a rough sea of consternation and doubt.

Earlier, he had called upon Marcia to invite her out for some refreshment, thinking such an outing would be a sovereign remedy for what ailed her, but she had taken to her bed. Following the shocking news of Virginie Ménard's apparent abduction and murder, Marcia had suffered a mild relapse, not from her consumption but rather from what Sir Henry diagnosed as "female hysteria." The doctor had prescribed a sedative and obtained the services of a nurse. Having thus quieted his patient and provided for her care, he had no qualms about spending the day at Chatou with Betsy Endicott.

The Exposition is an unprecedented success, presaging a new century of progress and enlightenment. He read that line for the fifth time, and then lost it amid his recurring concerns about Marcia's mental and physical decline, Betsy's seeming indifference, and Sir Henry's increasing detachment from,

126

and questionable treatment of, his patient. *He doesn't give a damn about Marcia; it's Betsy he's after, and she seems infatuated with him.*

Arthur put down his paper, stubbed out his half-smoked cigarette, and habitually lit another. *We've all bought our one-way ticket to the slaughterhouse.* Arthur had written that line in a play, and then judiciously scratched it out as too dismal and disturbing for his audience. But eliding such comments on the human condition from his work did not keep them from repeatedly nettling his conscience.

"Well this is certainly a chance meeting. Good afternoon, Arthur."

He looked up with a start into the veiled face of the onetime Venus of Belgravia. Lady Agatha Fitzroy smiled slyly at her old friend's wide-eyed look of astonishment at her sudden appearance.

"My goodness, Arthur, do I look as bad as all that? You stare at me as though I were one of the ghosts in that deliciously wicked story of yours."

He rose from the table, tipped his hat, and made a slight bow. "Pardon me, Lady Agatha, I was preoccupied and you came up so—so unexpectedly. Of course, you're looking splendid, as always, and I'm both delighted and surprised to see you."

She laughed at his formal flattery, laughter that he had once compared to that of a tinkling silver bell, demanding one's attention in a manner that was both charming and intrusive. "Why are you so stiff? I'm the same Aggie you've known these past ten years and more. Now, will you *permit* me to join you, or should I just plop down and impose myself like a fellow American?"

"Oh, please do be seated, Aggie. I'll call the waiter. I'd like another coffee and an aperitif. Will you join me?"

"Thank you, Arthur; that would be delightful." Aggie sat across from him and lifted her veil. Venus had certainly withered, but she had not yet quite decomposed. Lady Agatha looked like a tastefully wrapped mummy of a type Arthur often encountered in society, a once-beautiful woman now well past her prime who tried to conceal her wrinkles, warts, and age spots beneath a layer of paint, powder, and rouge. Typically, such relics had been belles coming out early in the reign of Queen Victoria and at the court of Louis Philippe. But those beauties of yesteryear were in their sixties; Aggie was barely thirty-nine. Years of casual promiscuity, drinking, and opium smoking had taken their toll.

Arthur offered her a cigarette. She accepted and leaned forward as he struck a match. He noticed the slight tremor in her gloved hand as she held his to steady the light.

Arthur called the waiter and their drinks were brought presently. The aperitifs had a tongue-loosening effect. After exchanging a few pleasantries Arthur asked, "So what brings you to Paris?"

Aggie downed her drink and requested another before answering: "I won't beat about the bush with an old friend. Frankly, I'm strapped for cash and selling artwork to raise capital. I've had some very good offers in London, but for certain pieces I might get a better price in Paris. And I have one item of particular interest to Betsy Endicott, my famous Mark Brownlow portrait. Someone—you'll forgive me if I don't reveal the name—has already offered me a thousand guineas."

Arthur's eyebrows lifted at the sum. "By Jove, a thousand you say? That's quite a handsome offer, even for a modern masterpiece."

The waiter interrupted with their drinks. Aggie took a sip and then fiddled with the liqueur, rolling the stem between her fingers, sloshing the drink, and spreading a green film on the inside of the glass. After a moment: "I expect Betsy would pay more than a thousand guineas, quite a bit more in fact. I know she and Marcia have a suite at the Grand Hotel, and you're staying there as well. I'm afraid that's a bit beyond my means these days. I was going to announce myself by leaving a card at the front desk, but I wonder if you'd do me a favor by sounding them out first?"

Aggie's frank disclosure of her financial difficulties coupled with her expectations of significant gain from the sale of her portrait to Betsy raised Arthur's suspicions. To his knowledge, only five people besides himself knew of the Mark Brownlow deception—Marcia, Betsy, Daisy Brewster, Princess Albertini, and Lady Agatha. Was Aggie's situation so desperate that she might attempt blackmail? Such things were not unknown in society when creditors came banging at one's door. The revelation that for more than two years Marcia had lived and painted as a man would be harmful to all concerned, including Arthur, who had acted as "Mark"'s agent and had promoted the young artist's works aggressively among his many social contacts and friends.

Arthur tried to disguise his apprehension behind a smile. He was privy to some information that might extricate him from his dilemma. Betsy would pay a premium for Marcia's work if she knew some of the money would be used for Marcia's care. Arthur immediately conceived of a scheme that would benefit Marcia and at the same time help Aggie without her being tempted to resort to criminal tactics. "I'll of course be glad to 'sound them out.' We're old friends, after all. And I believe Betsy would indeed pay a fine price for your portrait, assuming you kept your demands within reason. By the way, did you know Betsy and Marcia were parting company?"

"No, I didn't know that. Has Marcia's illness anything to do with it?"

"Her illness—and other things. At any rate, she's currently under the care of a noted physician, Sir Henry Collingwood. I believe you're acquainted with the gentleman?"

Lady Agatha's eyes narrowed, revealing a network of wrinkles through white face powder like the crazing on an old pottery glaze. "You needn't be coy, Arthur. We're not in a London drawing room. My *former* relationship with Sir Henry is quite well known."

"Ah yes, but now it seems Sir Henry has turned his attention to Betsy, and that is one of the 'other things' I mentioned as the cause for separation."

Lady Agatha laughed, but it sounded more like a rasping file than a tinkling bell. "Oh, I'm sure they'll make a jolly pair." She paused a moment and sipped some liqueur to clear her throat. She did not want to meet Sir Henry, a fact Arthur had counted on, and she made up an excuse which fit perfectly with Arthur's off-the-cuff scheme. "I forgot to mention I've been invited to Nice, and must leave Paris presently. You remember my friend, the count? He was once a famous sportsman; I believe you did some shooting with him? Now he's in his dotage, poor dear, almost blind, bound to a wheelchair, and his heirs hover round him like vultures. He can't stand the sight or smell of them. At any rate, he remembers me as I was and enjoys my company immensely, so I must go to him when he calls. I provide diversion, and he rewards me with little tokens of his appreciation. *C'est un prêté pour un rendu, n'est-ce pas?*

"Would you be willing to act for me in my absence? Negotiate with Betsy for the purchase of my painting. I could make it worth your while if you get me the right price."

Arthur smiled, but was careful not to seem overly eager. "Well, I don't know, but *perhaps* I could. You'd have to give me a figure to work with."

"I told you I was offered a thousand in London, but I think the painting's worth fifteen hundred—that's guineas, my dear, not pounds or dollars, and *certainly* not francs."

Arthur whistled in feigned astonishment at her stated amount. "That's a great deal of money, Aggie. Still, it *might* be done, but will you come down to, say, twelve-fifty? I might need some leeway to close the deal."

Lady Agatha sighed. "Oh, all right, if necessary I'll take twelve-fifty, but not a farthing less. And here's an incentive. If you get me fifteen hundred or more, I'll cut you in for a ten-percent commission."

"That's very generous of you, Aggie. I promise I'll do my best. Now, I'll need your address, a place I can wire."

Lady Agatha opened her purse and withdrew a silver pencil and a little scented notepad. She scribbled a few lines and handed the ecru slip to Arthur. "Here's my address in Paris. I'll be leaving for Nice tomorrow and you may wire me there." She glanced down at a small gold watch pinned to her breast. "Ah, this has been delightful, but I fear I must leave. I shan't be gone long; a couple of days, no more, and I'd like this business concluded by then. It's been lovely seeing you again. *À bientôt!*"

Arthur watched as she vanished into the crowd streaming up and down the boulevard. *Contemptible hag.* He ordered another coffee and aperitif, lit a cigarette, and returned to his newspaper. He'd get her price and more and use the commission to help defray the cost of Marcia's care in England. *I've become a regular Major Pendennis when it comes to squaring things and cleaning up after people.* He turned to the article about the Exposition and for the sixth time read: *The Exposition is an unprecedented success, presaging a new century of progress and enlightenment.* "Rubbish!" he muttered, and then turned the page to read about an execution in Marseilles.

⁂

Jeanne sat up in bed and smiled at Achille. She had Adele's bright green eyes and light brown hair, an adorable expression when she was pleased as she was now, and for the most part, a sweet temperament. He had just finished reading *Beauty and the Beast*.

"That's my very favorite story, Papa," she declared enthusiastically.

He put the book on the bedside table, turned down the lamp, leaned over, brushed away a few curls, and kissed her forehead. She smelled of clean fresh linen and scented soap. "Why is it your favorite, little one?" he whispered.

"Because the beast turns into a handsome prince, he marries Belle, and they live happily ever after."

"But do you know *why* he became a handsome prince, and *why* Belle became his queen?"

Jeanne's sweet, contented smile changed into a perplexed pout, a typical reaction to her papa's questions that often seemed beyond her comprehension. She thought a moment, and then the smile returned with what she believed was the correct answer: "Because the good fairy made the beast into a handsome prince so he could marry Belle and be rich and happy!"

Achille tried to formulate a response his four-year-old daughter would understand. He gave her a quick, simple plot summary until he reached the moral of the story. "Belle was rewarded because, unlike her wicked sisters, she preferred virtue to wit and beauty. Appearances are deceiving, Jeanne; people are not always as they seem. Belle had a pure and virtuous heart, and that allowed her to look beyond the beast's appearance, to see his noble soul, the handsome prince within. Now, do you know how to get a pure and virtuous heart?"

Jeanne looked very serious. "Will the good fairy give me one?"

Achille smiled and stroked her hair. "Perhaps she will, but I know a better way, and it's not hard. All you have to do is say your prayers every day, be a good girl, and listen to mama and nanny. Do you think you can do that?"

She smiled and threw her arms around him. "Is that all? That's *so* easy. I do that already."

Achille lifted her out of bed and hugged her. "Of course you do, darling," he whispered.

There was a knock on the door. Adele entered with Madame Berthier and the nanny, Suzanne, a dark-eyed, sprightly little spinster of thirty from Provence. Suzanne slept in a cot next to Jeanne's bed.

Achille tucked Jeanne under the covers while Adele and Madame approached. Suzanne placed a candle on the dresser, and then turned her attention toward the family, silently observing their bedtime ritual with amused interest.

Adele bent over and kissed the child. "Did papa tell you a nice story?"

"Oh yes, mama, a lovely story. And he said if I get a pure and virtuous heart I can marry a handsome prince."

"He did? Well, that's very wise advice. Now kiss grandmamma and say good-night."

Madame leaned over slowly and stiffly with aching joints and a loud creaking of whalebone stays. She touched her lips to the child's forehead;

Madame couldn't quite reach the upturned little mouth. "Good-night, my pretty little cabbage."

Jeanne smiled angelically. "Good-night, Grandmamma."

Suzanne then bid them all good-night. The family filed out of the bedroom, Madame Berthier first, followed by Adele and Achille. Once in the hall and out of the earshot of Suzanne and Jeanne, Madame remarked: "She's such a sweet child. You must give her a little brother or a sister at the very least. What are you waiting for?"

Achille stared at his slippers. Adele replied: "We'll give you another grandchild soon enough, Mama."

Madame frowned. "Remember Adele, you had two brothers and a sister. Only you and your eldest brother lived past twenty and he was killed in the Tonkin war. Now, you're all I have left. Think about it. Good-night." She turned, creaked and rustled down the hall to her suite.

Later in bed Achille whispered, "For once, your mother makes sense. We ought to try again; a boy or another little girl, it makes no difference to me."

Adele smiled and stroked his cheek tenderly. "I agree, darling, but do you think you can, with this case on your mind day and night?"

He stared at her for a moment. "I'm sorry, you're right. When this is over, I'll demand a holiday. Féraud owes me. We'll go somewhere romantic by the sea; perhaps Nice. It'll be lovely, just you and I, as we were today at Chatou before the Englishman came." In the dim light he could read the disappointment in her eyes, as though she had lost faith in his promises. "Good-night, dear." He kissed her, rolled over, and put out the lamp.

❦

Rousseau sat on the edge of the bed in a small Montmartre flat. Louise, his mistress of twenty years, knelt behind him. Her strong hands kneaded his shoulders; her pendulous breasts rubbed against his broad back.

"You're so tense, my dear," she whispered. "Your muscles are like knotted ropes."

"It's this damned case," he muttered.

Louise kissed his hairy neck. "You've worked hundreds of cases. I've never known one to bother you like this."

Rousseau closed his eyes and had a vision of Féraud and Achille. After all his years of service, he was being cut out. There seemed to be nothing left for him but retirement and the life of an aging pensioner. He spoke without looking at her: "You don't understand, my dear. I'm coming to the end of the line and I want to go out in style. And I want to do it my way—the old way. But the professor's running the show. Féraud's backing him and his newfangled methods to the hilt."

Louise laughed. "Is that all? Lefebvre's green as grass; you said so yourself. You can brush him away like a fly."

Rousseau got up and turned on her with a scowl. "Achille's a good man—he's clever, honest, and decent. I admire the bastard, yet I hate him for showing me up. And I hate myself for hating him. I'm in hell, Louise."

"I'm sorry, darling. What are you going to do?" She left the bed and put her arms around him.

Rousseau groped the familiar flesh of her behind and thighs. "I don't know; I can't think straight. I won't hurt Lefebvre, but I don't have to be too helpful. Maybe I'll leave him on his own, and crack the case myself." He paused a moment. Then: "I need you again, but first a drink."

She smiled and rested her head on his chest. "Of course, darling; you'll work it out, somehow. You always do."

11

OCTOBER 19, MORNING, AFTERNOON, AND EVENING

About three hours before dawn. Jojo peered through the sooty window of his dark, fourth-floor garret. The moon was barely visible through a thick cloud cover; the only light source a flickering gas lamp on the other side of the narrow street. His sharp eyes scrutinized a cramped passageway between two buildings directly opposite, dimly lit by the lamp's yellow glow. *The snoop's still there. I can smell your flat feet, you fool!* Jojo had an appointment. He had some concern about the upcoming meeting, but little worry about shaking his too-conspicuous shadow.

Jojo opened the door and passed into the dank hallway, stepping lightly over the creaking, buckled floorboards. There was a rickety step-ladder leaning against the damp, mold-splotched wall. The ladder led to a trapdoor that opened onto the roof. He scaled the ladder; his long arms pushed up on the door. The trap squeaked on rusty hinges; he propped it with a stick, swung up and popped through the tight opening with acrobatic ease.

Hunkering down, Jojo scampered across the iron roof to the cornice molding. He glanced back in the direction of the snoop, and then hauled himself over the cornice onto a ledge. Bracing himself, he took a deep breath before making a circus leap over the air space to the roof of the neighboring building, landing with a dull thud.

Grasping the tiles, he caught his breath, and then turned back toward the snoop. The detective half-emerged from his hiding place and looked up in the direction of the garret. Jojo grinned. He scuttled noiselessly to the other end of the roof. Grabbing hold of the guttering with his large, powerful hands, he went over the side, worked his way to the drainpipe, caught onto it and shinnied down to the alley below.

Dressed in black, lurking through shadows, he sneaked his way uphill along the byways and backstreets, climbing two steep stairways, until he reached an abandoned mill in a sparsely populated neighborhood hard by Sacré-Coeur at the summit of the butte. Jojo scurried round the back through a clump of tall weeds until he reached a boarded-up window. He gave a prearranged knock in code, and then waited until the board slid away.

The dirt-floored interior stank of rot and decaying rubbish, pitch dark except for a taper glimmering on a table on the other side of the millstone and cogwheels. Several dormant bats hung from the rafters.

"I trust you haven't been followed?" The *sotto voce* question was posed by a man in a black cloak. A broad-brimmed slouch hat was pulled low over his forehead, and he concealed his identity behind a false beard and thick spectacles.

"No, monsieur. There's a pig on my tail all right, but he's an idiot. He's picking his nose and staring up at my empty flat. But we do have a problem."

"And what is that?"

"The cops picked up Lautrec, but they released him the same day. There's been no arrest. And it appears I'm under suspicion."

"That is a problem. And what do you hear from your friend, Inspector Rousseau?"

"Rousseau has nothing to say, and he isn't running the investigation. He's been put under Inspector Lefebvre. Lefebvre reports directly to Chief Féraud, and he's as clean as they come. And he's smart too; the cops call him 'professor.' But more than smart, they say he's incorruptible."

The cloaked man laughed; a dull, bitter rasp. "*Incorruptible*, eh? Just like old Robespierre, I suppose. Well, Jojo my lad, everyone's got his price, but I'm not sure I'm willing to square the honorable Lefebvre; after all, there's a limit to my resources. And how does Rousseau like working for this paragon of virtue?"

"Not at all. Rousseau's been scrapping his way up for twenty years. Now he's taking orders from a college boy."

"Hmmm, I'm beginning to see a way of dealing with honest 'professor' pig."

Jojo stared silently for a moment before asking: "What's your plan, monsieur? If it involves my services, I'm afraid——"

"I know, I know," he broke in," you'll be compensated. In the next day or two I'll send you a message at the circus. Just keep cool and wait; that's all you need to know for the present. Now, you best be off before the sun gets up."

Jojo returned to his flat by a circuitous route varying from the one he had taken to the abandoned building. He lowered himself through the trapdoor and entered the hall outside his garret before first light. Once in his room he checked the window; the snoop hadn't moved an inch. *As stiff as a palace guard, and twice as stupid.* Jojo laughed until he noticed a *chiffonier* working his way up the street, stopping and picking through the overflowing *poubelles*. *Did he see me?* He worried for just an instant, before answering himself with a shrug: *Well, what if he did?*

⌒∞⌒

"Did you and the wife have a pleasant Sunday, rowing at Chatou? You certainly had perfect weather for it."

"Thank you Chief; we did. And I also had an interesting encounter with the English doctor, Sir Henry Collingwood. He happened to be at the restaurant with Mlle Endicott, the rich American art collector."

They had an early morning meeting in Féraud's office. The chief seemed to be in a good mood, but he frowned at Achille's reference to the Englishman and his wealthy, American companion. He leaned back in his chair, stared at the ceiling, and began fiddling with his death's-head charm. "So tell me more about this 'encounter'."

Achille communicated the details concisely, focusing on how his attempt to get an impression of Sir Henry's fingerprints had been thwarted by the Englishman's gloves. He was beginning to relate his plan to obtain the prints when the chief interrupted:

"We have no legal basis for holding Sir Henry. He's a British subject, and could hop on the boat train for Dover any time he pleased." The chief leaned forward, planted his arms on the desk, and looked Achille in the eye.

"Of course, Chief, that's why I want to redouble our efforts to obtain evidence for the *juge d'instruction*."

Féraud displayed a little tic, an almost imperceptible "snick" at the corner of his mouth. "What does Rousseau think?"

This was a touchy subject. Achille's confidence in the "old boy" was eroding, but he'd need to tread lightly when expressing such concerns to the chief.

"Rousseau seems fixated on Lautrec, and I fear this might be hampering the investigation. For example, he hasn't detailed his best men to shadow Jojo, and I firmly believe the clown could lead us to the murderer. And as far as I'm concerned, the artist's in the clear. A thorough search of his flat and studio turned up nothing. We've looked into his various haunts and habits, and can account for his whereabouts for almost all the time in question, enough to support an alibi. In other words, it appears he didn't have the opportunity to commit the crime. As for the means, according to our foremost expert on the subject, only a doctor could have removed the uterus and cervix and then stitched her up so neatly. And her head and limbs weren't hacked off; they were surgically amputated.

"There's not much of a motive. He's freely admitted to having been a jealous lover, but after questioning him I don't believe he's the sort of individual who could carry out such a cruel, premeditated murder over a mere disappointment in love. Moreover, he's highly intelligent, so why would he conceive of, plan, and execute such a crime and then leave a trail of evidence ostensibly pointing back to him?

"Finally, we have fingerprints and the opium cigarettes. There are prints on the canvas and cigarette case that don't match Lautrec's, and we have no evidence of him being a habitual opium smoker. I believe—"

"Damn this case!" Féraud broke in. "No witnesses. The evidence is *all* circumstantial, and bloody thin at that. And your primary suspect is a foreigner, a well-heeled English gent who could bolt at any time." For a couple of tense minutes the chief returned to his silent, meditative posture. Then: "All right, Achille. Where do we go from here?"

"I want to wire a trusted contact at Scotland Yard to see if they have anything on Sir Henry. It'll be a routine, discreet inquiry. Next, I want to talk to the American artist, Marcia Brownlow. She knew the victim, and her companion has apparently formed an intimate acquaintance with Sir Henry. Moreover, I have reason to believe Mlle Brownlow may be one of Sir Henry's patients. This will be very delicate; I'll handle it myself, and I believe I can use Lautrec to make contact with Mlle Brownlow without tipping off the Englishman.

"Finally, I've got another way of nabbing Jojo, and it doesn't involve Rousseau. In fact, I don't want him to know about it."

Féraud frowned, his face reddened, and the tic returned. "Do you realize what you're saying? I've known Rousseau for twenty years. He's built up our network of snoops and paid informers in the Montmartre-Pigalle district. I depend on him."

Achille remained calm. "I understand, Chief, but there's a serious conflict of interest. Jojo's one of Rousseau's informers. I think their relationship's too close for comfort."

"Listen, Achille, Jojo's an ex-convict. He's scum. If he farts in a public place, we'll haul him in and put on the screws. If you have anything, I mean *anything* at all on that little shit, we'll beat a confession out of him. But you must have *something*, and you're telling me you don't trust your brother officer, one of my veterans, to get it for you." Féraud stared hard at Achille a moment before pursuing: "So let's say you're right. How would you go about it?"

"We have Delphine Lacroix, the victim's best friend. I've been looking into her background. She worked for Jojo when she was a kid, and she was one of the girls he beat up. And she has reason to dislike Rousseau too; she won't give anything up to him, or anyone working under him. But she has strong connections to the *chiffoniers* and *zonards*. She's part of Jojo's underworld. If he's an accomplice as I think he is, I believe I can persuade her to inform on him, and then Jojo can lead us to the killer."

Féraud smiled wryly and shook his head. "I don't think you know what you're getting into, my boy. You talk about an 'underworld', but you haven't been there. You can't know it the way Rousseau and I do. You have to live among these people, talk like them, act like them, stink like them, to even begin to understand them. That's why I split the assignment the way I did." The chief paused a moment for emphasis. Then: "But I have confidence in you, my boy. Rousseau will put in a few more years and retire. He'll never rise any higher in the brigade. But some day you could occupy this office, and then perhaps even a higher position. You're our future; the old boys and I are the past. So I'm going to back you up, at least for now. But I don't want Rousseau to feel he's being left out. Give him routine duties, enough to keep him busy. Agreed?"

Achille felt as though he'd crossed the Rubicon. Like Caesar, he'd confidently gambled on his future; there was no turning back. This case would make or break him. "Thank you, Chief. I agree."

⌇

Marcia reclined on the drawing room settee, her back propped up by a velvet bolster. She wore a scarlet kimono; the luxuriant silk fabric, her long, lush auburn hair, and lively green eyes all in sharp contrast to her gaunt face, which seemed as if it were rendered in grisaille, a gray monochrome surrounded by an overabundance of color.

Arthur sat in close proximity to Marcia, his smiling face attentively inclined toward hers, his hands resting on kid gloves and stick. Sir Henry had deemed Marcia well enough to receive; Betsy and he were on another pleasant outing; the nurse was occupied running errands.

"I'm relieved to find you looking so well, my dear. Assuming a continuation of this fair weather, tomorrow you must come out with me to a café."

She smiled at the suggestion. "That would be delightful, Arthur, provided my keeper gives me leave to go."

The reference to Sir Henry as Marcia's 'keeper' irked him, since under the circumstances the word had disturbing connotations. "You mustn't allow yourself to remain under his thumb for too long. You had a shock recently; it affected your condition, but a diagnosis of 'female hysteria' is no joke, and frankly I don't approve of Sir Henry's treatments. I understand he's prescribed a strong sedative."

"I appreciate your concern, Arthur, and I share your misgivings about Sir Henry and his treatments. But his prescription helped me through a rough patch." She smiled and took his hand before adding: "I promise you, I'm in no danger of addiction. As you recall, we both indulged in Aggie's opium cigarettes without succumbing to the drug's evil influence."

He stroked her frail hand, leaned forward and kissed it gently. Arthur wanted to say something profound; to tell her he loved her and would care for her for as long as she lived. But like his protagonists he could not betray himself with such a commonplace declaration. Instead, he restricted himself to expressions of concern and friendly advice. "I fear there's something *louche* about Sir Henry. Yesterday, I had a chance meeting with Lady Agatha at the Café Riche—"

"Aggie's here, in Paris?" Marcia interrupted with a spark of piqued curiosity in her voice.

Arthur noticed Marcia's interest with distaste. "I fear she's in Queer Street and looking to flog off your Mark Brownlow portrait to the highest bidder. She's approached me to negotiate with Betsy for the sale and she's gone to Nice to spend some time with her friend, the count. You know the villa well, I believe?"

Marcia indeed recalled the villa; eleven years earlier she had spent a magical weekend there with Lady Agatha that had inspired the famous painting. "Poor Aggie," she sighed. "If she's that hard up, I'm surprised she hung on to the painting this long. I believe it meant a great deal to her." Marcia could have added that it meant a great deal to her, too.

"I'm sure it does mean a lot to her, as it would anyone in the art market. Ruskin, Leighton, Sargent, and others have proclaimed it a modern masterpiece, a fact of which you should be justifiably proud. And it will certainly fetch a handsome price if I have anything to do with it. But I digress. When I met with Lady Agatha, I mentioned Sir Henry and his interest in Betsy. You should have seen the look on her face when I uttered his name; she winced as though she'd swallowed a glass of raw lemon juice. I won't speculate as to the nature of their relationship, but I imagine it had its unpleasant aspect."

Marcia laughed. "Knowing Aggie as I do, it must have involved some protracted examinations and treatments of a highly stimulating nature."

Arthur frowned. "This is no joke, or rather, a diagnosis of hysteria is nothing to laugh at. In England, there's a board in Chancery, made up of several gentleman holding the rather ludicrous title of Master in Lunacy. I've heard stories of independent, free-thinking women, no madder than you or I, who were diagnosed as hysterical, declared lunatics by the Masters, and then packed off to asylums for 'treatment,' leaving complete control of their persons and property to their husbands or guardians.

"Now, as American citizens, both you and Betsy would not normally come under the jurisdiction of English law. But that could change if Sir Henry and Betsy married and resided in England and you somehow came under his guardianship. I don't want to alarm you, but I advise you to remain on your guard. I can hardly imagine how difficult this must be for you, but please don't give in to narcotics, soothing words, and pampering. Assert yourself, but do it reasonably and with good humor. Tell Sir Henry and Betsy that you're feeling much better, even if you aren't. Then, if Sir Henry raises no professional objection, you'll go out with me tomorrow. But if he does object, don't argue too much, and for heaven's sake, don't become emotional. We'll work something out, I'm sure.

"At any rate, I suggest you break with them as soon as possible and come to England with me. Besides, if you stay here much longer I suspect you'll be questioned by the police concerning your relationship with Mademoiselle Ménard."

"But Arthur, I *do* want to talk to the police. I must, if there's anything I can do to assist in the investigation. Surely, you understand."

He thought for a moment. If Marcia believed she was helping the police in their effort to locate the killer, it might put her mind at ease. Then he could negotiate the sale of the painting, settle up with Betsy and Lady Agatha, bid farewell to Sir Henry Collingwood, and get Marcia on the boat train to Dover. "You're right, my dear. Let me handle this. I'll find out who's in charge of the investigation and set up a clandestine meeting. You surely don't want any publicity. We can do it on the pretext of an outing to the Luxembourg Gardens, or some such thing. And I think it best to keep Betsy and Sir Henry out of it."

She responded to his suggestion with a warm smile. "Thank you, dear. As one of your English chums might say, you've been a brick. Now, why don't you ring for tea?"

Marcia contemplated Arthur wistfully as he walked to the service bell. She sometimes wondered if he had loved Mark, Marcia, or both? But she would not embarrass him to satisfy her curiosity; the question would remain unasked.

∽

"Is it true this is the toniest restaurant in Paris?" Betsy put the question to Sir Henry as they dined on Tournedos Rossini accompanied by an excellent Château Haut-Brion at the Maison Dorée. Immense chandeliers blazed with light; gilt cornices sparkled; Aubusson carpets cushioned the steps of modishly shod feet; salon paintings of gods, goddesses, fauns, and nymphs decorated richly papered walls; tables covered in crisp, dazzlingly white linen, set with the finest silver service, china, and crystal, displayed haute cuisine, the creations of master chefs served with the choicest wines from one of the world's premier cellars. The terrace dining room was a study in Gilded Age opulence; the perfect setting for showing off Betsy's Parisian haute couture and diamonds from the Rue de la Paix.

"Yes, it's rather smart, isn't it?" Sir Henry replied as he savored his Haut-Brion. "And you haven't seen the private dining rooms, reserved for royalty, nobility, and the immensely rich." His monocle magnified the wicked gleam in his eye as he pursued the subject in an insinuatingly hushed voice: "They're the perfect venue for a discreet tête-à-tête between an emperor, king, or magnate and his paramour."

Betsy picked insouciantly at her foie gras. "I'll admit it's impressive, but I wouldn't put it above Delmonico's or Sherry's."

Sir Henry laughed. "Do I detect a hint of Yankee pride?"

Betsy's face glowed through her powder and her inhibitions had been lowered by three glasses of Haut-Brion. "I guess you do. Frankly, there's nothing you have over here that, given time, we can't equal or excel. Take my father, for example. We come from an old New England family, Mayflower genealogy and all. But we don't rest on the laurels of our ancestors. Each generation made their own distinct contribution to the family fortune. My father gambled on railroads; he had a good turn of luck on Wall Street, and he never stood pat. When the bubble burst in the '70s he sold short and doubled his fortune. Now I collect art, and my purchases have all appreciated in value.

"Marcia comes from a similar background, but her father wasn't as shrewd or lucky as mine. He went under in the crash and subsequent depression. Fortunately, she possesses a singular talent that's enabled her to climb to the top rung of her profession. But that's just the marketplace acting according to the scientific rules of evolution set down by Darwin and Spencer—survival of the fittest."

Sir Henry was taken aback; he was not accustomed to women injecting market economics and Darwinism into a politely intimate conversation, at least not in such a bluntly provocative manner. "I see your point, but isn't that an awfully harsh way of viewing the world?"

Betsy smiled tipsily in a way that was both enticing and subtly calculated to put him off guard. Her words were ironic and an intended challenge to Sir Henry's complacency. She might have viewed him as one of Oscar Wilde's Liberals who counted among the Tories because he dined with them. "Oh it's harsh, all right, but realistic and in some circles considered progressive. That's why *we* dine at the Maison Dorée while others root through dustbins for a crust of stale bread or a scrap of rotten cheese."

He found this discussion distasteful and at the same time disturbingly stimulating. Sir Henry felt a sudden urge to carry her off to one of the private rooms. He wanted to change the subject to regain his equilibrium, but he couldn't help making an observation. "I think we'd better make some provision for those scrounging unfortunates. As Dickens warned, we oughtn't to behave like bad old Scrooge prior to his Christmas conversion. Otherwise, those who, according to Mr. Spencer and others, are less fit to survive might rise up and cart off their betters to the guillotine. Remember, the Universal Exposition celebrates the Revolution's centennial; Liberté, Egalité, Fraternité, and all that."

"Ah, I'd almost forgotten the Fair's historical reference to a utopian ideal. I was much more impressed by the exhibits of progress, the Tour Eiffel, the focus on improvements in hygiene and public sanitation, and especially the new wonders of our industrial age. Take the Daimler, for example. The automobile's in its infancy, like the locomotive sixty years ago. That little motor car is a seed that will sprout and grow until it spreads out and towers like one of our giant California Sequoias. By the way, Marcia told me she'd love to ride in an automobile before she dies. Poor dear, I doubt she'll get her wish."

Betsy's reference to Marcia's condition provided a welcome opening for Sir Henry. "Oh yes, poor Marcia. I'm afraid the news of that unfortunate young woman's disappearance and suspected murder has given her quite a turn, which leads me to a delicate subject. We needn't pursue this now, but some thought should be given to the disposal of Marcia's estate. As I recall, she never married and has no children, immediate family, or close relations with a claim?"

The reference to her friend's estate had a sobering effect. Betsy may have been slightly fuddled with Haut-Brion and taken with Sir Henry's good looks, charm, and elegant manner. She enjoyed sparring with him, asserting herself as a free-thinking American woman. But she was never a fool when it came to money, and she replied cautiously. "Not that I know of; I've never given the matter much consideration."

"I see. Do you know if she has a will, or insurance? I believe she's left quite a few valuable art works at your home in San Francisco."

Betsy sensed a significant shift in the tenor of the conversation; their pleasant dinner deluxe had begun to resemble a high stakes poker game. "Marcia has kept a studio in my home for several years. I've purchased many of her most important works, as have other American collectors.

And she now has a contract with Goupil to represent her in Europe. Why do you ask?"

Sir Henry attuned himself to her shifting mood. He played his next card carefully. "I fear that in the near future Marcia's condition might deteriorate such that she may no longer be competent to make decisions concerning her medical treatment or the management of her estate. I've had considerable experience with such cases. Has she left many works in her studio that remain unsold; any written instruction as to their disposition?"

Betsy knew of several oils, watercolors, and drawings in her possession that could fetch several thousand dollars in the American market. He might indeed be offering sound advice as a physician and friend; on that account, she was willing to give him the benefit of the doubt. But when it came to matters involving great sums of money, experience had taught her to play her cards close to her vest, even when you thought you were playing with friends. "Oh," she remarked nonchalantly, "there might be a few, I suppose. I've never had them inventoried. At any rate, she's going to England with Arthur. He's always been savvy in business matters, and, should the need arise, I can easily put his solicitors in contact with mine." She smiled disarmingly, and then casually placed a shot across his bow to keep him honest. "By the way, have you heard of Nellie Bly?"

He suspected a diversionary tactic. That was all right with Sir Henry; he'd play along—for the time being. "No, I haven't. Sounds like a stage name. Is she an American actress?"

"Nellie Bly's a nom de plume all right, but she's not an actress. She's a reporter for the New York World. Not long ago she went undercover, had herself committed, and wrote an exposé of the deplorable conditions at the Women's Lunatic Asylum on Blackwell's Island. Her article raised quite a fuss in the States. There was a thorough investigation followed by a shake-up in the hospital administration and vast improvements in the living conditions and treatment of the inmates. Considering your practice, I thought you might have heard of it?"

Sir Henry smiled coolly. He decided to pay her back in kind. "No, in my practice I've had very few patients who required commitment, and in those cases they received the best private care. I haven't heard of this American matter, but I'm certainly glad to learn that the conditions at the asylum were improved and the lunatics afforded better treatment. By the by, I wonder what your survival of the fittest chaps would make of it?"

"Oh, I suppose *they'd* consider it a problem in public sanitation and waste disposal." She took a sip of Haut-Brion and eyed him with a suggestive smile.

Sir Henry returned her smile and said nothing. But for a moment Betsy evoked in him the troublingly erotic image of a fractious mare that needed breaking.

∞

Achille met Lautrec in a smoke-filled, murky *boîte* off the boulevard near the foot of the hill. The inspector tried to dress and act inconspicuously but the moment he crossed the threshold everyone smelled cop. Consequently, the regulars departed furtively in ones and twos until no one was left except for Achille and the artist.

The proprietor, a squat, black-bearded bulldog of a man, served them with icy politeness; he was angry over the loss in business, but under no circumstances would he betray his contempt nor dare ask an inspector of the Sûreté to take his business elsewhere. And there was another factor adding to the proprietor's indignation. He was a snitch, another strand in Rousseau's underworld spider web. Achille had ordered Rousseau to lift the tail from Lautrec and concentrate efforts in shadowing Jojo. Rousseau complied reluctantly, and the widening rift between the two inspectors had become known on the street.

The proprietor grinned acrimoniously as he filled the two glasses with cognac and left the bottle. He had served them what was by far the best liquor in his stock, and he'd charge accordingly to compensate for his loss in the evening's trade.

Lautrec sniffed his glass, sipped, rolled the fiery liquid round his tongue, and then swallowed. He winced. "They *label* this stuff 'cognac.' As to its age, I believe it entered our world about the time the Fair opened. If I were rating swill, I'd place this cognac *manqué* in the superior category, fit for the most discriminating pig. Thank you for buying it, and I trust you'll pay our host generously. I'm one of his regulars and would like to remain in his good graces. Your unwelcome presence has managed to clear the premises in record time. A raging fire or a swarm of plague rats could not have done a better job."

Achille shook his head and grimaced. "Yes, apparently I'm not the master of disguise. The great Vidocq must be turning in his grave. On the other hand, my unwished for appearance in this establishment has provided us with an opportunity to speak freely, so perhaps my disgrace is not complete."

"I assume you wish to discuss your case. Have you made any progress?"

Achille scanned the room before speaking. They were indeed alone except for the proprietor, who appeared to be out of earshot and preoccupied behind the bar with the rearrangement and cleaning of bottles and glasses. Nevertheless, Achille leaned forward and lowered his voice to a near whisper. "The investigation is ongoing. I'd like your assistance in arranging discreet, informal meetings with two persons acquainted with the victim whom I believe are known to you: Delphine Lacroix and Mademoiselle Brownlow, the American painter."

Lautrec smiled shrewdly and rubbed his beard. "Delphine's no problem. She models for me from time to time, and we can arrange a surreptitious tête-à-tête at my studio. Mlle Brownlow is a different matter. She's quite ill, you know, and under Sir Henry Collingwood's care. Her companion, Mlle Endicott, might prove to be an obstacle too. But there's another way to approach her. She's intimate with Arthur Wolcott, the

American author. I'm acquainted with M. Wolcott and believe I can persuade him to act as go-between. Actually, he's quite well known for his discretion in such matters. Is there a particular message you wish to convey to him?"

Achille thought a moment before replying. "Please tell him that it's an urgent matter relating to my investigation. I'll try not to impose too long on Mlle Brownlow. We should arrange to meet somewhere inconspicuous, away from the hotel, and without the knowledge of Sir Henry or Mlle Endicott."

"Very well, Inspector; I'll do what I can. Delphine's dancing tomorrow evening at the Moulin Rouge. I'll make arrangements for a meeting the following day. And I'll get a message to M. Wolcott at his hotel. How shall I communicate with you? I fear if we keep meeting like this we'll put the *boîte* out of business."

"Have you access to a telephone?"

Lautrec laughed. "I'm afraid not, Inspector. I also lack the means of flying round the Eiffel Tower."

Achille smiled, but in fact the issue of discreet and efficient communication was no joke. The proprietor would most likely report this meeting to Rousseau, especially if he thought there was something in it for him. That would alert Rousseau, leading him to believe that he was being excluded from an important part of the investigation; he might then put another tail on Lautrec, despite Achille's orders to the contrary. He sipped brandy and gave the problem some thought. This clandestine meeting would be reported to Rousseau, but he did have a means of discreet communication going forward. Achille could trust Sergeant Rodin to convey a message without leaking its contents. At any rate, he was willing to take the risk. "Do you know Sergeant Rodin?"

"I've come across him a few times. Not a bad fellow, for a cop."

"Very well, Monsieur. Pass all your messages through Rodin, but make it clear that they are for my eyes or ears only. I'll contact the sergeant and explain the situation beforehand."

Lautrec eyed Achille with a knowing grin. "Pardon me, Inspector, but might one infer from your precautions that there's dissension in your ranks?"

Achille frowned. "It's dangerous, Monsieur, to make such inferences based on insufficient knowledge of the facts."

Lautrec nodded and adopted a more serious tone and demeanor. "Perhaps you're right, Inspector. Nevertheless, if there *is* an individual involved in the investigation who happens to be the cause of your concern for security, and that *certain individual* also happens to be someone very well-known in these precincts, you should know that many of my local acquaintances would gladly come to your assistance."

Achille had no doubt Lautrec had referred to Rousseau. For an instant, he did not know how to reply. Then: "Thank you, Monsieur. I'll keep that in mind."

12

Jojo's up to something, all right." In the early morning hours, Le Boudin sat at the table in his "shop" across from Moïse, one of his most trusted men. A light rain pattered on the roof shingles, dripping here and there through the open slats. Out back, a rooster perched on a fence near the henhouse crowed, as if in response to Le Boudin's suspicious declaration; goats stirred and bleated in their pen.

Tallow from a guttering taper flowed down the sides of its brown bottle holder, forming a little waxen pool on the tabletop. The flickering candle revealed the young *chiffonier*'s face in chiaroscuro, sharply contrasting highlights and shadows, like a Rembrandt. Long, oily locks framed

Moïse's lean, hawk-like face; the beginnings of a black beard shaded the youth's upper lip and jaw line; shrewd dark brown eyes gazed at Le Boudin directly.

"It was hard work shadowing him, that's for sure. Jojo was shaking some dumb flatfoot, one of Rousseau's men. Nathan and me tailed the clown all the way up the hill, twisting and turning, like chasing a friggin' monkey through the jungle. He met someone in an old mill up by the big church at the top of the butte. Nathan hung round and followed the other guy while I clung to Jojo's tail, all the way back to his digs. Nathan says the other guy was tricked out like an actor: cloak, slouch hat, fake beard, and spectacles. Nathan says the bloke ran like a bat out of hell, all the way downhill to the boulevard where a coach was waiting."

Le Boudin's eyes narrowed. "And Nathan lost him?"

"Yeah, he tried to jump on the back of the coach, but it pulled away too fast."

"The guy didn't suspect Nathan was shadowing him, did he?"

Moïse shook his head confidently. "No, boss, Nathan's too sharp for that."

"Hmmm, I guess so, but it's too bad he couldn't keep up the tail." Le Boudin looked down and drummed his fingers for a moment. Then: "Did you boys pick up anything else on Jojo or the mysterious bloke?"

Moïse scratched his fuzzy cheek and thought a moment. "Yeah, the clown's been living it up the last week or so, spreading his gelt round the *boîtes* and whore houses, more than he could earn at the circus, that's for sure. He's probably done a job for that shady cove. But so far, nobody's seen or heard of Jojo's new pal. Anyway, it's a good bet he ain't from Montmartre or Pigalle."

Le Boudin pulled out a purse, opened it, and emptied a few silver coins onto the table. "That's for you and your brother. Keep shadowing Jojo and see what you can find out about the other guy. And get word to Delphine. I want to see her here today if possible, or tomorrow for sure. But not a word to her or anyone else about what you've found out. You boys keep your traps shut. And watch out for Rousseau. If the cops pick you up, you don't know nothing. If they put the screws on, tell them you'll talk to Inspector Lefebvre, and no one else. You follow?"

Moïse smiled, scooped up the coins and shoved them into his pocket. "Don't worry, boss; Nathan and me, we've dealt with the cops before. We know the ropes. And we've heard Lefebvre's a square guy."

Le Boudin's brow knitted. "It ain't you boys I'm worried about, it's Delphine. She's got a hot temper and sometimes she acts before she thinks. She's a tough girl, all right, but she ain't a match for Jojo." A few dim morning rays seeped into the shed through the cracks and unglazed windows, striking Le Boudin's face. His hard-boiled features glowed like a savage mask in firelight. He recalled the beating Delphine had taken from Jojo and imagined what had been done to her friend, Virginie.

Le Boudin balled his one huge hand into a hammer-like fist and rested it on the table next to his hook; looking down at these two weapons he swore an oath: "Moïse, I've killed men in battle under the French flag, but I've never committed murder. But as God is my witness, if that bastard ever hurts my girl again, I'll gut him with my hook, rip out his evil heart, and feed it to the crows."

❧

Arthur and Achille sat at a window table in one of the quieter, less conspicuous café-bars, not far from the Quai des Orfèvres. Rain beat down steadily on the pavement, driving the sidewalk trade indoors. Still, the place was not crowded and the two could speak freely. Arthur had contacted Achille's office that morning and set up the appointment. He would have included Marcia, but the inclement weather had kept her at the hotel.

Achille admired the author; he had read some of his stories in English and decided to take some time to get to know the man better. He hoped that by establishing a good rapport with Wolcott he would gain Marcia's confidence and thereby obtain something he needed desperately, an object with Sir Henry's fingerprints.

Arthur seemed tense; he fidgeted with his gloves and kept glancing out the window, as if he were being followed. Achille tried to put the author at ease with small talk. "The coffee and pastries are quite good, don't you agree?"

Arthur turned to Achille with a surprised look. "Oh—yes, of course, Inspector. Rather good, and reasonably priced too."

"I'm glad you agree. I come here often when I'm deeply involved in a case, and want a quick meal. It's a short walk from headquarters. The beer and sandwiches are pretty good too."

Arthur didn't mind the pleasantries, but he hadn't come out in foul weather to discuss the bill of fare at what seemed to him a second rate café for the lower middle class. He was about to lay his cards on the table, but on reflection decided it was best to remain polite. "Indeed, I'm sure the beer and sandwiches are superb, and will keep that in mind when I'm next in the neighborhood."

Achille smiled and continued his effort at breaking the ice by reference to one of Arthur's stories. "Last year I read your story about the detective who tracks down a lady jewel thief and falls in love with her. I thought it was excellent, as good as anything by Maupassant."

"Thank you, Inspector, that's very kind of you." Arthur forced a smile; he hated the story. He had written it hastily at the urging of a magazine editor who regularly published his work and paid top dollar. Arthur wanted to use a nom de plume, but the editor convinced him that would hurt sales. Not surprisingly, the story was a great success, which made the publisher and Arthur's agent quite happy. Moreover, since its publication, nine out of ten readers who complimented him mentioned this story, which he considered a meretricious potboiler. Maintaining his smile, he pursued: "That detective story is quite popular, and I'm very pleased you enjoyed it, but it's not really my line of country."

They were speaking English. Achille was fluent, but something Arthur had said puzzled him. "Pardon me, Monsieur, what is your 'line of country'?"

"I'm sorry, Inspector, I'm afraid that's an Anglicism that's crept into my speech. I should have said not my *métier*."

"Ah, I see, well for something that's not your métier you handled it splendidly."

Achille's calculated flattery had worked its magic. Arthur relaxed and enjoyed his coffee and brioche. Rain battered the plate glass window, washed over the pavement and filled the gutters to overflowing. *No use rushing in such weather*, he thought. *It's a cozy place, the coffee and brioche aren't bad, and this policeman seems like an intelligent fellow. I wonder if he reads anything besides romantic detective novelettes.* "Perhaps you could satisfy my professional curiosity, Inspector. Have you a favorite writer or novel?"

Achille seized the opening. "With all due respect to your work, Monsieur, which I do indeed esteem greatly, my favorite novel is Dumas père's *The Count of Monte Cristo*. I say this because it had a significant influence on my choice of career."

The author was now intrigued by the policeman, Achille's literary allusion having made a further inroad into Arthur's confidence. *An interesting individual*, he thought. The inspector was more than a flattering casual reader; he had transformed into a 'character,' grist for Arthur's fictive mill. "If I may inquire, Inspector, in what sense did the novel influence you?"

Achille smiled, now confident that he had accurately analyzed Arthur's personality; his calculated effort to ingratiate himself with the author seemed to have been a success. He proceeded to reveal something about himself that was sincere while at the same time self-serving in the sense that it was intended to help secure Arthur's unequivocal support. "I was a boy of thirteen when I read the book. I was deeply moved by the story of Edmond Dantès, an honest, decent man who through no fault of his own became the victim of treachery, greed, and the corruption of justice.

Through either chance, or more likely the intervention of Divine Providence, he transformed into an avenging angel, an instrument of Divine retribution, a strict *lex talionis* that, in the end, was tempered with mercy.

"Of course, there were elements of adventure, mystery, romance, violence, and intrigue that would appeal to a young boy. But above all, Dumas' story inspired in me a passion for justice, a dogged determination to pursue the guilty and defend the innocent."

"That's a noble sentiment, Inspector, and a fine ideal for a man of your profession. But what do you think of Hugo's Javert?"

Achille felt like an angler; Arthur had taken the bait, it was now time to tug the line and drive the hook home. "You know, M. Wolcott, many believe Hugo modeled Javert on the Sûreté's founder, Eugène François Vidocq. But Vidocq spent his career pursuing and capturing dangerous criminals; he did not hound poor individuals who stole bread to feed their starving families, and neither do I.

"Yet in many ways I am like Javert; I'm not a Divine avenger, and I'm more a realist than an idealist. I don't make the laws; I assist in their enforcement. Justice is imperfect as is our world; citizens can make improvements, but we will always fall short of an ideal. As for my youthful passion, it's been tempered by experience and the constraints of my profession. I now subscribe to Rochefoucauld's maxim: "The love of justice is simply, in the majority of men, the fear of suffering injustice.""

Arthur nodded his silent agreement. He sipped his coffee and nibbled some pastry. Then: "Tell me Inspector, what can I do to assist your investigation?"

"At the moment, there are two things, Monsieur. First, if her health and circumstances permit, I would like to speak to Mlle Brownlow, informally and away from the hotel. You may be present. Hopefully, she can tell me something about Mlle Ménard that will be of some significance. Women often share confidences, even with casual acquaintances, that they would keep from their husbands or most intimate male companions."

Arthur did not disagree. He knew Marcia had spoken intimately with Virginie and she had not yet revealed the details of their conversation to him. "Very well, Inspector, I'll try to arrange such a meeting as soon as possible. You mentioned something else."

Achille frowned and spoke solemnly to emphasize the gravity of the situation. "Monsieur Wolcott, I know you by reputation to be a man of honor. What I'm about to say must be held in the strictest confidence. I must have your word as a gentleman that you'll not reveal what I'm about to tell you. If you break your oath, there could be grave consequences."

Arthur nodded. "You have my word of honor, Inspector."

"Very well, Monsieur. While this remains unofficial in the sense that no evidence has been presented to the magistrate, I suspect that Sir Henry Collingwood may have some involvement in the disappearance and death of Virginie Ménard. At present, and for reasons you do not need to know, I want a writing of Sir Henry's, a note, letter, or perhaps a prescription. Could you obtain such a document?"

Arthur's eyes widened. He had had his own suspicions about Sir Henry, but they had not gone so far as murder. Moreover, he had recently obtained a letter from the doctor relating to Marcia's illness and recommendations for further treatment in England. "I do have something in my possession. May I ask why you need it?"

"I'm afraid not, Monsieur. The less you know about this matter, the better."

"I see. Will you return the letter to me?"

Achille shook his head. "Depending on what I discover, I may need to keep it in evidence. If that's the case, I'll provide you with a copy. By the way, Monsieur, have you noticed if Sir Henry always wears gloves?"

Arthur found the question perplexing; he thought a moment before answering, "I've seen him without his gloves on occasion. And I suppose if I ask why you need this information you'll tell me to mind my own business."

"I apologize for being so secretive. Permit me another question. Were you with him when he wrote the letter? If so, was he wearing gloves?"

Still puzzled, Arthur replied "I was indeed present and he wasn't wearing gloves."

Achille smiled with relief. "Thank you, Monsieur Wolcott. You've been most helpful. There's one more thing. When you arrange the meeting with Mlle Brownlow, you may do so on the pretext of taking her to the Bois, a gallery, or whatever. But instead, you'll bring her here. You may contact my office by telephone to make arrangements."

"All right, Inspector. But before I leave, I insist you tell me something. Do you believe Mlles Brownlow and Endicott are in danger?"

The question raised concerns that had troubled Achille's conscience day and night. Regardless, he answered honestly: "For the time being I believe not, Monsieur. But the sooner my suspicions are either confirmed or refuted by hard evidence the better for all involved."

⚬∞⚬

The rubbish-clogged drainage ditch burgeoned into a swollen stream, overflowing its muddy banks and rising to the level of the rickety foot-bridge. The steep trail winding uphill from the old military road to Le Boudin's compound had transformed into a waterfall, cascading into the flooded channel. Delphine chose a longer, more circuitous route round the gradual incline of the reverse slope.

She grabbed a stout fallen poplar limb to aid in her climb. Her bonnet and waterproof cape provided protection from the elements; leaning forward with the wind and rain at her back, she lifted her skirts in her left hand while her right worked the staff; her leather boots slogged on through the muck as Delphine made slow and steady progress to the summit.

She picked up her pace as the ground leveled. Her eyes scanned the ridge for signs of life, but all the inhabitants, human and beast alike, had sought shelter indoors. Only Bazaine remained outside, crouching in a dry spot on the leaky porch, faithfully guarding his master's doorway.

Delphine bent over and patted the dog's upturned head. "You haven't forgotten me, have you old boy?" She stroked Bazaine's muzzle and he licked her hand in greeting. Then she knocked on the door and shouted, "Hey Papa Le Boudin, it's me. Let me in before I drown!"

"Come in Delphine," he called out "and shut the door behind you!"

She found Le Boudin at his table, eating a light meal and reviewing his receipts with one of his women. Delphine recognized her immediately. "Hello, Marie. You remember me, don't you?"

The portly, ruddy-cheeked, good-natured woman of forty welcomed Delphine with a gap-toothed smile. "Of course I do, my dear. I'd kiss you, but I don't want to get soaked. We were just going over the accounts. Business is good; we'll make a fine profit this year." She got up on her feet and scrutinized the girl, from dripping bonnet to mud-caked boots. "Now, you better get out of those damp clothes and hang them up to dry. I'll fetch one of my dresses, though God knows it'll be big enough for two of you."

Le Boudin laughed and patted Marie's broad backside. "Three of her at least, and with room to spare!"

Marie slapped the offending hand and grinned. "You old bastard." Then to Delphine: "Now take off your bonnet and cloak and have a seat. I'll be back," she turned to Le Boudin with a gleam in her eye, "with one of my little daughter's dresses."

"Take your time, old woman. The girl and me have some personal business to discuss."

Marie nodded knowingly, covered herself with a woolen blanket, and ran out into the storm. Delphine shook out her hat and cape and hung them on the back of a chair. She sat down and was about to speak when Le Boudin piped up: "Wait a minute. I've got rum. You need a stiff drink to keep out the chill." He fetched a black bottle and then filled two glasses with the fiery liquor. "Now take it down in one gulp. It's like medicine."

She drank, then coughed and cleared her throat. "What is this stuff? Tastes like lamp fluid mixed with roach poison."

Le Boudin laughed and re-filled their glasses. "It's rotgut, sure enough, but it ain't as bad as all that. Do you want me to send out for vintage champagne?"

"All right, Papa, make it Veuve Clicquot, 1878. Seriously, I'm sure you didn't bring me out in this weather to see who could crack the lamest joke."

Le Boudin frowned. He stared at the liquor in his glass for a moment, swirled it round and took another swig. "Frankly, I didn't expect you so soon, but it's just as well you came. You were right about Jojo. He's up to no good, and the cops are already onto him. Rousseau's having him shadowed, but he's put a fool on Jojo's tail. And the clown's working for someone. Moïse and his brother Nathan tracked them to an abandoned mill near Sacré-Cœur. Nathan tailed the other guy down to the boulevard, but he lost him.

"We're going to keep shadowing them to see if we can figure out their game. And I want to remind you of your promise. Take the information to Lefebvre and keep your nose out of trouble. Jojo's bad enough, but we don't know anything about this guy he's working for. He may be the bastard who killed your friend. If that's the case, you'd best leave him to the cops."

Delphine looked down at her hands; she fiddled with the catch on her bag. "I gave my word, Papa. But if he is the guy, I'd like to get him alone, just long enough to give him a taste of my razor."

Le Boudin leaned over the table and lifted her chin so he could look her in the eye. "I understand, Delphine, but get those thoughts out of your head. Remember what I told you about revenge." She stared back at him and he saw tears running from the corners of her eyes. He wiped them away gently and stroked her cheek. "That girl must have meant an awful lot to you."

"She did, Papa. She did." Delphine was silent for a moment. Then: "When I left here I felt awfully sorry for myself, and it wasn't your fault. You and mama were good to me. But—but I always wanted something more. I imagined a world outside the barriers; somewhere away from the Zone. I thought nothing could be worse than this place, but I was wrong. You warned me about the world, and so did others, but like most kids I wouldn't listen. So I ran away straight into the arms of Jojo—and others.

"I learned the hard lessons of the streets, how to fight, roll with the punches, make do, and survive. Then I met Virginie. I thought I knew suffering, but she opened my eyes to real agony, unspeakable cruelty—" Delphine could not continue. She covered her face with her hands. "We're in hell. There's no justice, no mercy, no love. Why bring a child into such a world as this?"

Le Boudin got up from his chair, walked round, and took her into his arms. "I'm sorry, my girl, so sorry." He let her cry for a while until she regained her self-control. Then, he looked at her and smiled. "You'll stay the night with us, won't you? Don't walk all the way back to Montmartre in this filthy weather."

Delphine took a handkerchief from her bag, wiped her eyes, and blew her nose. "I'm sorry, Papa, I'm dancing tonight at the Moulin."

He grimaced and shook his head. "For the love of God, you'd go back out into this shit for a few francs? Those degenerates can do without ogling your legs and behind for one night."

Delphine smiled sadly. "I'm sorry, Papa. It's my living, it's what I do. Anyway, we have a few hours to visit and talk of old times. Hopefully, the rain will let up before I have to go."

Marie entered the room, dumped her soaked blanket on a chair, and removed a patched brown dress from a canvas bag. "Try this on, dearie. I think it'll fit all right. My Jacqueline's just about your size."

Delphine walked over and embraced Marie, her arms barely able to encircle the big woman's waist. "Thank you, my dear, and please thank Jacqueline for me. I'll make it up to her."

"Oh, it ain't nothing, dearie; just an old rag."

Delphine laughed. "Well thanks anyway. And you can kiss me now. I'm not as wet as I was."

"Bless you, girl, you're quite dry, but now I'm soaked through!"

⌒∞⌒

An intense white beam streamed down from an arc light situated high up in the rafters. Standing far below within the lamp's gleaming aura, the ringmaster, a tall, stout man tricked out in white tie and tailcoat, and sporting an enormous handlebar moustache, snapped his whip with authority. A large white horse trotted round the perimeter of the sawdust-covered ring, its canter accompanied by a brass band playing a sprightly galop. A female acrobat in ballerina costume rode the horse bareback. Following the initial circuit, the woman rose to her feet gracefully, circled the ring once more, then executed a handstand, first on both hands and then on one to a round of enthusiastic applause.

Jojo capered about the ring in an ape costume, his simian antics garnering peals of laughter, especially so when he examined a pile of horse dung, stuck in his finger and sniffed. But laughter turned to applause when the clown performed a series of back flips, vaulted onto the horse's crupper, and mimicked the acrobat's every move, including spectacular twin somersaults that made the audience gasp.

The rain had let up and there was a decent crowd on hand for the evening performance. The one-ring circus was located in a high-domed wooden building with colorfully decorated rafters. The audience sat in rows of seats that rose precipitously from the ring, providing a superb view along with an intimacy and engagement in the performance not commonly experienced in the larger arenas. Artists frequented the Circus Fernando to sketch the acts, among them Toulouse-Lautrec. But Lautrec was elsewhere this particular evening.

The equestrienne and Jojo were followed by another popular act, a young woman who hung from an iron ring by her teeth. Dangling

163

precariously, she was hauled up high into the rafters to the level of the trapeze, with no safety net below. Spectators craned their necks and thrilled to the danger as she started to spin round like a whirligig, while far below, clowns trembled and covered their eyes.

Jojo rested on a stool in the dressing area, taking a short break between acts. He pulled off his mask and mopped sweat from his face and neck with a towel. Then, staring into the gas-lit mirror, he mocked himself with an ape-like grin. He reached for a packet of cigarettes and a box of matches. A slip of paper lay hidden beneath the matchbox. *What's this; another bloody job? It better pay well.* Jojo examined what appeared to be a blank sheet. He struck a match and held it behind the note. The following appeared: "Meet me usual place at 3:00 A.M." Jojo burned the note and lit his smoke. He inhaled deeply, exhaled slowly, and then stubbed out the cigarette. It was time to get ready for the next act.

⚮

Lautrec sat at his favorite table at the Moulin Rouge, sketching the crowd and dancers while consuming a prodigious quantity of cognac. His life had become more complicated and his worries multiplied in consequence of his involvement with the investigation. He drank more, sought more diversions, and enjoyed them less. Earlier, he had surreptitiously slipped a note to Zidler to pass on to Delphine, urging her to meet him at his studio the following day, and he requested she acknowledge and confirm the appointment through Zidler; Lautrec did not want her to reply to him directly. He disliked such furtive behavior, but he could not shake the disquieting sense of being under constant surveillance, the sort of feeling he imagined one might have in a police state like Tsarist Russia. He believed an honest citizen of the French Republic ought not to fear asserting his rights of free expression and association, nevertheless he was afraid.

"Good evening, Monsieur Lautrec."

Lautrec looked up with a start; his hand trembled, smudging the sketch.

Arthur noticed the artist's reaction and could sense anxiety in his blank stare. "I apologize for coming upon you so suddenly. I trust I haven't spoiled your drawing?"

Lautrec relaxed at the sight of a familiar and not unwelcome face. "It's nothing, M. Wolcott. Will you join me?" Lautrec rubbed out the stray mark from his charcoal sketch while Arthur took a seat. He was glad of the company; anything to distract him from the murder case.

Arthur had his own troubles; he had been similarly affected by the investigation. The storm had passed. With the change in the weather and some improvement in Marcia's condition he had arranged a meeting at the café-bar near Sûreté headquarters, and he would bring Sir Henry's letter. He was well aware of his pledge to secrecy; he would not discuss his suspicions about Sir Henry with anyone except Achille and perhaps Lautrec. And he would be similarly discreet when discussing Virginie Ménard and her relationship with Marcia.

Arthur lit a cigarette and ordered more cognac. The orchestra had taken a break; the dance floor was empty; customers were milling about the mezzanine, bar, and gallery, keeping up a constant buzz of conversation. Arthur looked toward the rafters and blew a couple of smoke rings. Then he deposited the cigarette in an ashtray and smiled at Lautrec. "I was at Joyant's gallery today. Your work is impressive, Monsieur; it's all excellent, but I was especially taken by your portrait of the unfortunate Mlle Ménard. I made Joyant a fair offer, and hope to close the deal should you not receive a better one. I'd like to make a gift of the painting to my friend, Mlle Brownlow."

Lautrec drained his glass and then re-filled it. "I'm honored, Monsieur. I'm well aware of your reputation as a connoisseur of fine art." There was no hint of sarcasm in Lautrec's reply. He respected Arthur and was grateful for his interest. Lautrec took a sip of cognac before inquiring: "How is Mlle Brownlow? I understand she has not been well."

"Thank you, Monsieur; she's as well as can be expected. Alas, Mlle Brownlow is dying. She's a dear friend, and I intend to make her remaining days as pleasant and comfortable as possible. She was indeed quite impressed by your portrait of Virginie Ménard. In fact, she was concerned that you might have been offended by her reference to the painting's 'prettiness.' In any case, you may rest assured she admires your work, despite the fact that it's quite different from hers. You see, Mlle Brownlow always found it difficult separating her life from her art. She once told me how she envied my objectivity, my cool detachment. But I've learned over the years that there's more than one way for an artist to get at the truth."

For a moment Lautrec gazed at Arthur without comment. He was not sure what the author was implying. Had Arthur made an oblique reference to Lautrec's relationship with Virginie? Was he suggesting that Marcia would have been more understanding and sympathetic? Unable to resolve this quandary he replied coolly: "I observe and record what I see, like a photographer with my own peculiar lens and singular set of plates. At any rate, I don't make moral judgments and market them as art."

Arthur smiled wryly. "I appreciate that, Monsieur. An old Royal Academician friend of mine used to quote Turner: 'I paint what I see, not what I know.' Marcia was always fond of that quote, but I don't think she ever quite believed it."

Arthur was about to venture a cautious query concerning the intimacy of Marcia and Virginie's relationship when Zidler came to their table, looking very prosperous in his dapper tailcoat. He greeted Arthur politely, then turned to Lautrec, bent over and whispered into his ear. Lautrec nodded his understanding; Delphine would meet him at his studio the following day. He would notify Achille of the meeting by way of Sergeant Rodin.

His business with Lautrec concluded, the manager turned his attention to his distinguished guest. "I trust you will stay for the Can-Can, M. Wolcott?" Zidler glanced at his watch. "It begins in little more than five minutes. I assure you the girls are very pretty and," he added with a sly wink, "quite uninhibited and provocative."

Arthur laughed. "M. Zidler, I wouldn't miss it for the world."

Zidler rubbed his hands and bowed unctuously. "Thank you, thank you very much, Monsieur. You won't be disappointed." Then he took off in the direction of his office to count his receipts.

The house lights flashed, the musicians returned to their stands and began tuning and warming up their instruments. Wandering patrons returned to their tables and chairs, and out of the corner of his eye Lautrec noticed Delphine waiting in the wings with the other dancers. He flipped his sketchbook to a fresh sheet, exchanged his charcoal for pastels, and fueled his artistic imagination with another glass of cognac.

13

OCTOBER 21, MORNING, AFTERNOON, EVENING;

OCTOBER 22, MORNING

The abandoned mill about three hours before dawn: Jojo stared at a huge black spider dangling from an immense web overspreading a pair of rotting cogwheels. He marked the spider's resemblance to the cloaked figure beckoning him from the shadows on the other side of the millstone.

The shady "spider" raised a silencing finger to his false-bearded lips and motioned for Jojo to approach, signaling halt with a raised hand when the clown had come within whispering distance. "You've been careless, Jojo," he hissed.

"Careless, Monsieur? I don't understand," Jojo replied in a perplexed whisper.

The mask grinned sardonically. "You've seen the spider but you missed the two little flies."

"Please Monsieur, you speak in riddles. Is there a problem?"

"There's a problem, all right, but thankfully I have a solution. We're being shadowed by a couple of rag-picking Jews. One follows me from the boulevard; the other tails you from your flat. I didn't notice them until this morning. I don't know who they're working for, but my guess is it's not Rousseau."

Jojo's eyes blazed. He reached into his pocket and flicked out a switchblade. "I'll fix the little rats here and now."

The disguised man's whisper hoarsened to an angry rasp. "Put away your stiletto and listen. Is the dumb flatfoot still watching your apartment?"

Jojo closed the blade, pocketed his knife, and nodded in the affirmative.

"Good. Tomorrow morning at three sneak out of your flat the usual way. The cop'll keep his eyes glued to your window and the front door but one of the Jews will tail you up the Rue Lepic. Two blocks on there's an alley. I'll lose my shadow and wait for you with a cart, the kind the rag-pickers use. The kids are both runts; in the dark you could pass for either of them. I'll chloroform your shadow. Once he's out, we'll put him in the cart under a pile of rags. You take the cart back down the street and drop a little package in a dustbin right in front of the cop's nose. You'll be very sneaky looking but obvious, enough to catch the fool's attention. You'll continue to an alley where you'll ditch the kid and the cart. There'll be just enough time before he wakes up, and when he does he'll be groggy and disoriented."

"What about the other kid?"

"I'll knock him out too. But I'll add an injection that'll keep him stupefied for an hour at least."

Jojo grinned. "You're going to frame up the Yids?"

"That's right. The cops wouldn't go after the son of a count, no matter how degenerate. But a rag-picking Jew from the Zone is the perfect suspect. And if what you've told me about your chum Rousseau is true, it'll shake things up at the Sûreté when he takes our bait and openly turns against Lefebvre. Imagine how he'll gloat when he cracks the case and shows up the professor.

"At any rate, I figure no one will help the Jew, especially when I set the rest of my plan in motion. But that's none of your business. You just play your part as written. Now get out of here, and try not to let on that you know you're being followed. I'll wait awhile, and then give the other kid the slip. And here's an incentive, a little something on account. Do this right, and there'll be more." He reached into his pocket, retrieved a few gold coins and dropped them into Jojo's outstretched palm.

Jojo's eyes gleamed at the sight of the gold pieces. "Don't worry, Monsieur. It's a cinch."

"It had better be, my friend. Remember—three A.M. in the alley, and no slipups."

∞

"So your friend at Scotland Yard has something?" It was five A.M. sharp. Féraud stared across his desk at Achille, his interest piqued by the news.

"Yes, chief, I received a coded message by wire this morning. They have two recent cases involving the torsos of unidentified females. The Yard doesn't think it's the Ripper's work, but the torso killer's *modus operandi* does resemble that of the perpetrator in our case. And of course the English press is connecting the bodies to the Ripper murders. Without more evidence, that's pure speculation."

Féraud shook his head and leaned back in his chair. "Did your contact give you any more information concerning the status of their investigation?"

"I'm afraid this is all my friend's willing to provide by cable, even in code. If we want more, I'll have to go to London and get it in person."

THE DEVIL IN MONTMARTRE

Féraud thought for a moment before replying. "I'd need to get authorization from high up for something like that. If word leaked out of what you were doing unofficially, things could get very sticky with the English. But you may share some information about the mutilated torsos through official channels without relating it to the Ripper. And you certainly don't want to stir up a hornets' nest with our own press. Now what else have you got planned for today?"

"I'm meeting M. Wolcott and Mlle Brownlow. The American woman might have important information about Virginie Ménard that I believe will point to Sir Henry. And M. Wolcott has a letter with Sir Henry's handwriting and latent fingerprints. The handwriting could be very useful, and there's a proven method for bringing out latent prints on paper. I can compare the prints to those on the cloth and cigarette case. If they match, he's our suspect.

"After I'm done with that meeting, I'm going to interview Delphine Lacroix at Lautrec's studio. She has important information about Jojo, and she may also provide more clues from her knowledge of the victim."

Féraud nodded. He shuffled some paperwork and ruminated for a moment. Then: "All right. Carry on, and get back to me if or when you turn up anything significant. What I'd really like is one credible witness, a lead from a believable snitch, or at the very least some strong circumstantial evidence that'll hold up in court. This fingerprint business is too experimental; it makes me nervous. What have you heard from Rousseau?"

Achille frowned. "Nothing, I'm afraid, and frankly I don't expect much."

Féraud shook his head and drummed his fingers in frustration. He stuck a cigar in his guillotine, lopped off the tip, and started chewing without smoking. "Very well, Achille," he muttered with the unlit cigar shifting round in his mouth, "you may go."

"How lovely," Marcia had observed as Arthur helped her up into an open carriage. "I doubt we shall have many more such days."

"A fine day indeed," he replied. They were on their way to the café-bar to meet Achille. Arthur had his qualms about their rendezvous with a policeman, but he consoled himself with the thought that the inspector was a man of discretion, a gentleman. Considering her health, he would not press Marcia if he sensed his questions were too upsetting. And Marcia was enthusiastic; she wanted to help, if she could. At any rate, she had insisted on going out on the pretext of visiting the Louvre followed by some refreshment at a boulevard café and Sir Henry had not objected. It was as though he had lost interest in his patient ("She won't survive the winter" was his undisclosed prognosis) and was now concentrating all his attention on Betsy.

Arthur had concluded his negotiations for the sale of Lady Agatha's portrait. He had wired Betsy's generous offer of seventeen-hundred guineas to Aggie, and she had replied immediately. He'd earn a handsome commission and use it all for Marcia's care, though he would not tell her that. Arthur would let her believe his physician friend was providing services at a reduced rate out of gratitude and repayment for favors rendered.

Lady Agatha would be up from Nice on tomorrow's train, to conclude the deal. As soon as this business was over, Arthur intended to spirit Marcia away to England. He wanted to extricate her from the entanglements of the investigation and Sir Henry and Betsy's affair, to provide her shelter in the safe harbor of his country garden.

He held her gloved hand as she sat beside him on the sun-warmed leather carriage seat. Dressed in white, with a flower- and ribbon-trimmed hat, and veil, a fringed parasol protecting her from the sun, she appeared innocent, as though twenty years of worldly experience had been erased from the slate of her less than stainless life. *If only I could give her one more spring, to see her painting the roses in my garden.* He had a vision of her working at her easel on the lawn as he looked on from the unobtrusive vantage point of a window seat in the angle of a bay.

He smiled and squeezed her hand. "I almost forgot to tell you, my dear. I've closed the deal for Lady Agatha's portrait. Betsy's agreed to seventeen hundred guineas without so much as batting an eyelid."

Marcia gasped at the enormous sum. "Goodness! I would have asked half that price. I hope Betsy won't feel cheated."

"You underestimate the value of your work. That's why you need a canny manager. We'll make a good team, just like in the old days."

"Oh Arthur, I'm afraid all you'll get from me now are a few watercolors, if that."

He laughed. "Nonsense, young lady. Just wait 'til I get you to England. The pure country air will brace you up, and then it's back to work. Malingering will not be tolerated."

She patted his hand. "I fear you'll be a hard taskmaster. What am I getting into?"

They both smiled and sat quietly for a few minutes, enjoying the sights of the boulevard, the horse-drawn cabs and omnibuses bustling up and down, the well-dressed pedestrians out for a stroll. As they neared the café-bar Arthur remarked: "If at any time you feel this is too much for you, we'll break it off. Inspector Lefebvre's a gentleman; he'll understand."

"Don't worry about me, Arthur. I'll be fine."

The carriage pulled up to the curb under a spreading, autumnal poplar. Arthur paid the fare and then assisted Marcia down from the step. He took her arm and immediately noticed Achille approaching from an outdoor table set up under a striped awning. They greeted one another, made their introductions, and proceeded to the table, which was purposefully set off from the other patrons, Achille having asked the owner not to seat anyone within earshot.

Arthur surreptitiously handed an envelope to Achille. "This is the document you requested, Inspector." He had not told Marcia about Sir Henry's letter.

"Thank you, M. Wolcott. I'll have a copy made and sent to you tomorrow." Then, to divert Marcia's attention from the letter, Achille recommended the freshly baked croissants and coffee. "Or a good house wine, if you prefer." They settled on a respectable *vin ordinaire*. Achille called the waiter, ordered, and then opened the inquiry with a compliment. "I'm honored to make your acquaintance, Mlle Brownlow. My wife and I viewed the American gallery exhibit at the Exposition and we very much admired your prize-winning landscape."

"You're most kind, inspector. The painting was done in the Impressionist style. Do you like the Impressionists?"

"Yes indeed, Mademoiselle. I'm especially fond of Renoir. Last Sunday. . . ." He was about to say they had gone rowing at Chatou, but he caught himself. He did not know if Marcia was aware Sir Henry and Betsy Endicott had been at the restaurant that day. "Last Sunday my wife and I visited a gallery and viewed one of Renoir's paintings of Chatou. It was charming. Alas, he's become so popular we can't quite afford him. We must content ourselves with the paintings of younger, less well-known artists."

Marcia smiled and nodded. "I know Renoir, and I'm familiar with the scenes at Chatou. I'm also familiar with an excellent Corot painted in the vicinity before they built the railway and the iron bridge. Anyway, Renoir paints delightfully. But I'm afraid the new generation of artists sees things differently and is changing their style accordingly. I've met some brilliant young painters here in Paris, and their work is quite affordable, but I doubt you'll find their creations as *charmant* as their predecessors."

Achille recognized her oblique reference to Lautrec. He decided to begin his circumspect interrogation by mentioning the painter. "I'm acquainted with one of the young painters of whom you speak, M. de Toulouse-Lautrec. I believe you know him from the *Atelier* Cormon and of course, your mutual acquaintance, Mademoiselle Ménard is the subject of my investigation."

The waiter arrived with the wine. They sat silently as he served them and did not continue their conversation until he had returned to the bar. Then: "Yes, Inspector, I know something about your investigation. How can I assist you?"

Achille wasted no more time with pleasantries. "Do you know if Mademoiselle Ménard had been threatened by anyone? Or did she ever tell you she feared, or had reason to fear, anyone in particular?"

Marcia sipped some wine to clear her throat before answering. "No one in particular, Inspector. She told me about her relationship with M. Lautrec. It had been intense, at times, and they quarreled, but she did not fear him. Frankly, I believe they were in love, but they couldn't stand living together. A not uncommon situation, if I may be permitted an observation. She was also intimate with Mademoiselle Lacroix." Before continuing, she glanced at Arthur and noticed him avoiding her gaze. "Frankly, I believe they too were lovers. Does that shock you, Inspector?"

Achille shook his head. "Not at all, Mademoiselle. *Homo sum: humani nihil a me alienum puto.*"

Arthur coughed nervously into his serviette but Marcia smiled. "You are very well-read and *sympathique* inspector. At any rate, far from fearing Delphine, Virginie felt safe with her. It seems Mademoiselle Lacroix knows the rules of the game, how to survive in the *demi-monde* jungle."

"I appreciate your candor. Were you also attracted to Mademoiselle Ménard?"

Arthur blushed; his hands trembled and he spilled some wine. "Really, Inspector, you go too far."

Marcia touched his hand lightly. "Please, Arthur, it's all right." Then to Achille: "Virginie was one of the most beautiful women I've ever known, and I'm noted for my portraits of *les belles femmes*. I was most certainly drawn to her aesthetically. As for sexual attraction, all I can say is there has always been a fine line between Eros and aesthetics in my art. But my vision of Virginie was formed in chiaroscuro, sharp contrasts in light and shade. I believe it's the dark side that interests you, is that not so?"

"Please elucidate, Mademoiselle."

"I'll try, Inspector. You asked if there was anyone Virginie feared. I would say, from a few conversations during our brief acquaintance, the person she feared most was herself. She was an orphan raised by an aunt and uncle who treated her like a slave. The aunt had been particularly abusive, and the source of much pent up anger and resentment. Virginie had two means of releasing that seething hostility: the wild, uninhibited Can-Can, which was positive, and fits of what the doctors call 'female hysteria', which was of course negative.

"At our final meeting, which was a few days before her disappearance, she said she had met someone she believed could help with her hysterical fits. But I'm afraid she didn't elaborate, and my sensitivity precluded me from pressing her for details."

Achille's eyes narrowed; his mind focused on his primary suspect. "Do you believe the individual who was 'helping' Mlle Ménard could have been a doctor specializing in the treatment of female hysteria?"

Marcia frowned; she stared at him for a moment before replying: "Are you referring to Sir Henry Collingwood?"

Arthur's eyes darted furtively from Marcia to Achille, but he remained silent.

Achille responded cautiously but forthrightly. "Not necessarily, Mademoiselle, but to my knowledge he is the only physician practicing in that field who had made acquaintance with Mlle Ménard."

Arthur instinctively held Marcia's hand as though she needed reassurance and support, but she remained cool and composed. "Inspector, you are of course aware that I'm presently under Sir Henry's care. You may also know that he is pursuing an intimacy with one of my dearest friends, Mlle Endicott."

Arthur broke in: "Inspector Lefebvre, you assured me that these ladies were in no immediate danger or at least that there was no present need for concern."

Achille nodded. "That is correct, M. Wolcott. At present, I have insufficient evidence to accuse anyone in this matter, but so far everything points to a doctor who had access to the victim, Mlle Ménard. You and Mlle Brownlow have provided me with useful information, for which I'm grateful. I have another appointment today, and some work to do at headquarters, after which I expect to be closer to solving the case. If I may ask, what are your plans for the next few days? Do you intend to remain in Paris?"

Arthur glanced at Marcia; she nodded as a sign, a tacit agreement that he could speak for her. "I have some business to conclude within the next two days, after which I intend to accompany Mlle Brownlow to England."

"Very well, Monsieur. And do either of you know Mlle Endicott's intentions?"

Marcia replied, "Betsy plans to stay for the closing ceremonies, and I assume she'll attend them with Sir Henry. Afterward, they'll both depart for London."Marcia's eyes widened with apprehension; she coughed into her handkerchief.

Arthur placed a hand on her shoulder. "Are you all right, my dear?"

Marcia nodded and took a sip of wine before continuing. She looked directly at Achille. "Of course, Inspector, if you suspect Sir Henry—"

"Mlle Brownlow," he broke in, "I have asked M. Wolcott to give his word of honor not to discuss this matter with anyone, and now I must ask the same of you. You may of course be concerned for your safety and that of your friend. Please be assured if I discover any further evidence against Sir Henry, I will see to it that you and Mlle Endicott are notified at once. Moreover, I'm going to request that Sir Henry be placed under surveillance, which will afford you and your friend additional protection. But I most urgently request that you not speak of this to Mlle Endicott or anyone else."

"You have my word on that, Inspector," she answered firmly.

Achille smiled, and he noticed more evidence of worry in Arthur's expression than in Marcia's. "Thank you, Mademoiselle. Now, I know you and M. Wolcott have other things to do, so I won't detain you any longer. I appreciate your cooperation and please, if either of you have any further questions or concerns, contact me immediately."

They parted amicably, but on the way back to the hotel Arthur muttered, "Don't worry my dear. The French are always jumping to conclusions. I'll be deuced if Sir Henry's a murderer. After all, he's a member of my club."

Marcia smiled faintly. She knew the seemingly fatuous comment was Arthur's way of putting her at ease. "I hope you're right. At any rate, we both know Betsy's quite capable of defending herself."

Arthur nodded. "Ah, yes; her concealed pistols. I've heard she's a regular Annie Oakley."

Marcia recalled several demonstrations of Betsy's marksmanship. "Yes, thank goodness she is," she replied. Then she turned and tried to divert her attention away from Betsy by watching the multi-hued falling leaves floating gently in the breeze.

⚬◦⚬

"These are quite interesting, M. Lautrec. I can learn a great deal about the subject from your sketches." Achille occupied a chair in Toulouse-Lautrec's studio. The artist had opened a portfolio, displaying several drawings of Virginie. He spread them out carefully on a long, narrow table near the center of the room. This area was bright and warm with sunshine flowing in through a large skylight.

The artist contemplated the policeman from a shadowy corner, his arms folded and his back resting on a shelf stacked with plaster casts. He reached into a vest pocket and pulled out his watch. "Delphine should be here shortly. Would you care for a drink?"

Achille looked up from a pastel he was admiring. "No thank you, Monsieur."

Lautrec walked to a cabinet near the table and retrieved a bottle. "Well, I'm sure you won't mind if I indulge. Let me know if you change your mind." He pulled up a chair next to Achille, uncorked the bottle, filled a glass with brandy, and continued silently observing.

After a few minutes, Achille returned the drawings to the portfolio. "I feel as though I'm getting to know Mlle Ménard. That's often important in my work, to understand the victim as well as the criminal."

Lautrec took a drink before asking, "Why is that, Inspector?"

Achille was about to answer when they were interrupted by a knock on the door. "That must be Delphine," Lautrec said. He got up from the table, walked to the entrance, opened the door and greeted her. Then he turned to Achille: "Inspector Lefebvre, this is Mademoiselle Lacroix."

Achille rose and made a slight bow. "I'm pleased to meet you, Mademoiselle."

She nodded curtly and stared at him with wide brown eyes. Delphine was not timid, but the streets had taught her to fear the police. To her way of thinking, Achille's customary politeness seemed like a ploy; it did not put her at ease. Nevertheless, after a moment of anxious silence, she replied, "Call me Delphine; everyone does."

Achille smiled. He offered her a chair. "Please be seated, Delphine." As she approached, he noticed her stiffness and hesitancy. He'd seen the same look and gait in prisoners on their way to interrogation. That gave him an idea. "M. Lautrec and I were about to have a drink. Will you join us?"

She sat and glanced up at him furtively. "Yes, thanks."

Lautrec produced two more glasses and poured for all three. Then he took a seat next to Delphine.

Achille retrieved a packet of cigarettes from his breast pocket and offered her one. She accepted gratefully and held his hand to steady the match. After a few minutes of smoking, drinking, and small talk he decided things had loosened up enough to venture a question: "So Delphine, I understand you have some important information about Joseph Rossini. Will you please give me the details?"

She drained her glass and held it out to Lautrec for a refill. Then: "Yes, Inspector. Papa Le Boudin is having Jojo shadowed."

"Excuse me, Delphine," Achille broke in, "Who is Papa Le Boudin?"

She stared at him incredulously. "Why, everybody knows Le Boudin. He's the King of the *chiffoniers*. Old clothes, pots and pans, scrap, junk, you name it. He's the biggest dealer in Paris."

"Pardon my ignorance, Delphine. I'd like to meet him some day. Anyway, please continue."

For an instant, she eyed Achille suspiciously. He seemed on the level, although a bit green. Delphine remembered what Le Boudin had told her about going to Lefebvre; she had no alternative but to trust him. "All right, then. Le Boudin put two of his men, Moïse and Nathan Gunzberg, on Jojo's tail. They shadowed him up to an old, abandoned mill on top of the Butte, near Sacré-Coeur. Jojo met some guy up there about three in the morning yesterday, and again this morning at the same time. Nathan followed the guy back downhill to the boulevard, but he lost him. The guy wears a disguise; Nathan can't give a good description of him.

"Jojo and his pal pass notes to each other. Jojo gets his messages at the Circus Fernando and the guy picks up his at a tobacconist on the Boulevard de Clichy near the corner of the Rue Lepic. You can bet they're up to no good. As for the cop watching Jojo. . . " She caught herself on the verge of saying something disparaging about the police.

"Please go on, Delphine."

She stared at her hands, her fear returning like a sharp shaft of light cutting through the amiable fog of brandy, cigarettes, and Achille's good manners. Finally, and without looking up she replied, "Well, Inspector, he just hangs around doing—nothing."

"I see. Thank you for your honesty. Now, is there anything else you want to tell me about Jojo and this man he meets?"

She shook her head. "The Gunzberg boys are still on the lookout, that's all."

Achille took a moment to digest her information. If the fingerprints on the letter matched one of the sets of prints he'd obtained at the crime scene, he could assume the man Jojo met at the mill was his suspected partner in crime, Sir Henry. A matching set of Jojo's prints could complete the connection. He would test the letter in Bertillon's laboratory later that afternoon. He decided to change the subject to Virginie. "Delphine, I'd like to ask you a few questions about Mlle Ménard. According to your initial statement to the police, you said that as far as you knew she did not feel threatened by any particular individual. Do you know if she was being *helped* by someone?"

Her brow knitted and she eyed him curiously. "What do you mean by 'helped'?"

"I've heard that Mlle Ménard was a troubled young woman and that she'd found someone who was assisting her with her troubles, a doctor perhaps. If that were indeed the case, I believe she would have said something to you. After all, you were quite close to her, weren't you?"

She glared at Lautrec, as if he were the source of the information. He responded with a shrug. He was itching for charcoal and paper so he could record the expression on Delphine's face, which he found most interesting. But to have done so would have been *outré*; instead he scratched his itch with another drink.

Delphine ignored the artist and replied to Achille. "We were very close, Inspector. Virginie was troubled, that's true. We all are, I suppose. But perhaps her troubles were worse than most. You see, Virginie was full of hate, but all she ever wanted was love. She hated those who had hurt her, and she hated herself for hating. This is hard to explain, but I think when people hate themselves as she did, they feel that no one can love them. So when the wrong person comes along they're—oh, I can't find the right word—"

"Vulnerable?" offered Lautrec.

She glanced at him and then looked back at Achille. "Maybe that's the word I was looking for. I don't know, Inspector. I'm an uneducated woman."

"I believe vulnerable is the right word, Delphine. The unscrupulous among us mark such people; they take advantage of their vulnerability. And sometimes the victims love their tormentors no matter how badly they are abused. Can you please tell me more? Who hurt her? What was the source of her troubles?"

Delphine looked down and silently nodded her head in agreement. She recalled how she had fallen for Jojo and the way he had mistreated her when she was barely fourteen. After a moment, Delphine related the story Virginie had told her about her childhood in Rouen.

"Virginie came to Paris at the age of eighteen. She was kept by a rich silk merchant who died last year. He left her a little money, but she supported herself by modeling and dancing at the Moulin. She took the merchant's name, Ménard, as her stage name. She was an orphan, raised in Rouen by Monsieur Mercier, her father's eldest brother, and his wife. The Merciers were butchers and *charcutiers*. They had no children of their own and agreed to care for Virginie with the understanding that she would help around the house and shop and learn the trade.

"Virginie was immediately put to work. At first she was grateful for the food, clothing, and shelter her aunt and uncle provided. But memories of that childhood in Rouen haunted her, especially a nightmare of the Merciers slaughtering and butchering her pet pig.

"When she was a girl she avoided the slaughterhouse, an outbuilding behind the shop that was connected to the pigpen by a gated chute. On certain days Uncle Mercier would select a pig, open the gate, and drive it toward the shed with slaps and prods to its backside.

"Feeding the pigs was one of Virginie's chores, and she didn't mind it. She liked the animals and named them; there was fat Alphonse, greedy Gaston, and her favorite, little Buttercup. 'You're such a pretty little piggy,' she would say as she patted Buttercup's snout. The bigger, stronger pigs were always pushing Buttercup away from the feeding trough but Virginie saw to it that her friend always got her share.

"One morning, Virginie had begun her daily work as usual by sweeping out the store. Her aunt came up and tapped her on the shoulder. 'Put down your broom and come with me. This morning you'll learn an important part of our trade.'

"She followed Madame Mercier to the shed. They entered through a creaking, rusty-hinged back door. Pale light streamed in through the open gated doorway leading to the chute and the pigpen. Virginie could hear her 'friends' grunting and squealing in the background.

"Madame Mercier left Virginie in the middle of the shed near the butcher's block. 'Stay here, watch but don't move,' Madame ordered. Then she grabbed a heavy mallet from the block and walked toward the gate. Virginie's eyes scanned the scene: the heavy wooden block with its assortment of knives and saws laid out like surgical instruments prior to an operation; the large iron pulley, block and tackle suspended from a ceiling beam; the zinc basins, buckets, barrels, and a wooden rack. These were unfamiliar to her, but she imagined what they might be used for. Her stomach knotted and her throat dried; her hands sweated and trembled.

"The gate swung open; Monsieur Mercier prodded the grunting pig one last time. It lurched forward into the shed and Virginie's eyes widened in recognition. 'It's Buttercup! Please, please don't hurt her!' she cried, just as her aunt brought the mallet crashing down on the animal's head. Stunned, Buttercup collapsed in a heap onto the sawdust-spread planking. Virginie ran to the pig and tried to help it onto its feet.

"Madame Mercier was a big, tough woman of thirty-five, twenty years younger than her husband. She dropped her mallet, grabbed Virginie by the shoulder, pulled her away from the pig, and spun her round. Then, with her other hand, Madame slapped the child's face so hard it made her ears ring and her eyes see stars. A trickle of blood ran down Virginie's cut lip.

"'If you dare do that again,' growled Madame, 'I'll give you such a hiding you won't sit down for a week. Now shut up, stop sniveling, and watch!'

"Still half-dizzy from the blow, Virginie backed away and watched her aunt and uncle slaughter the pig. Madame tied one of Buttercup's back feet to the block and tackle and hoisted her off the floor while Monsieur ran to the butcher's block, grabbed a long, sharp knife, and then hustled back to the dangling pig. Virginie watched in silence as her uncle made a deep thrust into the center of the neck in front of the breastbone. Buttercup squealed and wriggled as her blood spurted and streamed into the collection vat, some of the fluid slopping over onto the sawdust-covered floor. After a few moments the pig lost consciousness and died.

"They forced her to watch and help in the butchering: scalding in a boiling vat, scraping, singeing and more scraping, skinning, gutting, removal of bladder and sex organs, the sawing, splitting and dressing, the racking and drying of offal. The stink of blood, guts, burned hair, shit, and piss, stuck in her nostrils and her memory. And as she worked, a hatred of her aunt and uncle grew inside her like a cancer, and that hatred made her stubborn. She would not slaughter and butcher pigs; she would not eat sausage, ham, or the Mercier's special delicacy, pork pâté.

"Virginie paid a price for her stubbornness which her aunt tried to cure with constant scolding, slaps, starvation, and beatings on the bare backside with a birch. That would be tough on any kid, even someone like me who grew up on the streets. But Virginie was delicate, sensitive. She needed a protector. Monsieur was an old monkey of a man. He was afraid of Madame, and wouldn't lift a finger to help his niece. When Ménard came along, Virginie was happy to run off with him to Paris. She would have done anything, short of murder, to get away from that place."

Delphine stopped; she shuddered, as if she'd been speaking of her own suffering.

Achille put his hand on her shoulder. "I'm sorry, Delphine, I know how difficult this is for you." He paused a moment before pursuing: "Did Virginie know Sir Henry Collingwood?"

Both Delphine and Lautrec stared at Achille. Delphine spoke first: "She posed for him at the *Atelier* Cormon, Inspector. And on occasion, we posed together for him in private."

"I didn't know that," Lautrec exclaimed.

Delphine eyed him coolly. "Yes, Monsieur, there are many things about Virginie you didn't know."

Achille followed up immediately. "Delphine, where did you and Virginie pose for Sir Henry? Can you give me the address?"

"Yes, Inspector. He rented a room in a cheap hotel here in Montmartre. If you have a pencil and paper, I'll give you the address."

Achille took down the address, and made a note to question the proprietor. Then: "You needn't go into detail, but was there anything about these modeling sessions of which Virginie might have been—ashamed?"

Delphine looked at him directly. "We posed together nude and in each others arms. Perhaps you think that's shameful?"

"Well I'll be damned," Lautrec muttered.

Achille shook his head. "I'm not here to pronounce moral judgment on you or Virginie. My purpose is to catch those responsible for her death and bring them to justice. Now, please think carefully. Can you recall any instances of private meetings between Virginie and Sir Henry?"

She thought a moment before answering, "I don't know, Inspector. And you mentioned shame. Virginie did things she was ashamed of, and she suffered for it. I know she hadn't gone to confession for some time. If she had met with Sir Henry she might have been ashamed to say anything about it—even to me." She paused, glanced at Lautrec, and then looked back at Achille. "Do you think the guy Jojo meets at the old mill could be Sir Henry?"

"I'm considering the possibility, Delphine. I'll need more evidence to prove it."

"The filthy swine," Lautrec muttered before downing another glass of brandy.

Achille decided he had enough information from Delphine, at least for the time being, and he was anxious to take the letter to the laboratory and make inquiries at the hotel. "You've been very helpful, Delphine. Unless there's something else you want to tell me, I'll let you go, but please keep in contact. M. Lautrec can act as go-between."

The artist put down his drink and nodded his agreement.

"Nothing else, Monsieur," she replied. "I'll keep in touch."

"Very well," Achille said. "There is one more thing before you go. I'd like to meet with Le Boudin as soon as possible. I want the Gunzberg boys to keep watching Jojo and his partner, but I want them to report directly to me. Can you arrange the meeting?"

"Yes, Inspector, but you'll have to accompany me to the Zone, and if possible try not to look and act like a cop when you get there."

He smiled warmly. "Thanks for the tip, Delphine. I'll do my best."

She said good-bye to Lautrec, who mumbled something in return, got up wobbly, made a perfunctory bow, and then staggered to the cabinet to retrieve another bottle.

Achille accompanied Delphine to the door. As she was leaving, he said, "I'm going to do everything in my power to see that justice is done."

She turned and looked up at him with a sad smile. "There's little justice in this world for the likes of Virginie and me, but I believe you'll do what you can. Good-day, Monsieur Lefebvre."

◦◦◦

Sir Henry leaned over a porcelain basin while vigorously scrubbing his hands in chlorinated lime solution. Following his ablutions he examined his fingers, paying special attention to the nails, bringing them up close to eye level for a meticulous inspection. The sun shone brightly outside, but the one window in the small room was tightly shuttered. A pair of candles glowed yellow on either side of the mahogany washstand mirror. After toweling his hands dry, he rolled down his sleeves, fastened his cuffs, and put on a pair of spotless white cotton gloves.

Betsy rested on her back; she lay nude and semi-conscious on sweat-dampened, rumpled sheets. He turned to admire the body he had so recently explored, focusing first on the silkily tufted pubic region he had massaged to orgasm. He smiled as his eyes wandered over Betsy's firm, glowing flesh, so youthful, he thought, for a woman in her late thirties. He admired her small, shapely feet, long beautifully-formed legs and thighs, flat stomach, and classically proportioned, rosy-nippled breasts.

Very handsome, sexually unfulfilled, in need of my professional skills, and immensely rich; I could not have wished for more.

He went to the bed, sat next to her, reached over and stroked the long un-pinned hair flowing over her shoulders and breasts. Her head turned on the pillow to face him; she sighed as if in the midst of an erotic dream. Sir Henry covered her with the sheet before whispering, "Be a good girl and wake up. It's time to go."

She responded with an incoherent moan, and then rolled over on her side with her back to him. Now impatient, he stroked a temptingly rounded buttock with his gloved hand before giving it a hard pinch.

"Ouch!" Betsy's eyes opened. She grimaced, rubbed her backside, and then turned round toward Sir Henry.

He grinned wickedly. "I see that got your attention. I was afraid I'd have to resort to smelling-salts to wake you up. We need to check out of the room."

Her hand went from her smarting behind to her forehead. "I'm groggy, like I've had too much to drink. What did you give me?"

He held her hand and kissed it. Then: "Just a little something to help you relax and get more benefit from my treatment, that's all. It's nothing to worry about. Now, take hold of my arm. I'm going to help you up slowly so you can swing your legs over the mattress and sit on the edge of the bed. Then I'll fetch the wash basin so I can sponge bathe and dry you before helping you dress. You're awfully damp."

Betsy rubbed her eyes and then felt her forehead. She sniffed something pungent and worried it might be her own odor. "I'm very warm; it's stuffy in here." He helped her to the side of the bed, keeping her half-draped with the sheet. She felt woozy as she put her feet on the floor and tried to sit up straight. After a moment, she said, "I'm better now. I think I can dress myself."

Sir Henry fetched the basin, a sponge, a towel, a bottle of eau de cologne, and a tin of violet powder. He got down on his knees by the bedside and placed the basin and toiletries at her feet. Taking one foot in his hand, he nibbled her toes and tickled the sole.

"Oh," she giggled, "stop that!"

Sir Henry laughed. "Indulge me, my dear. I enjoy playing with you, and pampering you as well."

The drug's residual effect had lifted her inhibitions, just enough so as to leave her susceptible to what upon sober reflection she would have considered his "foolishness." Betsy looked down at his handsome face, reached out and tousled his hair. "Silly boy," she sighed.

He replied by dipping the sponge in fresh water, sprinkling it with cologne, and then slowly sliding it up her ankle, leg, and thigh.

∽

Achille's cab turned a corner onto the Rue des Abbesses. He leaned out the window and glanced up the street in the direction of a narrow, dun-colored two-story building with an arched entrance. He noticed a well-dressed lady and gentleman exiting down a low step to the pavement where a carriage was waiting. They seemed out of place in such a seedy neighborhood.

Achille signaled his coachman to pull over to the curb and wait. The driver reined in his horse and the cab halted. Achille watched as the couple entered their brougham and continued up the street. Further scrutiny confirmed his first impression; the chic pair was none other than Sir Henry Collingwood and Betsy Endicott. He left the cab and walked up the block to the hotel.

He passed through a squeaky-hinged door with a tinkling bell attached, into a dimly lit lobby that reeked of stale cabbage. A threadbare runner covered a long, narrow hallway leading to a back door barely visible in the shadows; to the right a stairway rose to the second floor; to the left there was a desk behind which sat an individual reading a newspaper by the light of a green-shaded kerosene lamp.

Upon hearing the doorbell, the concierge looked up, scrutinizing Achille with bug-eyes peering through thick spectacles. He put down his paper, rose to his feet, and croaked a greeting: "Good afternoon, Monsieur. How may I help you?"

Achille approached the desk and pulled out his tricolor badge. "I'm Inspector Achille Lefebvre of the Sûreté. I have some questions about one of your guests, the gentleman who just left with the lady."

The stubby man trembled; little beads of sweat popped out on his splotchy, bald head. "We run a respectable establishment, Monsieur. Have you spoken to Inspector Rousseau? He'll vouch for us. The license is in order, I assure you."

Achille could guess at the man's "arrangement" with Rousseau. "I work with Inspector Rousseau. I have some routine questions about the individual I mentioned. I trust you have a registration card for him?"

"A card? A card? But of course, Inspector." The concierge mopped his brow with a handkerchief and then retrieved a lidded wooden box from a dusty shelf. He placed the box on the front desk, opened the lid with shaking hands, and retrieved the registration. "Here it is, Inspector." He handed the card to Achille, adding: "You see, everything is filled out properly."

Achille read the registration, Sir Henry Collingwood, London England, with five separate date entries, two indicating "and guests" and three indicating "and guest." Achille smiled. "I presume, Monsieur, that all of the gentlemen's 'guests' were ladies?"

Now shaking visibly, the man pleaded: "Please, Inspector, I'm a poor man with a large family: a wife, four young children, and an infirm mother. I've already squared everything with Inspector Rousseau. Please have pity, I beg you."

"Calm yourself, Monsieur. I won't threaten your livelihood, as long as you do as I say and answer my questions honestly. First, do you know the ladies' names?"

The man took a few deep breaths before answering. "Two of them are locals: Delphine Lacroix and Virginie Ménard. The English gentleman brought them here twice, as you can see on the card. Then, he brought

Mademoiselle Ménard alone, on two occasions. As for the lady today, I swear I don't know her, but she isn't French. From her accent I'd say she's an American."

"Did Inspector Rousseau ever question you concerning the gentleman's relations with Mlle Ménard?"

The bug-eyes widened; he hesitated before answering, "I know there's an investigation concerning the young woman's disappearance, but Inspector Rousseau never asked me about it."

Achille's confidence in Rousseau was now fully eroded. "Very well, Monsieur. I'm taking this card as evidence. Do you keep duplicates?"

"No, Inspector, this is all I have."

Achille frowned and put a hint of menace in his voice. "Now listen carefully. If you want to stay out of trouble and keep feeding that needy family of yours, say nothing about my inquiry to *anyone*, and that includes Inspector Rousseau. If the English gentleman returns, you're to notify me at once. Do you understand?"

"Oh yes, Inspector, absolutely. You can count on me." He continued bowing and repeating, "Thank you, thank you very much, Monsieur," even as Achille turned and walked out the door.

⌖

"*The Devil in Montmartre*, eh? That'll make a catchy headline all right, especially if you add an exclamation point. The writing's not bad either, and the salacious stuff will surely entertain your readers." Edouard Drumont, author of *La France Juive* and founder of the *Anti-Semitic League of France* smiled shrewdly. He smoothed his bushy beard and pushed his gold-rimmed spectacles back up his nose before advising his friend, M. Cauchon: "You understand that publication might cause some trouble with the police? After all, the letter contains a veiled reference to the Virginie Ménard case and it implies that the Sûreté is intentionally bungling the investigation because it's been infiltrated and corrupted by the Jews."

Pierre Cauchon, editor and publisher of *L'Antisémite*, sat across from Drumont at a sidewalk café table. Pink-faced, portly, with beady blue eyes, a fringe of graying blonde hair, twelve children, a long-suffering wife, and fifteen-year-old mistress, his enemies had nicknamed the anti-Semitic editor *le vieux Cochon*. Earlier that day, Cauchon had received a letter signed "Angelique" from an anonymous source. The mysterious missive had been dropped off at the newspaper's office; there was no postmark or return address.

Angelique claimed to be a Catholic girl of eighteen, the eldest daughter of an old Provençal family that had been impoverished due to the machinations of a Jewish banker. While the banker occupied their foreclosed manor, Angelique, her parents, and two younger siblings were reduced to living in a peasant's cottage on their former lands.

Angelique was pretty and the Jew took an immediate interest in her. He offered her employment as a maid; despite her misgivings and her parents' entreaties, she accepted his offer to aid her starving family. At first she was well-treated and her employer made no unwelcome advances, thus creating in her a false sense of security. Then, one night as she slept, the Jew and his accomplices stole into her bedroom and chloroformed her. Bound, gagged, and stupefied with drugs, Angelique was transported to a secret location in Montmartre. Once there, she tried to resist her abductors, insisting that her parents would go to the police when they realized she was missing. The fiends laughed; her parents would be told she had run away, and if they went to the police no one would waste much time or energy looking for her. Angelique continued her resistance; she was starved, beaten, and thus forced into slavery as a temple prostitute for the Illuminati.

According to Angelique, the Illuminati were an international cabal of wealthy Jews and Freemasons who, through manipulation of currencies, financial markets, and political corruption, had conspired to rule the world from the shadows. The spider had spun an immense worldwide web, but the organization's headquarters, commanded by a Sanhedrin of six Jewish High Priests of global finance, was located in

Paris. There, they employed a system of bribery and extortion intended to gain influence, subvert, and manipulate the highest levels of government. Moreover, the Illuminati enticed and abducted innocent Catholic girls to be used as sex slaves in their satanic rituals.

Angelique had escaped her tormentors, but another young woman who had fallen into the spider's web had not been so fortunate. Having been lured into performing a Can-Can at one of their Baphometic orgies by promises of an enormous fee, Virginie Ménard fled the Illuminati and threatened to expose their foul practices. The following evening, she was abducted and ritually slaughtered by a shohet (kosher butcher) to silence her permanently and as a warning to others.

"Of course I know the risks of publication, M. Drumont. I believe it's my duty to publish this letter as a service to France, but I intend to preface the article with a disclaimer."

Drumont nodded. "A disclaimer is good. We must exercise some caution, since you can't produce the girl as a witness. We should avoid embarrassment to the League, especially with all these foreigners in Paris for the Exposition. Of course, there's no problem with credibility among our followers who'll believe anything against the Jews, but we must remain plausible when going to print if we are to gain new adherents to our cause.

"The letter doesn't name anyone specifically, and it makes no direct accusations except against a shadowy organization. Moreover, it does not blame the police directly for incompetence in the Ménard investigation. So I don't think there's danger of a suit for libel.

"You are publishing matters of public interest and concern so you can certainly rely on the Press Law of 1881 if the police clamp down. In my experience the present government respects our right to publish freely; they'll leave you alone as long as you comply with the requirements of the law. When do you go to press?"

Cauchon smiled broadly. "Thank you for your advice and support, my friend. I've already given orders to set type. I intend to have a special edition ready for distribution by tomorrow morning."

Drumont nodded affirmatively. "I hope Baron de Rothschild gets hold of a copy. I'd like to see the look on his face when he reads it. I'll bet it makes him choke on his matzoth."

The Jew-baiting journalists had a hearty laugh before settling the bill and parting company to embark on their next great crusade.

❧

Achille bounded up three flights of steep stairs to Gilles' studio and knocked impatiently on the door. He heard a faint "I'll be with you in a moment" followed by a clatter of paraphernalia and the rapid clomping of footsteps on the bare wooden floor. Presently, the door opened a crack and a pair of excited eyes greeted him: "Ah, it's you Inspector. You came at just the right time. There's something here I must show you." Before Achille could say "fingerprints," Gilles was leading him to a work bench in a back corner of the loft, a shaded area away from the late afternoon sunshine flooding through an immense skylight.

The photographer halted abruptly and pointed to a small black box resting on the tabletop. "There it is, Inspector, an invention that will revolutionize photography. It's just arrived from America."

Achille was anxious to discuss the latent prints on Sir Henry's letter, but his curiosity intervened. "What is it, Gilles?"

The photographer smiled proudly and presented the wonder to Achille for closer inspection. "It's the new Kodak No. 1 box camera. It has the latest modifications, including an advanced shutter and celluloid roll film, an improvement over the paper stripper film. It's light, hand-held, and simple to operate; perfect for detective work. And you don't need to focus through a ground-glass. Do you see that "V" shaped device on top of the camera?"

Achille examined the object. "Yes, it looks like a sighting mechanism."

"Exactly so; almost like you'd have on a firearm. Now please give me the camera and back up into the light." Achille returned the Kodak and did as Gilles asked.

"There, that's it. Perfect! Now, I set the shutter with this string, line you up in the sight, push the button, and *voila!* I've just taken your photograph in a matter of seconds; I wind this key and I'm ready for the next exposure, one hundred in all on a single roll of film."

Achille immediately saw the camera's potential. He approached to get a better look at the Kodak. "You're right, Gilles. As long as you had enough available light, this would be perfect for surreptitiously photographing suspects."

Gilles frowned and returned the camera to the work bench. "It would indeed be ideal for that purpose, but there is a major drawback. The new film and the method for developing and printing it are patented; the whole camera must be returned to the Eastman Company in Rochester, New York for processing and reloading. That might be all right for a detective in the eastern United States, but for us the time involved in shipping and handling makes it impractical."

Achille pondered the problem for a moment. "Do you think the Eastman Company would be willing to negotiate a contract with our government to permit the processing of the film here, in Paris?"

Gilles rubbed his chin. "I don't know, Inspector, but it might be worth pursuing."

Achille made a mental note to raise the issue with Féraud and Bertillon. Then: "I've come to you on urgent business." He pulled an envelope containing Sir Henry's letter out of his breast pocket and handed it to Gilles. "This envelope contains a document with a suspect's fingerprints. Please handle it with gloves or tweezers."

Gilles smiled. "Ah, Inspector, this is another of your fingerprint experiments."

"Yes it is, and at first I was going to perform it myself at the laboratory, but I believe the method used to develop the latent prints would be better suited to your skills."

"Oh, and what may I ask is that method?"

Achille reached into another pocket, withdrew a notebook, and turned it over to the photographer. "I've written it down here. The process was discovered more than twenty years ago by the chemist, Coulier, but to my knowledge it's never been used in forensics."

Gilles studied the notes carefully for a few minutes. Then, muttering to himself: "This is interesting. Coulier used iodine fuming to bring out the prints. A small quantity of iodine is mixed with finely grained sand. The mixture is placed in a developing tray with the document fastened to a lid placed over the tray. The document is then exposed for a period of time to the iodine fumes. The fumes act as a reagent with the oil and sweat residue from the fingerprints. The latent images emerge and can be fixed with silver nitrate. This is all familiar to me; it's a process similar to developing and fixing an image on a photographic plate. The trick is to get the iodine mixture and exposure time right." He looked up at Achille. "Is this your only document with the suspect's fingerprints?"

"At this time, that's all I've got."

"I see. Well, then, I'd like to run a couple of tests first, using my own prints. I don't want to muck it up on the first try. And even if I get it right, some or even all your suspect's prints might be blurred. It depends on how he handled the document."

Achille nodded his understanding. "Very well, Gilles. Can you have your results at my office by tomorrow morning in time for my meeting with Féraud?"

Gilles winced. "At five A.M. inspector?"

Achille smiled sheepishly. "Sorry, I'm afraid so."

The photographer clapped the inspector's shoulder. "That's all right, my friend. I'll do my best. No rest for the wicked, eh?"

Achille laughed. "Yes Gilles, Satan never sleeps and neither does the Sûreté."

⌘

Shortly before three A.M., Jojo surfaced from the murky depths of a passageway sandwiched between two tenements. Emerging like a furtive cockroach from a cracked skirting board, he scurried onto the narrow, winding Rue Lepic. Pausing for an instant, he glanced back down the shadowy street in the direction of his flat; as usual, the unimaginative cop hadn't stirred from his hidey-hole.

Pulling up his collar against the pre-dawn chill and misting drizzle, Jojo sneaked up the street on boots caked with mud from the passageway, toward his alley-way rendezvous. He sensed he was being tailed, but according to his instructions, having evaded the policeman's notice, he acted as though he were now in the clear.

A thick cloud cover occluded the moon and stars; the pale glow of flickering gas lamps marked the way uphill with tiny points of light, growing smaller and dimmer in the distance until they merged near the summit in a dull, diminutive vanishing point. A few meters from his destination a yowling black cat leapt from its *poubelle* and scampered across his path. Startled, Jojo stopped and muttered a curse. *A bad omen*, he thought before walking on.

A few steps past his encounter with the foreboding feline, he turned into the alley. Several paces on, he heard a muffled hissing from a dark passageway. Approaching cautiously, he noticed his confederate's eyes glowing beneath the pulled-down brim of his slouch hat. The man motioned for Jojo to join him in his hiding place.

"The kid's right behind me," Jojo whispered.

The man nodded. He clutched a bottle and a handkerchief in his gloved hands. "You grab him and I'll chloroform him," he murmured.

Moïse turned the corner, walked a few paces, and halted. Wary of danger, he stared up the dark alley. Seeing nothing, he sensed trouble. *Damn! It's a trap.* He started to turn round, as if he were about to run back to the Rue Lepic.

"Now, before he bolts!" the man snarled.

Jojo sprang from his hole, ran a step or two, tackled Moïse from behind, and threw him to the ground. Straddling the youth's back, Jojo grabbed him by the chin hairs and yanked his head up. His partner covered the squirming boy's face with the chloroform-soaked handkerchief. Moïse struggled for less than half a minute. His eyes closed, his body grew limp, and then lay still.

"He'll be out for at least ten minutes. Quickly now, put on his jacket and hat, and then we'll throw him into the cart."

Jojo switched clothes. He lifted Moïse under the arms while his partner grasped the boy by the ankles. They carried him to the *chiffonier's* cart and hid him under a bunch of rags. Jojo threw his jacket on top of the pile. The man handed Jojo a round, cloth-wrapped package. Jojo gripped it with hands muddied from his scuffle in the unpaved alley.

"You haven't much time 'til the kid comes round."

"What about the other one?"

"Don't bother about him. He's sleeping it off in a passage down near the boulevard. Remember what I told you. Drop the package in a *poubelle* near your flat so the cop can see. Then go down the street to the next alley, change back to your jacket, ditch the kid and the cart."

"And the rest of my money, Monsieur?"

The man glared at him. "You'll get it soon enough," he growled. "I'll send you a message. Now go!"

Jojo nodded with a sly grin, grabbed the cart handles with his powerful hands, and pulled his burden back out onto the street. Iron-shod wooden wheels rattled and rumbled on the cobblestones, announcing the ragman's approach to the sleeping neighborhood. As he neared his flat, he spotted a *poubelle* within the shadowing flatfoot's line of sight.

He stopped, lifted the cart's handles, tilting it back gradually so as not to upset his unconscious freight onto the pavement, and then took out the package. Jojo casually walked over to a *poubelle*, opened the lid, and dumped the object into the rubbish. Then he returned to the cart and continued rattling and rumbling down the street.

The covert policeman's eyes followed Jojo until he disappeared from view. *Now why would a rag-picker dump something into a poubelle?* That puzzling thought rattled round his stolid brain for a couple of hours while his feet barely shuffled and his eyes remained dutifully glued to Jojo's flat.

14

Y ou see, Chief, these are the patterns Galton identified and categorized. All fingerprints fit within one of five types, but according to Galton's calculations, the odds against two persons having the exact same lines are so overwhelming we can say duplication is impossible." Achille pointed to a fingerprint chart set on a table in Féraud's office, next to Gilles's photographs. They viewed the evidence by gaslight supplemented by the illumination of two kerosene lamps and reflectors. "On each finger there are many lines organized in patterns around a nucleus, and over that central point are one or two secondary points. Following Galton's method, I've identified two distinctive types found at the crime scene. Gilles did a fine job photographing the prints on the cloth and the enhanced latent prints on the cigarette case."

Féraud examined the photographs under a magnifying glass. "Yes, Achille, I can see how one set of prints matches."

"Now, please look at the prints on Sir Henry Collingwood's letter and compare them to the prints on the cloth, cigarettes, and cigarette case."

Féraud spent a few minutes examining the fingerprints. Finally, he put down the magnifying glass and looked at Achille. "I can see how the prints on the letter match the prints on the opium cigarettes and the blood-spattered cloth. And there's clearly a different set on the case."

Achille nodded confidently. "That's right, Chief. I believe the other fingerprints are those of Sir Henry's accomplice, an individual of short stature who would match the shoeprints I found at the scene. Lautrec has been ruled out; I believe Joseph Rossini's our second man."

Féraud gestured to Achille and returned to his desk. Once seated, he said, "Let's review what you've got on Sir Henry and Jojo."

Achille took his seat across from the chief and began his summary of the evidence. "First, there's the victim's body. According to Dr. Péan, the pathologist, and Chief Bertillon, the suspect was a physician of considerable skill. The head and limbs were surgically amputated, and the uterus removed by a rarely used technique. In fact, our foremost gynecological surgeon, Dr. Péan, has only performed the operation twice. Sir Henry witnessed one of the operations, and he specializes in gynecology.

"Second, Sir Henry is the only physician attending Dr. Péan's clinic who had relations with the victim. That relationship has been confirmed by Delphine Lacroix. Moreover, I have evidence that Sir Henry met with the victim at a hotel in Montmartre the day before she disappeared.

"Third, according to Mlle Lacroix, the Gunzberg brothers, *chiffoniers* who work for Le Boudin, have been shadowing Jojo. They've. . . "

Féraud raised his eyebrows. "You didn't tell me that," he interrupted.

"No Chief, I just found out about it when I interviewed Mlle Lacroix. I want them to continue the surveillance and report directly to me. The man Rousseau put on Jojo's tail is incompetent."

Féraud eyed him with a skeptical squint. "What makes you think that?"

"According to Mlle Lacroix, the Gunzbergs shadowed Jojo to an abandoned mill near the summit of the Butte. He meets an individual there, and they pass notes to each other at the Circus Fernando and a tobacconist's shop near the corner of Rue Lepic and the boulevard. The *chiffoniers* can't identify the man, at least not yet, but I believe he's Sir Henry Collingwood. It fits with my theory."

Féraud smiled wryly. "Yes Achille, *your* theory. So to make the evidence support your theory you'll take the word of a slut and a pair of ragpickers over that of a brother officer?"

"Remember, Chief, Jojo's an acrobat. He could easily evade an inattentive detective by climbing to the roof, leaping to the next building, and then shinnying down a drainpipe. I recall that happening in another case involving a trapeze artist."

Féraud shook his head. "Yes, I remember the case well. But you're forgetting something. Delphine has a grudge against Jojo. After all, he was her pimp and he beat her up."

Achille replied firmly. "I found her credible, Chief. I believe she wants justice for her friend, and is willing to assist in our investigation."

Féraud leaned back in his chair while weighing the pros and cons of using the ragpickers for surveillance. He had always trusted Achille's judgment, but he worried that the young inspector was too committed to his theory and may have been overly influenced by Delphine Lacroix. Finally he said, "I think your evidence against Sir Henry is compelling, though I don't know what the *juge d'instruction* will make of the fingerprints. Still, all things considered, I'm willing to bring the Englishman in for questioning. Do you have any suggestions?"

Achille had a plan, but he knew it was a gamble. "Chief, we'd have a stronger case if we could get a confession from Jojo. He'd lead us to Sir

Henry in exchange for a reduced sentence. I'm sure he'd cooperate if he thought he was facing the guillotine or life in *Le Bagne*."

Féraud grunted in frustration. "But what have you got on him besides conjecture?"

Achille replied patiently. "First, we have the shoeprints. They're a close match to the measurements in Jojo's records. We could bring him in for questioning on that alone, measure his feet and his gait and make the comparison; I believe Chief Bertillon would back me up. In addition we have fingerprints taken at the scene, his evasion of our surveillance, and eyewitnesses to the suspicious meetings at the old mill. If the fingerprints and shoeprints match, he's the accomplice, and I believe he'll crack under pressure."

Féraud frowned and began a washing motion with his hands, usually a bad sign. "You're counting on Jojo's fingerprints and shoeprints matching what you got at the crime scene. As for the meetings at the mill, you have the word of two ragpickers by way of Delphine Lacroix, which directly contradicts one of our men's eyewitness reports."

The telephone rang. Féraud lifted the receiver. "Chief Inspector Féraud." He listened for a moment, then: "Yes; yes; I see." He glanced at Achille with a worried frown. "Yes, Inspector Lefebvre is here in my office. I'll send him out directly with the photographer. Have you set up a barricade? Good." Féraud hung up. "That was Sergeant Rodin. Rousseau's man found a neatly severed female head wrapped in a muddy cloth. At about three A.M. this morning a ragpicker dumped the head in a *poubelle* on the Rue Lepic, near Jojo's flat. They suspect Moïse Gunzberg; Rousseau's already working with the police to track him down. Well Achille, I guess that blows a hole in your theory?"

Achille remained cool; he spoke calmly and met Féraud's piercing eyes with a steady gaze. "Not necessarily, chief. I'll fetch Gilles and get to the scene as soon as possible. When I'm done, I'll take the head to the Morgue for identification. We should know soon enough if it's Virginie Menard. If it's another woman—" Achille checked himself. "Please notify Chief Bertillon."

Féraud shook his head and muttered, "This is the devil of a case."
Then: "I'll do that, and report back to me immediately when you've
finished with Bertillon." As Achille opened the door, the chief added: "If
it's a second murder, the press will be screaming 'Ripper'. If that happens,
we'll be up to our necks in shit."

Achille glanced back at Féraud, replied with a determined nod, turned,
and walked out into the hallway.

⸎

Shortly after dawn, Achille and Gilles met Sergeant Rodin and the Morgue
attendant at the crime scene barricade. The cloth-wrapped head had been left
on the pavement near the *poubelle* in front of Jojo's flat. Achille knelt by the
dust-bin; he examined the muddy fingerprints on the cloth and a faint trail of
shoeprints. He looked up at Rodin: "They were clumsier this time, sergeant."

"*They*, Inspector? You don't think Gunzberg was alone?"

Achille rose to face Rodin. While dusting some dirt off his jacket he
replied, "I don't suspect Moïse Gunzberg. I believe he was set up. What
do you know about him?"

The sergeant pursed his lips and scratched his beard as he pondered the
question. "Not a bad kid, really. There was some trouble with his license a
couple of years ago, but Le Boudin squared it all right. Anyway, Gunzberg
works this street regularly, and your man shadowing Jojo is a witness.
Rousseau plans to question everyone on this block, including Jojo."

Achille nodded, inwardly wincing at the thought of Jojo as witness.
He caught the sergeant's attention with a sweeping gesture. "Do you see
the muddy shoeprints?"

Rodin glanced round. "Yes, quite a trail of them. You really can see
them clearly since the sun came up."

"Yes, and there're muddy handprints on the cloth. The stuff's quite
sticky and it dried nicely. Where in this neighborhood would someone
pick up all that mud?"

202

"Oh, there are plenty of unpaved alleys and passages hereabouts."

Gilles joined them. He smiled at Rodin. "Excuse me, Sergeant." Then to Achille: "I've got some good photographs, Inspector. Your suspect tracked plenty of mud around the scene, that's for sure."

"If I can locate where he stepped in that muck maybe I can get a good cast of the impression. Anyway, please tell the attendant he can take the head now. We've got some more work to do around here, and then we'll follow him to the Morgue."

Gilles nodded. "All right, Inspector. I suppose you got a good look at her forehead?"

"Yes, Gilles, I did. I'll discuss that with Chief Bertillon at the Morgue."

Gilles understood from the inspector's terse reply that the mark on the forehead was something not to be bandied about. He changed the subject. "So where do you want me to photograph next?"

Achille glanced up at the garret window. *Is Jojo watching us?* Achille looked back at Gilles. "Gather your equipment and follow me." Then to Rodin: "Sergeant, I'd like you to accompany us."

As soon as Gilles returned with his camera, tripod, and plates, he and Sergeant Rodin followed Achille into the narrow passage between Jojo's tenement and the next building. A few paces in, Achille halted and motioned toward the rooftops. "Have you seen Jojo perform at the circus, Sergeant?"

"Indeed I have, Inspector."

"Do you think he's capable of making the leap from the roof of his tenement and then catching hold onto the roof of the adjacent building?"

Rodin looked up four stories, raising his right hand to shade his eyes from the early morning sun. "I believe he could do it easily, Inspector."

"I wouldn't be surprised if we found some shoeprints up there. We'll check later."

Gilles sighed audibly.

They followed the passage until it ended in a cramped, unpaved back alley, its borders demarcated by the rear of the building and a high wooden fence. Achille pointed up to the guttering. "Can you see how someone with Jojo's skill could work his way round to the drainpipe without being observed from the street?"

"Of course," the sergeant replied. "That's a typical cat burglar's trick."

Achille appreciated Rodin's perspicacious response. "Too bad Rousseau's man lacks your perception and experience, Sergeant." They turned right into the alley, Achille cautioning Rodin and Gilles to be careful not to step on shoeprints. As they walked up the path, a large watchdog started barking, growling, and thumping its bulk against the other side of the fence.

"That'll get the neighbors waked up," the sergeant observed.

Bringing up the rear, Gilles cursed under the burden of his equipment and almost stumbled as he skirted round a bloated rat carcass crawling with maggots. The muddy alley was littered with rubble, rubbish, and rank with weeds. Flies swarmed and buzzed; the sharp stench of backed-up sewage and rotting trash permeated the stagnant air. "My God, the stink," Gilles muttered. "It's like an open sewer running through a graveyard; makes you want to puke. I wouldn't be surprised if we discovered a decomposing body or two."

Presently, Achille raised his right hand. They stopped near the drainpipe that emptied into the alley. "Just as I thought. Look at these shoeprints." He approached cautiously and crouched beside the prints. "Nice, deep, dry impressions. I'm going to set up a boundary line for a casting." Achille reached into a shoulder satchel and pulled out a few wooden stakes, twine, and a mallet. He pounded the stakes firmly into the ground and strung the twine as Gilles set up his camera.

"I can see they're the prints of a small man, Inspector. Just like the casting you got from the horse turd near the cesspit."

Achille glanced up from his work with a satisfied smile. "I believe so, Sergeant." When he had finished staking out the boundary Achille said, "Sergeant, I'm going to return to make my plaster cast. Please have this alley barricaded and detail a couple of men to guard it day and night." This would certainly tip off Jojo that the police were on to his game, but it didn't matter, since Achille expected the magistrate to issue a warrant for Jojo's arrest by the end of this day, or the next at the latest.

Sargent Rodin agreed to extend the barricade and assign men to guard it; Gilles photographed the area. Achille got up and dusted off his trousers and jacket as best he could. "Very well, gentlemen, let's follow the shoe-prints and see where they lead."

Gilles was packing his equipment. He shot a look at Achille and mut-tered: "Oh yes, by all means 'let's follow the shoeprints,' even unto the ends of the earth. Be thankful you don't have to lug all this equipment around, Monsieur."

Rodin laughed. "You're a very amusing fellow, Gilles."

He nodded grumpily as he folded his tripod. "Rodin, my friend, one must have a sense of humor to do this bloody job."

Achille smiled sympathetically. "I'm sorry, Gilles. I don't think we have much farther to go."

"That's easy for you to say," the photographer grunted as he hoisted his heavy gear onto his back and prepared to continue their forensic expedition.

Achille led them through another unpaved passage back onto the street, his eyes glued to the pavement. After a few steps he halted. "You see that, gentlemen? Two faint, but distinctly different sets of prints. I deduce from the evidence that this is where Moïse Gunzberg began tailing Jojo." They followed the tracks up the street; as they neared the next alley the shoeprints faded until they were barely perceptible. Achille stopped again when they reached the entrance. He approached the passageway where the pavement ended, his keen eyes scanning the unpaved area thoroughly. Then he gestured to delineate the crime scene. "It's as I suspected. You see three sets of prints, clear impressions in the mud and dirt. And there's a larger impression, evidence of a struggle. Let's enter, but be very careful to go round the area I indicated."

Rodin and Gilles followed him, stepping gingerly to avoid the impressions. After a few paces they stopped and Gilles asked: "Shall I set up my camera here?"

"Yes, I want this area photographed and I'm going to erect another barrier for casting." Then to Rodin: "Sergeant, do you see how two sets of prints emerge from that small passage near the back stairway?"

"Yes, Inspector. It's obvious."

"Very good, Sergeant. That's where Jojo and his confederate hid, waiting in ambush for Moïse. You can also see where the boy entered the alley, stopped, and then tried to double back onto the street when he sensed trouble."

Rodin nodded his agreement.

"Now, please concentrate on where the scuffle occurred." He approached the scene and crouched. Then he looked back at his companions and pointed to wheel tracks. "You see the tracks? I believe they were made by a ragpicker's cart."

"The tracks are plain enough, Inspector. There are two sets; one runs out to Rue Lepic, and the other goes up the alley toward the north exit," Rodin replied.

Achille nodded his agreement. "Excellent, Sergeant. Jojo's pal wheeled the cart in from the north, and we should be able to follow his shoeprints up to the next street." He rose to his feet and turned back toward Gilles and Rodin: "Here's my scenario, gentlemen. The confederate wheeled the cart into this alley and waited for Jojo. Jojo entered the alley and joined his partner in crime in the hiding place, with Moïse not far behind.

"The boy entered cautiously, walked a few paces, and halted. Smelling danger, he turned to flee, but the two jumped him before he got more than a step or two back toward the street. There was a struggle and they knocked him out, probably with a strong drug, most likely chloroform. Then they dumped him into the cart, and Jojo proceeded up the street to the *poubelle*, where he ditched the head. I imagine he exchanged some clothes with the kid to fool Rousseau's man, who I'm sorry to say is not among the most observant on the force."

Sergeant Rodin snorted. "Pardon me, Inspector. With all due respect to the Sûreté, I always thought that fellow was an ass."

Achille shook his head. "I must regretfully agree with your assessment of the man's capabilities, Sergeant." Then to Gilles: "We've got a lot of work before we finish up here and go to the Morgue. First, I want to have a look at the tenement roof. I bet we'll find more muddy shoeprints leading down to the landing and right up to Jojo's doorway. I must telephone Chief Bertillon to say I'll be delayed. He'll understand when I tell him what we've discovered. I also need to contact Chief Féraud." He turned to Rodin: "Sergeant, I'm going to request a warrant for the arrest of Joseph Rossini. I want your men to keep an eye on him. Don't let him leave his flat. If he demands to know the grounds for his detention, tell him he's being held under suspicion of murder in the case of Virginie Ménard. Let him sweat."

"You can count on me and my men, Inspector. What about Rousseau? He's called out the dragnet for Moïse Gunzberg."

"If you see or hear from Rousseau, tell him to report directly to me. I'm going to speak to Féraud about Moïse. I believe I can bring him in voluntarily as a witness for the prosecution."

A wide grin spread across Rodin's prodigiously bearded mouth. "Now we're getting somewhere, Inspector."

⋙⋘

As was her custom, Mme Berthier accompanied cook on her early morning marketing. They were out at the crack of dawn when the stalls were well-stocked with the freshest and choicest comestibles. Immense wicker baskets dangling from their arms, the two women circled the marketplace like vultures before swooping down on the vendors advertising the best priced items for the family's table. But no matter how fair the posted prices might be, Mme Berthier was determined to beat them down.

The sellers knew Madame well and many cringed at the familiar rustling of her black widow's weeds signaling her approach, because she had gained a reputation for tenacious and obstreperous haggling. When she was unable to negotiate what she considered a fair price, Madame loudly condemned the quality of the merchandise, the sanitary conditions of the stall, and the merchant's honesty, patriotism, and moral character. She would then turn her back and start marching toward a competitor. Nine times out of ten the mortified vendor would call her back and agree to her price. Upon seeing her, one old fruit-seller lamented, "I'd rather have a tooth pulled than bargain with that penny-pinching old witch."

Nevertheless, she was not without friends at the market, most particularly old Mme Gros, who was renowned for the quality of her cabbages and the ardor of her rightist sympathies. She was also a purveyor of Cauchon's *L'Antisémite*.

Mme Gros greeted Mme Berthier with a wrinkled, toothless grin. "Good-morning, Madame. How nice to see you again. As always, I have the loveliest and freshest cabbages at the best price, just for you." She winked, lowered her voice, and beckoned. As Mme Berthier leaned over the stand and drew nearer, the vendor whispered: "That's not all I have, Madame." She pulled a copy of *L'Antisémite* from her apron. "Here's a special edition hot off the press, all about the Judeo-Masonic conspiracy and the ghastly murder of that poor young girl up in Montmartre."

Mme Berthier grasped the newspaper, read the headline, and murmured with keen interest, *The Devil in Montmartre!* Intrigued and eager to finish marketing so she could run home to read the article, Mme decided to dispense with her customary haggling. "Thank you, Madame, this is indeed most interesting. And since you're the fairest vendor in this market, I'll not dicker. You may give me two of your freshest, finest cabbages at the advertised price—provided you include this copy of *L'Antisémite* at no additional charge."

Mme Gros smiled broadly. "Bless you, Madame. It's an honor and pleasure to do business with the distinguished widow of one of France's heroes, the late Colonel; God rest his soul."

"You're most kind, Mme Gros." Mme Berthier stuffed the proffered cabbages into her basket along with the newspaper and then addressed cook with urgency: "All right, let's finish our marketing. I'm in a hurry to return to the apartment."

Immediately upon arrival, Madame handed her basket to cook and rushed off to her boudoir with the newspaper. She did not as much as bother to stop by the nursery to greet Adele and Jeanne.

Closeted in her sanctum Madame loosened her stays, removed her boots, rubbed her aching feet, and reclined on a settee. She took her spectacles from a case, adjusted them on her aquiline nose, struck a match, and lit a table lamp. Now comfortable and with adequate reading light, she devoured every word of *The Devil in Montmartre!* in record time. As the narrative unfolded, she clicked her tongue, gasped, shook her head, and muttered, "Poor thing," and "it's just as I suspected" at each gruesome detail and awful revelation.

At last, Madame set the newspaper down on a side table. She sighed deeply, leaned back on the bolster, and stared at the ceiling in the direction of heaven. Her lips moved in hushed prayer: "We renounce the devil and all his works and all his ways."

There was a gentle knock on the door. "Mama, are you all right? May I come in?"

"Just a moment, Adele," Madame replied. She sat up slowly and swung her legs over the side of the settee. Bending over with a grunt, she lifted her voluminous skirts, stepped into her boots, and laced them. Then, puffing from exertion, she said, "You may enter."

The door squeaked open; Adele entered the dimly lit, stuffy room hesitantly. She approached the settee and offered a hand to her mother.

"Thank you, Adele; I'm still capable of rising without your assistance." Madame braced herself on an armrest and pushed up with another audible grunt.

Adele was concerned that the shopping excursions had become too much of a burden for her aging mother. "I worry about you, Mama. You really ought to leave the marketing to cook."

Madame sniffed. "Nonsense; she'd be cheated and think nothing of it. After all, it's our money, not hers." She paused a moment before pursuing: "Of course, you could accompany her, but I'm afraid when it comes to bargaining you're no better than our simple cook."

Adele ignored the insult. "Jeanne asked for you. She wondered why grandmother hadn't come to kiss her good morning."

Madame smiled. "That's sweet, how the little one cares for her poor old grandmamma. I'll come to her before breakfast. I fear I was preoccupied this morning." She grabbed the newspaper from the side table and handed it to Adele. "This is a special edition of *L'Antisémite* that came out this morning. You should read it, my dear. You'll find the featured article quite illuminating."

Adele handled the newspaper gingerly, as though it were smeared with dung. "Mother please, you know how Achille despises this sort of thing. He doesn't want it in the house."

Madame sniggered. "Oh, I'm sure he'll hate it all the more when he reads this edition. It appears that Chief Féraud and your brilliant husband have been on the wrong track."

Adele looked down; she fumbled with some ribbons on her dress. After a moment, she looked her mother in the eye; she tried to remain calm but Madame's insinuations had provoked her and it was evident in her expression and tone of voice. "What do you mean by that, Mama?"

Madame was vexed by what she considered her daughter's impertinence. She narrowed her eyes and hissed, "Oh, I think you get my meaning, well enough. Your husband's bungled the case. It's clear from the article that the Jewish bankers and their Freemason allies murdered the girl to keep her mouth shut and as a warning to others who might betray their secrets. Perhaps M. Lefebvre's failure is due to his incompetence as an investigator, but I can think of another explanation."

Adele's face reddened; her hands trembled. Feeling the sting of an insult to her husband, Adele's throat tightened. She swallowed hard before sputtering, "Please be direct, Mother. You have something to say, so come out and say it."

Madame was an officer's widow and the granddaughter of one of Great Napoleon's Old Guard. She came at her daughter with calculated insults like a hot-tempered soldier seeking a duel. "Very well, then. *Perhaps* your incorruptible husband has been bought by the Jews, and *perhaps* he's used their money to keep a mistress in Montmartre, which would explain his long absences better than his feeble excuses about the demands of his job. What's more, it would also explain the fact that after five years of marriage you've produced only one child. Have you considered the possibility that M. Lefebvre has been planting his seed in another field?"

Adele was like a boiler that had blown its safety valve. Her voice quavered but her words hit their mark with blunt force. "How dare you make such unfair accusations against my husband? Show me the evidence, Madame. You have none, just as that gutter press rag you read has no basis in fact for its vile slanders. And I'll no longer tolerate your corrupting my innocent child with your vicious prejudices."

Madame stood her ground. "You forget yourself. I'll remind you, Adele, that you are *my* daughter and owe me your respect. I ought to slap your insolent face."

"You can try, but then I might re-pay you in kind." These words, spoken in the heat of the moment, negated a lifetime of filial obedience.

Madame shook her head and laughed bitterly. "I see how it is. It's the tragedy of old age. I had a husband and children who loved me but they're gone and I'm left with *you*."

Adele realized that she had opened a vast gulf between them that might never be crossed, at least not in this world. "You needn't suffer my presence much longer. Our rent is paid to the end of the month. After the first, Achille, the child, and I will make our home elsewhere."

Madame sank back onto the settee. She spoke without looking at her daughter. "Do as you wish. See how well you manage on an inspector's pay, and that's assuming the Sûreté lets M. Lefebvre keep his job. Now please go and leave me in peace."

Adele left the boudoir, closing the door behind her. Madame sat for a moment, silently staring at her hands. *Why have I lived so long?* She turned down the lamp, and lay back on the settee, imagining she was already in her grave. Tears welled in her eyes and streamed down her wrinkled cheeks, but she made no sound.

⸿

On the outskirts of the forest of Fontainebleau by the banks of a placid river that flows into the Seine sits a medieval town known for its natural beauty, historical monuments, and rural charm. No more than an hour by train from central Paris, the place attracts many visitors, including painters inspired by the history, medieval architecture, ancient ruins, and scenic environs. Many artists have captured a vision of the ancient fortifications, church, monastery, and stone bridge, white walls, shining towers, slate roofs, and spires rising against the background of a cloud-stippled cerulean sky.

Valois, Capet, Angoulême, Orléans, Bourbon, Bonaparte; all had some connection to this place. Wars of religion, internecine feuds, revolutions, invasions, the roar of cannon, the rattle of musketry, the stench of powder smoke, drums rumbling and bugles blaring, the screams of wounded men and horses, the triumphant cries of victors as they charged the fleeing enemy, through all this sound and fury the little town had endured, survived, and even prospered.

At least one great king had kept a mistress lavishly in this place; those out of favor, the victims of intrigue and betrayal, had found less congenial accommodations in the castle dungeon. There, if lucky, they were left to languish and die naturally in obscurity. The less fortunate suffered torture and violent death hidden far away from the king, exiting the bloody stage of royal politics as in the old adage, "Out of sight, out of mind".

Grass and flowers had overgrown the carnage and waste of centuries; whitewash had covered generations of spattered blood. The pain and sorrow of a thousand years had been recorded in the history books and stored deep within the collective memory of the region's inhabitants. "History repeats itself." These scenes would be replayed by a new generation of players, if not within the remainder of the waning century, then surely within the next.

But on this particular morning, all was calm as the meandering river ran slowly beneath the ancient bridge, its surface adorned with fallen leaves tinted russet and old gold. A soft breeze rustled willows, poplars, and tall reeds lining the muddy banks. Morning bells rang; birds sang in the trees, monks prayed, and people went to market as they had since the time of Louis VII and Eleanor of Aquitaine.

On the second story of an *auberge*, secluded within a circle of acacias, Betsy Endicott lay in bed, her hand gently toying with Sir Henry's golden chest hairs as he slept quietly by her side. As arranged, she had come alone the previous evening; Sir Henry joined her early that morning. They immediately went to bed and made love. Then he drifted off into a deep sleep, as though he had been up all night.

Betsy's eyes wandered round the room, past the shadows of branches swaying on the ceiling, toward the white, wind-ruffled curtains and the dim light streaming in through half-opened shutters. *Does he love me?* She wondered. Betsy had lived with Marcia for more than a decade; until her relationship with Sir Henry, she had never been intimate with a man.

Am I in love with him? That was another question for which she could find no answer. He had stirred something within her; he aroused a passion that she had believed was not there, at least not within the experience of her thirty-nine years. *Am I pregnant?* That query was at once exciting and frightening; it would soon be answered by her anticipated period. A first pregnancy at her age could be dangerous for both mother and child. *Does he want a child? Does he want me?*

Betsy trembled, her heart raced, her mouth dried. *I'm suffocating; I can't breathe.* She turned away from him and sat up on the edge of the bed. Her naked body dripped with perspiration; it had soaked the sheets. She stepped down onto the cold wooden floor, walked to the washstand, sponged off, and wrapped herself in a large towel. Gazing into the mirror she was almost surprised to see how youthful and lovely she looked.

She turned from the mirror to Sir Henry. His seemingly untroubled sleep annoyed her, as though none of her reasonable doubts and fears had so much as crossed his mind. *Can I trust him? Is he as strongly committed to me as I am to him?* Betsy finished drying herself, gathered her clothes, and began dressing. As she concealed her vulnerable nakedness beneath layers of linen, lace, and silk, Betsy pondered her plight. Were she and Sir Henry inseparable, *Faithful and bound to each other for as long as we both shall live?* Or should she remain free with the flexibility to adapt to a sudden change in circumstance? She stared hard at her reflection, sighed, and finished dressing without reaching a firm conclusion.

15

The tearoom quintet played a sugary rendition of *Sous le dôme épais* from *Lakmé*. A faint murmur of polite chatter, clattering silver, china, and crystal added counterpoint to the sobbing violins. Lady Agatha and Marcia Brownlow sat at a quiet corner table, enjoying an early afternoon tea served by a handsome young waiter.

"What a charming boy," Lady Agatha observed as she eyed the withdrawing waiter from behind. Then, smiling wistfully, she turned to her friend and took a bite of muffin followed by a sip of tea. She returned her cup to the saucer, brushed away some crumbs and wiped her gloves fussily with the serviette. "Why *do* we wear gloves when taking tea? I always smear butter on mine."

Marcia laughed. "I doubt whether future generations of women shall bother with such niceties."

Aggie grinned wickedly, leaned forward, and whispered, "Future generations of women, my dear, will guzzle gin, smoke cigars, dance like bacchantes, swear like sailors, fight like the *apache*, and show their naughty bits in public. I regret you and I shall not live to see it."

Marcia smiled sadly and nodded at the reference to changing times and encroaching mortality. She had acclimated herself to her friend's decline as she had adjusted to her own. To her painter's eye, the former Venus of Belgravia, subject of one of Marcia's loveliest and most admired society portraits, was like a clipped rose pressed between the leaves of a book; there was still just enough color and fragrance in the remains to revive a memory of the flower in full bloom. "At any rate, I'm so glad you decided to call on me before leaving Paris."

"Of course, darling; I'm off to Vevey on the morning train. I should have despised myself had I missed the opportunity of seeing you after all these years. And I'm delighted to find you well enough to come out to tea."

"Yes, I do seem to have improved tremendously. Perhaps that's due to an anticipated change of scenery. Arthur's arranging our departure; we should be on the boat train to England the day after tomorrow."

Aggie smiled and patted Marcia's hand. "It's awfully sweet to see you and Arthur together again. Just like old times. But what does Betsy think of that?"

"I fear Betsy's so taken with Sir Henry Collingwood she thinks little of me, or not at all. They're off together in the country, where I don't know. I'm not sure I'll see her again."

Aggie frowned ominously. "I'm sorry to hear that, my dear. I'll not mince words. Sir Henry's a cad."

Marcia fidgeted nervously with her teacup. Despite Achille's assurance that the couple were under surveillance, she could not shake off the alarming thought that her companion and former lover might be intimate with a brutal murderer. "Do—do you know that from experience, or are you merely repeating gossip?"

"I was one of his patients, and a bit more than that I'm afraid. Have you submitted to one of his infamous *treatments*?"

"No, that is to say I haven't—" Marcia caught herself. The thought of Sir Henry therapeutically manipulating Betsy and Aggie's private parts made her gag. She coughed into her serviette.

"Are you all right? Perhaps you should drink some water, though Lord knows I never touch the filthy stuff. My father, God rest him, lived past eighty and he never drank anything but whiskey and good English beer. He used to say water makes frogs in one's stomach."

Marcia shook her head and cleared her throat. "Don't worry; I'm fine." She took a couple of deep breaths before continuing: "He did give me some medicine to help me through a rough patch."

Lady Agatha nodded knowingly. "Ah, yes. Sir Henry's medicine. As you know, I was already an opium smoker when I first consulted him. Aside from using my person shamefully, he introduced me to stronger drugs—much more potent than my tainted cigarettes." She sighed before confessing: "I'm hopelessly addicted, my dear."

Marcia looked down at her hands. *Poor Betsy*, she thought. Then, without looking up: "I'm sorry to hear that."

Aggie laughed bitterly. "Don't trouble yourself, Marcia. That's all history. At any rate, I always keep a vial of the stuff in my handbag, a jolly mixture of morphine, cocaine, and chloral hydrate. Perhaps someday I'll be careless and take a wee bit too much. 'The thought of suicide is a great consolation: by means of it one gets successfully through many a bad night.' That's Nietzsche, a German philosopher."

Marcia stared at Aggie with a puzzled expression. Her friend's morose observation was shocking, but its source even more so. Society had attributed many qualities to Lady Agatha, but erudition had not been one of them. To avoid the unpleasant topics of suicide and drug addiction, Marcia resorted to a bland remark. "I didn't know you read philosophy?"

Aggie smiled. "I don't, my dear. I received that nugget of wisdom from our mutual friend, Arthur Wolcott."

"Yes, that sounds like him. I'm afraid morbid German philosophy is Arthur's forte, though I'll admit he's been awfully sweet to me of late."

Aggie now regretted her gloomy tone. She did not want to burden Marcia with her own troubles. "And I'm glad of it, darling," she said optimistically. "You'll be quite happy together, I'm sure." Then, on a more somber note: "I was sorry to part with your painting. I treasured it; I believe it's the finest thing I'll ever own. But I'll confess that with the passing years I found it hard to look at. It reminded me of what once was and could never be again.

"I had everything, you see: youth, health, beauty, and wealth. The first three must go surely; such is life. But I thought I could at least hold on to my money. I married for advantage twice. The first time worked out wonderfully; within three years the old baronet went to his reward leaving me a title, property, and a handsome annuity. But the second time was a bust. How was I to know that Fitzroy was in so deep to the bookmakers? His credit was blown, and the bailiffs were at the door; they hounded him to his grave. And I had to use much of my own fortune to pay the lawyers and satisfy Fitzroy's creditors. So you understand my dear, I simply had to sell your lovely painting. I didn't want to but—but Betsy's offer was so generous. . . ." Lady Agatha choked up. She opened her handbag, withdrew a lace handkerchief, and wiped a tear.

"Of course I understand, my dear. You did what anyone would do under the circumstances."

Aggie blew her nose and returned the handkerchief to her purse. She smiled through the tears. "That's frightfully good of you, my dear. But then, you were always so *sympathique*." She sipped some tea; then pursued: "But I suppose you are concerned about Betsy now that she's taken up with that bounder Sir Henry."

Marcia thought a moment before replying. "I do worry, of course, but I guess I know Betsy better than anyone, having lived with her all these years. We got along, for the most part, because I rarely contradicted her and she never felt threatened by me. But there were tense moments, and some fearful rows, especially when we were drinking. She could be awfully jealous. In fact it was my interest. . . ." Marcia caught herself. She did not want to mention Virginie Ménard. "Rather, it was Betsy's *misapprehension* of my interest in a model that caused our present rift and perhaps made her more susceptible to Sir Henry's charms.

"At any rate, Betsy's quite capable of taking care of herself. She's a crack shot. I've seen her cut dead center on an Ace, five times out of six with a revolver at ten paces."

"Why, she's a regular Miss Annie Oakley!" Lady Agatha broke in.

Marcia smiled. "Not quite, perhaps, but she's fearfully good. She carries a .38 caliber Smith & Wesson pocket revolver in her handbag, and on occasion she backs it up with a derringer concealed in a garter holster."

"A pistol concealed in one's garter? How exciting. I *must* get one of those. One never knows when it might come in handy."

Marcia nodded. "And Betsy's quite capable of using her firearms in a tight corner. On one particular occasion, her cool marksmanship may have saved our lives."

Lady Aggie munched her muffin excitedly and washed it down with half a cup of tea. She patted her rouged lips with the serviette; her eyes lit up with anticipation. "Oh, do tell me what happened."

"Several years ago, when it seemed that I'd fully recovered from my illness, we were on the spree in one of the less reputable districts of San Francisco, a place where ladies never ventured unescorted during the day, let alone at night. Before long, we were accosted by a couple of bully boys exiting a saloon, a pair of ugly, cigar-chomping mugs with black derbies tilted askew and turtleneck sweaters bulging with muscles.

"They blocked our path on the sidewalk. Grinning like an ape, one demanded, 'You gals is on the wrong side of town, ain't ya? Anyways, you'll pay us a toll to walk our streets, or you'll lift yer skirts for us in that there alley.' He pointed a thumb toward a dark, evil smelling passageway behind the saloon. Betsy calmly replied, 'You'll have neither our money nor our bodies. Now I advise you to let us pass.'

"The mugs nearly doubled over with laughter. The meaner-looking of the pair whipped out a large knife and waved it menacingly. 'Sister, yer a card. I think I'll carve a heart on yer pretty little ass, somethin' to remember me by.'

"I was trembling, perspiring, and felt as though I were about to faint. In a moment, I would have dropped to my knees and begged for mercy. Still cool, Betsy said, 'Since you put it that way, I suppose I have no choice but to pay you.' The bully-boy grinned. 'Now yer actin' wise, sister.'

"The rest happened so quickly, but I recall every detail as if time had slowed somehow. Betsy opened her purse as if to pull out a wallet. Instead, she drew the Smith & Wesson and shot the knife-wielding thug directly between the eyes. He keeled over onto the boardwalk like a poleaxed ox in a slaughterhouse. The other man stood frozen, stiff as a cigar store Indian. Betsy aimed and pulled the trigger; he joined his companion, face down in a pool of blood."

"How absolutely ripping!" Lady Agatha interjected.

Marcia nodded. "I was shaking; I felt my gorge rise. Doubling over, I vomited down my dress. Having heard the shots, a murmuring crowd streamed out of the saloon to see what had happened. I heard Betsy mutter, 'Calm yourself. Don't let them see you're afraid.' The crowd milled round the bodies. Betsy, smoking revolver in hand, shouted above the commotion to a burly bouncer: 'Will you please call a policeman? We shall wait right here until he arrives.' We didn't have to wait long. The cop on the beat had been at the bar all the while, partaking of free beer and sandwiches.

"Of course, it was self-defense, no charges were filed, and Betsy became something of a heroine in the local press. She was even commended by the mayor for her bravery and skill with a pistol."

Lady Agatha's face flushed with excitement, her breast heaved and she breathed heavily. Presently she sputtered, "What a fabulous story. And I had no idea what a remarkable girl she was. How I wish I'd been there. At any rate, it seems Betsy should have nothing to fear from that rotter, Sir Henry."

Marcia stared pensively for a moment before answering: "I certainly hope that's the case, Aggie." Then she poured more tea and buttered another muffin, adding a large dollop of refreshing raspberry jam.

∽

Based upon Achille's evidence, and with the backing of Chiefs Féraud and Bertillon, the *juge d'instruction*, Magistrate Leblanc, issued a warrant for Jojo's arrest and an order for his investigative detention in *La Conciergerie*. The infamous prison adjacent to the *Palais de Justice*, formerly referred to as the "antechamber to the guillotine," had been rebuilt during the Second Empire. Following the reconstruction, the mostly modern structure had retained the forbidding aspect of a medieval fortress along with its grim reputation. Deep in the bowels of that dreaded prison, its slate towers looming over the banks of the Seine as a warning to all criminals, Joseph Rossini, *aka* Jojo the Clown, sat despondently on a hard, narrow wooden bench in a dank cell. He stared at the stone walls and iron bars like an animal in the slaughterhouse pen. But unlike a dumb beast Jojo had a guilty conscience, and that sharp human knowledge of guilt tormented him with images of swift justice and harsh retribution.

Jojo rested his elbows on his knees, closed his eyes, and covered his face with his hands. *Why did I do it? I was making good money at the circus. I was popular, a featured act.* The answer of course was gold, and he hadn't been paid for the last job, the one that had got him caught. *It isn't fair.* Jojo recalled a life of neglect and cruelty. He blamed his deformity for his misfortunes, and he had taken out his resentment on those weaker than himself, most particularly the young girls who had worked the streets for him. But now all his pent up rage and bitterness against an unjust world was turned on his employer. *Why should I take the fall? I didn't harm the girl. I was nothing but an errand boy, and an ill-used one at that.*

Thumping boots echoing down the arched corridor, the clicking of a key turning the lock, the sliding of a bolt and the creak of a heavy iron door swinging on its hinges interrupted Jojo's ruminations. "C'mon Jojo, my lad" barked the guard, "it's time for a friendly chat with the Magistrate."

⁓◯⁓

Sir Henry and Betsy exited the *auberge* and proceeded down a gravel path winding through the acacias until they reached a gateway that opened onto a narrow cobblestoned street. Betsy wore a gray traveling coat, a jaunty little veiled black hat and scarf, and she carried an umbrella. The air had a singular freshness to it, a crisp autumnal bite and unmistakable fragrance that betokened rain. A bracing breeze stirred, scattering un-raked leaves, rattling semi-nude branches, and fluttering her scarf and the black-ribbon furbelow on her coat. Sir Henry was elegantly turned out in a Savile Row suit and bowler hat. He took her arm possessively as he escorted her through town in the direction of the old bridge.

As they passed by bright yellow- and white-walled shops and stalls, many of the townspeople took a moment from their occupation to admire the handsome couple; but they didn't gape or let the visitors' presence overly distract them; they were used to well-heeled tourists down from Paris for a day or two's sightseeing.

They stepped onto the arched bridge and crossed halfway before stopping to admire the view. Betsy removed her gloves and touched the rough, cold masonry as if by doing so she could connect with the place and experience centuries of history in a moment. *We have nothing like this in America*, she thought. She glanced up through her veil at a cobalt sky filled with immense white clouds shaded gray round the edges. The dif-fused autumn light shimmered over steep spires, towers, and slanted slate roofs. Beneath the ancient walls and stone embankments the burnished silver river flowed, reflecting the town's image on its smooth, barely rip-pling surface as it lazily meandered toward the Seine.

222

"A lovely subject for a painting," she remarked.

His eyes scanned the scene and he spoke while concentrating on some undefined object in the distance. "Indeed yes, and artists have come here for years. We're not far from Barbizon, you know. I imagine the place as Corot would have painted it; earth tones under a cobalt sky, all visualized through a glimmering coat of amber varnish. But the Impressionists have a different way of expressing it."

Betsy smiled and eyed him provocatively. "I'd like to see how *you'd* paint it, Henry."

"Oh me," he replied with a self-deprecating laugh. "I'm just an amateur. Painting's not my pigeon."

"Yes, not like Marcia. She's a genius. Next to her I've always felt so—so ordinary."

He turned to gaze directly into her eyes and took her by the hand. "Nonsense my dear; you're an extraordinary woman. I've known that since the first day we met."

Her veiled eyes were questioning, challenging. "What's so extraordinary about me, aside from the fact that I'm immensely rich?"

"You underestimate yourself. You're a distinguished collector. Without the support of people like you, the creative arts would wither and die."

"Perhaps you're right. After all, we wealthy Americans *must* be good for something." She paused a moment to study his expression, as if searching for some telltale reaction. Seeing nothing but his familiar amiable smile she pursued: "Henry, we've known each other for scarcely a fortnight. We've become intimate, and . . . ," she paused and lowered her voice to a whisper, ". . . there's that *other business*."

He winced in response to her reference to "other business" but said nothing.

She stared at him searchingly for a moment before continuing: "Yet I know so little about you. For instance, where do you come from? Why did you choose to become a surgeon instead of an artist?"

There was just a wrinkled hint of a frown around his lips and his eyes. "I was born in Abingdon in Oxfordshire, not far from the University. It's fine country for farming and raising fat, wooly sheep. Our market town is ancient; in many respects it resembles this place. We have a medieval church and abbey, and an old stone bridge like this one, spanning the Thames.

"As for surgery, it wasn't all a matter of choice, my dear. My mother loved the arts; she taught me and encouraged me, but she died when I was very young. Father was a physician, and he tended to make my choices for me."

Betsy could tell from his facial expression and tone of voice that he was reticent, yet curiosity moved her to press further. "Would you mind telling me more? I'd like very much to know about your mother."

He stared at her; he had never discussed the subject with anyone, not even under duress. Packed off to school by his father shortly after his mother's death, he had suffered the abuse of a brutal prefect who fagged him endlessly: "Collingwood, fetch water! Collingwood, black my boots! Collingwood, polish my silver!" The prefect used the slightest provocation, the merest failure in an assigned task, as pretext for a merciless caning. "Take down your trousers, Collingwood, bend over the back of that chair and prepare for six of the best." Every beating was followed by an admonition: "There's something about you I don't like. I can't quite put my finger on it, but I shall surely beat it out of you before the end of term."

Young Henry stoically endured the senior boy's bullying until an incident occurred that might have changed the course of his life. Early on a winter morning Henry sat on a wooden bench in the corridor outside the prefect's study. Dawn peeped through a frost covered windowpane. There, in half-darkness, he performed one of his routine chores, polishing his tormentor's boots. Lonely and miserable, aching hands chilled to the bone, he paused for an instant, reached into his pocket, and pulled out a miniature portrait of his mother. The miniature had been painted as a memento of his mother's eighteenth birthday, just prior to her wedding.

Henry sighed, his warm breath forming a small, vaporous cloud in the unheated hallway. "Dearest, I miss you so. Why did you leave me?"

"Shirking again, Collingwood? We shall have to brisk you up." The prefect emerged suddenly from his lair, gleefully grinning at the prospect of administering yet another beating to his chosen victim. "What have we here?" The bully snatched the portrait from Henry's open hand and examined it with an odious leer. "Oh my, she's a pretty one, ain't she? Is she your sweetheart, boy?"

Henry fought back tears. "No sir," he replied in a voice choked with emotion, "she's my mother. Please give it back to me."

The prefect laughed. "Your mother, indeed? So now I've discovered your secret. 'Idle hands are the Devil's playground.' You've been avoiding useful work to indulge in incestuous fantasies. I shall flog you twice as hard for that, you filthy little beast."

Henry exploded with pent up rage. The prefect was almost a foot taller and outweighed the younger boy by more than three stone, yet he was completely unprepared for what happened next. Henry leapt from the bench and, in a blur of violent motion, uncoiled like an overly taut spring. Releasing all the force of his small body, he slammed a fist into his tormentor's groin. The prefect screamed, grabbed his crotch, and crumpled to his knees. But Henry did not stop there. He launched a second hard right aimed at the senior boy's face that broke his nose with an audible crack.

The prefect writhed in agony on the floorboards, choking and gagging on his own blood. Henry sprang on top of him and continued his furious pummeling until several boys came and pulled him off. Had they not arrived promptly he might have killed the older boy, or at least have done him irreparable harm. As it was, the prefect spent a week in hospital, and Henry was permanently expelled from school. According to the headmaster, the boy was mentally and emotionally unstable. But Henry's father was determined to get his only son into Oxford. He hired a tutor and, away from the society of other boys, young Henry proved himself an apt pupil. By the time he was ready for university, he was also better prepared to socialize with his peers.

"Henry, are you all right? You've been staring at me for the longest time." Betsy had watched his blank face with amazement, as he appeared to have gone into a trance.

He shook his head and flushed with embarrassment, realizing that he had drifted off. He gazed into the eyes of the woman to whom he felt inextricably bound by fate, passion, and a secret that could destroy him, and perhaps her as well. "I'm sorry, my dear. I fear my mother's a subject I—I never discuss with anyone. The memory's too painful." He paused a moment before adding: "But then, with you it's different. Here, let me show you something." He reached into his waistcoat pocket and withdrew a gold watch. Opening the case to a miniature portrait, he handed the watch to Betsy. "That was she at the time of her eighteenth birthday."

Betsy studied the young woman's portrait for a minute before returning the watch. "She was very beautiful. I'm sorry, darling. You must miss her awfully."

He nodded sadly as he tucked the watch back into his pocket. Then, with a faint smile: "Yes, but now I've found someone to fill that void in my heart." His words were spontaneous, and their sincerity surprised him even as he spoke. He continued without waiting for her reply. "She suffered, most particularly in her final year; my father and his colleagues could do little or nothing for her. Since it was my fate to become a doctor, I decided that I would devote my practice to women, to use the latest methods of medical science to preserve their health and alleviate their suffering."

She smiled in response. The story of his mother had touched her deeply. But she was skeptical by nature, and did not altogether trust him. Without comment, she turned to gaze at the river, listening to its rippling as it flowed beneath the arches and round ancient piers.

Henry moved closer to her. He put his arm round her waist and stared silently into the distance. *We're adrift in a sea of lies*, he thought. But at that moment he was certain of one thing; he would propose marriage to Betsy Endicott; the only question was where and when.

∽∾

The loudly ticking wall clock produced the only audible sound in Magistrate Leblanc's office. Light streamed through tall windows opening onto the courtyard of the *Palais de Justice*. The Magistrate, a stout, gray, grandfatherly man in his sixties, with antennae-like brows and mutton-chop side-whiskers spreading beneath his temples down to the jaw line, sat hunched over a great mahogany desk stacked high with documents, photographs, and files. Above and behind him on gray painted walls hung the symbols of the Republic, the *Liberté, Egalité, Fraternité* motto beneath a profile of Marianne surrounded by the tricolor. The wall also displayed a portrait of President Carnot on its otherwise bare surface.

The Magistrate's brow furrowed and his thin lips pursed as he examined Gilles's photographs of Virginie Ménard's head, taken that morning at the crime scene and the Morgue. Tugging his whiskers nervously, he concentrated on the odd insignia tattooed on the decomposing forehead, a Masonic compass and square superimposed over a Star of David. "What sort of monster could have done this?" he muttered under his breath, though loudly enough to be heard clearly by the officers assembled before him. As his slightly trembling left hand held the photographs up for closer scrutiny, his right descended from his whiskers to the large Masonic symbol dangling from his gold watch chain.

The Magistrate set down the pictures. His sharp blue eyes darted behind his spectacles, looking from one stiff, silent officer to the next: Chiefs Féraud and Bertillon, Inspectors Lefebvre, Rousseau, and Duroc, the hapless detective detailed to shadow Jojo the Clown. The questioning eyes finally came to rest on Achille. "I commend you, Inspector Lefebvre, for your skill in marshalling evidence in this case. You are also to be commended for bringing in the Gunzberg brothers as witnesses. Their

testimony backed by your forensic evidence will prove invaluable at trial."
He paused a moment before admonishing: "But in future I trust you'll
inform your chief and me before permitting untrained boys to traipse
around Paris playing detective."

"Yes, Monsieur Magistrate," Achille replied respectfully.

Leblanc then turned to Rousseau's man, Duroc. "As for you, M.
Duroc, I hope you improve your powers of observation prior to under-
taking another such assignment."

Duroc glanced at Rousseau and was met with a scowl. He did not
dare look at Chief Féraud. Hanging his head like a whipped schoolboy,
he answered, "Yes, Monsieur Magistrate."

The *juge d'instruction* grunted an acknowledgement and then shuffled
through his papers, focusing on Sir Henry Collingwood's letter and a
document recently obtained by warrant from the editor of *L'Antisémite*.
"M. Bertillon, in your opinion as one of our leading graphologists, were
these two documents written by the same person?"

"I've made a careful analysis of the handwriting on both documents,
M. Leblanc, and I'm convinced the authors are one in the same."

"That's good enough for me, M. Bertillon." Then to Achille: "I find
your fingerprint evidence compelling, Inspector. However, it remains a
novel concept, untested at trial, and by itself would be insufficient to send
the case to the prosecutor. Fortunately, I believe you've uncovered sufficient
evidence aside from the fingerprints to support your theory of the case.

"Moreover, I agree with your conclusions concerning the tattoo on
the victim's forehead and *The Devil in Montmartre*. They are fabrications
intended to confuse the public, confound the police, and frame an innocent
boy. The perpetrator committed an atrocious crime. First he tried to fix
blame on M. de Toulouse-Lautrec. Thanks to your excellent detective
work, the initial ruse failed. The perpetrator then resorted to another
deception. In doing so, he relied upon a common human weakness, a ten-
dency to ignore facts when they conflict with our deeply rooted prejudices
or preconceived notions.

"But in this instance the perpetrator has condemned himself. By attempting a second diversion he has provided us with additional evidence that will convict him and send him to the guillotine. Following the trail of persuasive facts, and discounting the diversions, I conclude the perpetrator is Sir Henry Collingwood and Joseph Rossini is his accomplice."

Féraud smiled broadly. "M. Leblanc, Chief Bertillon and I agree that much of the credit in this case should go to Inspector Lefebvre."

"Yes Chief Inspector. Aside from M. Duroc's blunders, I'd say your bureau has performed splendidly."

At that moment, both Rousseau and Duroc would have gladly slunk out the door on all fours. Achille felt sorry for them.

"Gentlemen," Leblanc continued, "I'm going to issue a warrant for Collingwood's arrest. However, before doing so I want to question Rossini. He might provide useful information if he thinks it will save his neck, and the prosecutor can use him as a witness against Sir Henry. Do we have Collingwood under surveillance?"

"Yes M. Leblanc," Achille replied. "He's registered at the Grand Hotel, but he's currently staying at an *auberge* in Moret-sur-Loing. There's an American woman with him, Mlle Endicott. I've wired the Prefecture of Police to keep an eye on them. We don't believe she's in danger, at least not yet. She's very wealthy, and it's likely Sir Henry intends to propose marriage. In my opinion, the suspect is more likely to choose his victims from among women without money, property, or social connections."

The Magistrate shook his head and frowned. "Ah, the woman complicates things. You'll need to be very careful when making the arrest. You and Chief Féraud should go there at once to supervise."

"We've already made arrangements with the *gendarmerie*. The Chief and I will leave by special train as soon as you issue the warrant."

"Very well; let's bring in Rossini." The Magistrate glared at Duroc. "Your presence is no longer required." The chastened detective bowed curtly and left without a word. Duroc would spend the rest of the day exploring opportunities in the Colonial police. Then to Bertillon: "Chief

Inspector Bertillon, I want to thank you and your department, for your expert services and advice in this case. I invite you to remain for the interrogation, unless you have more pressing matters to attend to."

"Thank you, M. Leblanc, I'll stay. Jojo's an interesting criminal type, a prime example of atavism, a primitive throwback to an earlier stage of human evolution. His measurements and photographs have already made a useful contribution to my rogues' gallery."

Leblanc nodded. "The rascal's where he belongs—in a cage. At any rate, let's see what the creature has to say for himself."

A burly guard brought in the manacled prisoner followed by a clerk to record the proceedings in shorthand. The guard kept Jojo standing until the Magistrate gave him permission to be seated. Jojo shook visibly; sweat beaded on his forehead. His eyes shifted round the room from one stern face to the next. The inspectors reminded him of the witnesses to an execution; the *juge d'instruction* displayed the cool detachment, efficiency, and grim visage of the public executioner; the clerk seemed like the executioner's assistant.

Leblanc's deep, powerful voice echoed through the room as he summarized the evidence against the prisoner. Finally, in summation: "According to law, as an accomplice to murder you are equally guilty and subject to the same penalty as the perpetrator. Have you anything to say before I turn the case over to the prosecutor?"

Jojo's lips moved but he couldn't speak. His mouth dried; his throat constricted.

The Magistrate grinned triumphantly. "You seem to be having some difficulty speaking. Would you like a glass of water and a cigarette?"

Jojo nodded his head rapidly. Leblanc gestured to the guard, who poured a glass of water from a pitcher on the Magistrate's desk and handed it to Jojo, who took it between his shackled hands. He gulped the water, coughed, cleared his throat, and drained the glass. "Thank you, Monsieur," he grunted. The guard took the empty glass and produced a cigarette and a box of matches. He placed the cigarette between Jojo's lips and gave him a light. Jojo inhaled deeply and exhaled slowly.

"That's better, eh? Now then, Rossini, is there something you want to say to me? Remember, my boy, confession's good for the soul." Leblanc gazed at Jojo with what might have easily been mistaken for a benign smile.

Jojo lifted his manacled hands and removed the cigarette. He had already decided that cooperation was the only way to save himself. "Yes, Monsieur Magistrate. I performed services for the American lady."

There was a shocked silence in the room as the Inspectors and Magistrate stared in bewilderment at each other before focusing all their attention back on Jojo.

The Magistrate continued. "American lady, you say? Do you know her name?"

"No Monsieur, I do not, but Claude Duval, the night porter at the Grand Hotel, sent her to me. He might know. She wore a disguise, a false beard and glasses, but I could tell her nationality from the accent. As for her sex, let's just say I could tell. But I played along with her. After all, she paid well and I had no reason to question her masquerade."

"How and when did this woman first contact you?"

Jojo thought a moment before replying, "That was Sunday, the 11th of this month. She came to my flat in Montmartre."

"You mentioned 'services.' What was the nature of these 'services'? Why would this woman come to you?"

Jojo took another drag on the cigarette before answering. "At first, nothing more than to locate a girl, Virginie Ménard. Then later, there were other things." He looked down at his trembling hands.

"What were the 'other things'?"

Without looking up, Jojo said, "On occasion I've been known to dispose of things people wanted to be rid of. The lady must have learned about my—disposal service."

The guard suppressed a laugh and drew a reproving glare from the Magistrate.

Leblanc frowned; his eyes hardened, his voice regained its harshness. "The 'things' you disposed of were human bodies and body parts, including the torso and head of Virginie Ménard. When did you first perform that little service?"

"I put the headless torso in the cesspit early the morning of the 15th, before the night soil collectors made their rounds."

"I see. And you left the torso in the cesspit along with a gold cigarette case you stole from M. de Toulouse-Lautrec in an attempt to fix the blame on him."

Jojo looked up with alarm. "Oh no, Monsieur, I didn't steal it. That was the Englishman's job. I swear it!"

"What Englishman? Can you give me his name?"

"Sir Henry Collingwood. I believe he and the lady were . . . are intimate. Anyway, they both wanted to get rid of the . . . the body."

The Magistrate stared at Jojo in stunned silence. Despite his many years of experience with criminals from all walks of life, he found it hard to believe that a wealthy socialite could be involved in such a brutal crime. Nevertheless, he would follow the evidence wherever it might lead. After a moment, he proceeded in a cold, accusatory tone. "Very well, Rossini, when that first scheme failed, you threw the victim's head in a dust-bin and tried to frame Moïse Gunzberg as an agent of the Jews and Freemasons!"

Jojo's eyes widened; his whole body shook and broke out in a sweat. "I swear before God, Monsieur, I had nothing to do with the girl's death or the schemes! I just did as the lady told me. I . . . I disposed of things and. . . ."

The Magistrate's eyes narrowed; his voice lowered to an audible whisper. "And what else, Jojo?"

Jojo looked down at his chained hands. "I . . . helped her ambush and chloroform the kid. Then I changed clothes with Gunzberg, put him in the ragman's cart, and dumped the package in the *poubelle* to fool the cop watching my flat. And there was more." Jojo glanced fearfully at Rousseau before continuing: "She told me to feed false information to Inspector Rousseau, to stir up trouble between him and Inspector Lefebvre."

Rousseau clenched his fists and glared at Jojo. "You little rat!" he growled.

"Control yourself, Inspector," the Magistrate admonished.

Rousseau stared at his shoes and mumbled an apology. "Pardon me, Monsieur Magistrate." The room was silent except for the ticking of the clock. Then the Magistrate ordered: "Look at me, Rossini."

Jojo raised his head slowly. There were tears in his eyes.

"Do you think you could identify the woman?"

"I . . . I'd recognize her voice, Monsieur Magistrate."

"What if you heard her speak and she were dressed in her disguise?"

"Yes Monsieur; I'm sure I could identify her."

Leblanc nodded. Then: "Guard, you may return the prisoner to his cell." He waited for Jojo, the guard, and the clerk to leave before addressing Chief Bertillon. "M. Bertillon, is it possible you made a mistake in identifying the handwriting on the letter to the newspaper?"

His customary self-confidence shaken for the moment, Bertillon replied, "It's possible, M. Leblanc. The woman might have done a good job copying Collingwood's handwriting. It's happened before."

He turned next to Achille. "Inspector Lefebvre, did you have any reason to suspect a woman was actively involved in this case?"

Achille frowned and shook his head. "No, Monsieur, I did not. I was aware that a wealthy American woman, Mlle Endicott, had formed a relationship with Sir Henry, but my chief concern was for her safety. Frankly, I was shocked when Jojo implicated her in the crime. Even now, I'm not convinced she's a willing participant. Perhaps Sir Henry has coerced her into criminal complicity?"

A wry smile spread over Rousseau's fleshy lips. He remained prudently silent while thinking, *A nice excuse for missing a suspect. So the professor's not perfect, after all.*

The Chief noticed Rousseau's knowing smirk and sensed Achille's discomfort. He immediately intervened on behalf of his favorite detective. "Gentlemen, this new twist in the case has taken us all by surprise. I say we bring them both in for questioning. At the very least, the woman could be a key witness in our case against Sir Henry. Anyway, the Magistrate will soon get to the bottom of it."

The Magistrate nodded his agreement. "Very well; I'm issuing a warrant for Sir Henry Collingwood's arrest. The sooner he's locked up and questioned the better. I'll also issue a warrant for Mlle Endicott. And pick up Claude Duval, the night porter at the hotel who allegedly referred her to Jojo. If both he and Jojo identify Mlle Endicott as this mysterious woman posing as a man—" The Magistrate paused a moment before continuing: "Well then, gentlemen, we'll cross that bridge when we come to it."

16

OCTOBER 22, EVENING

Féraud and Achille arrived at the Gare de Lyon shortly after sunset. They hustled through the crowded entrance hall to the train shed where the passengers queued. The inspectors officially jumped the queue, flashed their credentials, and moved on rapidly in the direction of a gated platform guarded by a *brigadier*. The guard saw them coming and looked up at the station clock. They were right on schedule. He checked their tricolor badges, saluted, opened the gate and passed them through.

A hissing, chuffing engine with one passenger car attached waited for them up the platform. An attendant spotted them and opened the compartment door. He handed a telegram to Féraud. "We just received a wire from the Prefecture of Police. You should arrive at the station in forty minutes. A *brigadier* will be there with a *diligence* to take you and Inspector Lefebvre into town."

Féraud stuffed the envelope into his pocket and thanked the attendant. Then he and Achille stepped up into the compartment and took their seats opposite each other, the attendant locked the door, and signaled the engine driver with a wave. The engineer checked his pressure gauges, released the brake, opened the throttle, and gave a blast on the whistle. High above the platform, in the control tower, switches were thrown; the engine chugged and rumbled its way slowly up the siding, gaining speed as it entered the great iron spiderweb of rails and switches that shunted and shuttled trains into, out of, and around the enormous iron and glass shed.

As the train exited the station, Achille said, "This might seem odd, Chief, but all things considered I feel sorry for Rousseau. It's too bad he couldn't come with us and see the case through to the end."

Féraud shook his head and smiled wryly. "You're much too generous, Achille. I've known Rousseau for more than twenty years. He was a good detective, but this final blunder has ended his career. He's off the case, and I expect to see his resignation on my desk when we return to headquarters. Rousseau let that little shit Jojo make a fool of him. I won't be too hard on him for old times' sake, but he's lost face with the brigade; he's finished, end of story."

Achille glanced down at his folded hands. After a moment he looked up with a troubled frown. "I completely missed the woman, Chief. I must take blame for that, although I still doubt she's a willing participant in the murder. Perhaps she's just in love and covering up for her lover?"

Féraud laughed. *"Cherchez la femme!* You're a romantic, Achille. At any rate, I guess that old adage will take on a new meaning for you after this case. Seriously my boy, you did splendid work. I'm proud of you, and it will be reflected in my report. After all, you *were* right about Jojo and Sir Henry. The clown is singing like a canary. We'll pick up the Englishman and the American woman, turn them over to the Magistrate for questioning, and let him sort things out."

Oblivious to the car's lurching and noise, Féraud stretched out, yawned, and pulled his bowler down over his eyes. "I suggest you try to get forty winks. It may be your last chance for some time." With that pithy remark the chief drifted off into oblivion. Like the Great Napoleon, the chief was famous for his anytime, anywhere cat naps.

How can he sleep at a time like this? Achille admired his chief's sang-froid. *What would I do in his position?* Could he take on Féraud's job? Could he manage the Sûreté or would he collapse under the pressure?

He worried about his family. Were they all right? Adele was still sleeping when he left the apartment at four A.M. He had sent a message telling her he would not be home that evening. It was not the first time, and it wouldn't be the last.

The fact that his forensic investigation had focused his attention on Sir Henry and Jojo to the exclusion of other possibilities troubled him, despite the Chief's reassuring words. *Virginie died of a morphine overdose. But who administered the fatal injection? Sir Henry performed the operation and the post-mortem amputations, but was he the murderer? Mlle Endicott had a motive. She was jealous of what she believed was Virginie's relationship with Marcia Brownlow and perhaps of her relationship with Sir Henry, too. And she could have had the opportunity when Virginie was lying helpless and already sedated. Why didn't I question her? Was it some pre-conceived notion that women like her don't commit such crimes? If so, it's a flaw in my thinking that must be corrected if I'm to excel as a detective.*

The whistle shrieked as the train entered a tunnel, the rumbling of steel wheels on rails at forty-five miles per hour echoing on brick walls, the incessant chugging, the pounding of pistons in cylinders, firebox flashing in the darkness, the rush and roar as the engine streaked out of the man-made cavern into a cutting. On and on they raced, beneath the streets of the brightly lit city, past the fortifications into the suburbs, across viaducts and embankments, into the dark, peaceful countryside of the Île-de-France, toward a rendezvous with a murderer. But who was the real killer? Were they accomplices in the killing, or did one commit the crime and the other merely act as an accessory in a coverup? There were still too many pieces missing from the puzzle; he would not jump to conclusions. As the Chief said, such vexing lacunae would be filled in during the interrogations. Or would they?

Achille stared at his reflection in the car window. For a moment, he thought he saw Collingwood's face gazing back at him with an enigmatic grin. *What did he do, and why did he do it? Why didn't he run when he had the chance? Does he know he's trapped? Could the woman have set him up for the fall?* Achille could not answer these questions. With Betsy entering the picture, Sir Henry's motives were unclear. Achille turned away from the window, shook his head and rubbed his eyes; he was tired, his mind was wandering. He would have done better to have slept, like his chief. Since Achille could not nap, he thought about the best way to take Sir Henry and Betsy. The problem at hand was to effectuate an arrest without endangering the innocent.

An idea was forming in his head, but it would depend on the circumstances. He would know more when they made contact with the local police. Achille took his watch out of his pocket and held the dial up toward the ceiling lamp. They must have been in the vicinity of Fontainebleau. He glanced out the window into the darkness and could make out the shadowy forms of a dense thicket lining the railway embankment.

A few minutes later he sensed the slowing of the engine, the diminished thumping of pistons, felt a perceptible decline in the rocking and swaying of the car. Féraud noticed it too. He snorted, lifted his hat, rubbed his eyes, and scratched his head. The train switched onto a siding, chugged past a water tower, hissed and squealed up to the platform where it came chuffing to a halt with a bone-shaking jolt.

The chief yawned loudly, sat up, and consulted his watch. He smiled at Achille. "We made good time. I'm anxious to speak with the colonel, but I'm famished. I could do with a sandwich and a glass or two of good wine. How about you?"

"I haven't eaten since breakfast. Anything would taste good right now. As for talking to the colonel, I've got an idea for making the arrest, assuming the circumstances are right."

Féraud lifted his eyebrows. "An idea, eh? That's my professor, always thinking, on or off the job. Well don't keep it a secret."

Before Achille could reply, the compartment door swung open. A spruce young *brigadier* with an enormous black handlebar moustache saluted smartly and greeted them. "Good evening Chief Inspector Féraud and Inspector Lefebvre. You're right on time. The *diligence* is waiting to take you into town to meet with my colonel. It's a short drive, a little less than two kilometers from the station."

They stepped onto the platform and followed the *brigadier* down a path around the station to the parked *diligence*. The two draft horses pulling the coach turned toward them curiously, shook their heads, snorted, and exhaled steaming breath into the cold night air.

During the drive into town along a well-paved country road, the talkative *brigadier* provided them with useful information. "The suspects had an early supper after which they took a stroll around town. Then they returned to their room at the *auberge*, where at present they remain together. Looking up from the garden to their second floor bedroom window, you can see the light is out. The curtain is drawn but the shutters are half opened." The handsome young policeman smiled slyly and winked. "According to the maid who tidies up and changes the bedclothes, the couple has, shall we say, been very—active."

Féraud nodded curtly without cracking a smile. "I trust the proprietor has been informed and that men have been stationed discreetly within the house and around the grounds? We must take precautions for the safety of the other guests, and the staff."

Chastened somewhat by the chief's seriousness, the *brigadier* answered succinctly. "Of course, Chief Inspector. You may go over the details with my colonel."

"Do you know when the suspects plan to leave?" Achille asked.

"Yes, Inspector. They're supposed to be on the morning train to Paris. The *diligence* will come for them at nine A.M. That is to say, that's the arrangement Sir Henry made with the *auberge*."

Achille turned to Féraud. "Their plans fit in with my idea for the arrest." Then to the policeman: "Is there any way out of the room besides the door and the window?"

"No, Inspector; they're trapped. The door of their room opens onto the second floor landing and we have two men posted nearby. An acrobat or cat burglar might get to the roof from the window, but we'd spot them immediately from our positions in the garden. There's no way up or down except the stairs, and no way out except through the doors. We have everything covered."

Achille nodded. "I see. Let's say they managed to evade or break through your cordon, what routes would provide their best chances of escape?"

The *brigadier* replied confidently: "We've guarded the railway station, the roads, and the river landings. They could try to make a break for it cross-country, but I doubt they'd get far."

Achille paused a moment before asking, "Do you know if they're armed?"

A hint of apprehension crept into the *brigadier*'s voice. "No Inspector, we don't."

"Do you think it's possible they might know the police are watching them?"

The *brigadier* couldn't be sure of his answer but he tried to hide his worries behind a smile. "I doubt it, M. Lefebvre. We've been cautious, and from our surveillance it appears that their attention is focused on each other, which isn't surprising. They're quite an attractive couple, you know."

Achille frowned. He expressed his concerns to Féraud. "I think I know something about Sir Henry's psychology. I doubt he'll go peacefully, and the more trapped and hopeless he feels the more desperate and dangerous he'll be. He might try to use Mlle Endicott as a shield, and if he has a firearm he could take hostages from among the guests and the staff.

"On the other hand, for all we know the lady might be the instigator of the crime and the deadlier of the pair. All things considered, I don't recommend entering the room to make the arrest. We can't assume they're asleep. They might be waiting for us. At any rate, it seems too risky, and we don't know how they'll react. Instead, I propose my playing the part of the coachman come to take Sir Henry and Mlle Endicott to the station tomorrow morning. On the way to the *diligence* someone will divert Mademoiselle's attention; perhaps a messenger telling her she has an urgent telegram from Paris. The point is to separate the lady from Sir Henry long enough for me, along with a couple of discreetly hidden *brigadiers*, to make the arrests."

The young *brigadier* smiled broadly and stroked his moustache. "I'd gladly volunteer to be one of those assisting you, Inspector."

"Thank you, *brigadier*," Achille replied. Then to Féraud: "What do you think, Chief?"

Féraud nodded his assent. "It's a good plan, Achille. We can discuss it further with the colonel—over supper, I hope." A loud internal gurgling punctuated his statement. "Excuse me, gentlemen. My poor stomach's groaning 'feed me,'" he added with a sheepish grin.

⟨∞⟩

Sir Henry couldn't sleep. Around midnight he lay on his back under the covers, staring at shadows on the ceiling. Betsy nestled beside him, warm and inviting even as she slept. He glanced at her, recalling an afternoon and evening of uninhibited sex. *Is she dreaming of our passion? What lustful visions are running through her unfathomable mind?*

The sleeping woman seemed so innocent and peaceful, like a schoolboy's fantasy image of a lovely girl on the verge of womanhood. But Betsy was hardly that. Sir Henry had unleashed a tigress; his body bore the scratches and bite marks to prove it. But there was something other than Betsy's furious lovemaking troubling him. Earlier, during their supper at the *auberge* and their postprandial stroll, he had noticed an unusual number of *gendarmes* about town. At first he thought nothing of it, but now upon reflection in the lonely moments of a still night, with nothing and no one to distract him, he worried. *What's happening with Jojo and our scheme? Are the police getting wise to us? Have we stumbled into a trap?*

He craved a cigarette. Careful not to disturb Betsy, he lifted the covers on his side of the bed, swung his legs over the edge of the mattress and quietly set his feet on the hardwood floor. Gooseflesh covered his naked body. Sir Henry glanced toward the window. The sash had been left up a few inches, admitting the chilly night air. Pale moonlight streamed through half-opened shutters, lighting a small corner of the room. Forgetting about his smoke, he walked toward the other end of the bedroom, intending to lower the sash. As he neared the window he thought he heard the faint murmuring of voices coming from the garden below. Looking out through the pane he saw a flash of light coming from behind a stand of acacias. *Is it a lantern? Could it be the police?*

He considered the possibility with fatalistic calm.

⚭

A pair of *gendarmes*, watching from behind the trees, glimpsed Sir Henry at the window. One leaned over and whispered to his comrade, "So he's up and about, eh? Look, he's closing the window and shutters. It must be getting cold up there."

"*He's* cold? At least the bastard's got something nice to keep him warm in bed," the other answered with a smirk.

⚭

Sir Henry glanced back at the sleeping woman. *I suppose I ought to have stayed in Paris or, better yet, quit the country. But these last two days have made it worthwhile. She's an extraordinary woman. Father always said I'd come to a sticky end. At any rate, a short exciting life's better than one that's long and dull. I'm not afraid to die, but I prefer to choose the time, place, and manner of departure.*

Within the span of two short weeks, fate had entered his world in the form of two women, altering the course of his life forever. Virginie came first. She had agreed to a radical operation, to be performed in secret. There was a social stigma attached to a hysterectomy; she would submit to the surgery only under conditions of strict confidentiality. Using an assumed name, Henry rented a small apartment in Montmartre. He scrubbed and disinfected the place scrupulously and brought in several kerosene lamps and a reflecting mirror so he could operate in the pre-dawn darkness.

In the early morning on October 11, Virginie left a note for her concierge. She would be out of town on business for three days, returning on the 14th, providing adequate time for recovery before returning to her flat.

Henry operated brilliantly. The procedure was a complete success and he had the satisfaction of knowing that his new technique for vaginal hysterectomy had preceded the great Péan by three days. Respecting his patient's need for privacy, he felt honor bound never to reveal his surgical triumph. But he didn't mind the constraints of secrecy; knowing that he had succeeded where others had failed was sufficient compensation. Then Betsy Endicott entered the scene.

On the day he had planned to take Virginie back to her flat, he was shocked to find Betsy, disguised as a man, standing at the bedside. She told him a story he never really believed. Betsy had hired Jojo to locate Virginie. She wanted to bribe the girl to keep her away from Marcia, and she used a disguise to avoid scandal. When she arrived at the flat she found Virginie sound asleep. Betsy noticed a bottle of morphine and hypodermic kit on the bedside table and assumed the girl was heavily sedated. She was about to leave when Henry returned from witnessing the operation at Péan's clinic. Henry examined Virginie immediately. She was dead, apparently from a fatal overdose.

Did he inadvertently administer the overdose earlier that day, or did Betsy intervene with malicious intent? He would never know for certain. Regardless, the operation had been a success but the patient was dead. Under the circumstances, he feared a scandal that would ruin his career. But worse than the charge of medical malpractice was the possibility of criminal charges, up to and including murder. Betsy offered him a way out of his dilemma. Jojo would dispose of the body; they could frame up someone else for the crime. She had it all worked out beautifully. And there were added incentives for going along with her scheme. There was Betsy, marriage, and a share in her fortune.

Sir Henry kept staring at Betsy as she slept peacefully in their bed. He smiled resignedly and shook his head. *The goddess of fortune's a capricious whore*, he thought.

He remembered the story Betsy had told him about the two Barbary Coast thugs she had shot in self defense. *Is the revolver in her handbag?* Sir Henry crept noiselessly to the chair where she had left her things. He opened her purse and felt for the weapon. Immediately recognizing the smooth ivory grip, the cool nickel-plated cylinder, barrel, and frame, he removed the revolver. *The gun and Betsy could be my ticket out of here*, he thought.

He dressed quickly, then struck a match and lit a candle on the dresser. In the dim golden light he opened the revolver to check the cylinder. *Fully loaded, just as I expected; she's a smart girl to be prepared.* Smiling at the sight of five brass cartridges, he closed the top-break revolver with a loud metallic snap.

Betsy moaned and stirred under the sheets. Sir Henry walked to the bed, sat on the edge of the mattress, and gently placed his left hand over her mouth while the right gripped the Smith & Wesson. Her eyelids fluttered and then opened wide; the sharp gray eyes stared at him questioningly.

"Hush darling," he whispered. "We're in a bit of a tight corner, I'm afraid. We'll have to leave at once."

Her eyes glared at him, and she noticed the gun. He withdrew his hand and she hissed, "What the devil's going on?"

Her petulance excited him. For an instant he wondered if he could have her once more before they left. He shook his head. "Sorry, my dear; I'm afraid the police have us surrounded. My guess is they picked up Jojo and made him talk." He got up from the mattress and pointed the pistol at her. "Please get dressed now, and make as little noise as possible."

Glaring at him, she whipped away the covers angrily, flashing a full view of her naked body. The sight of her firm, rosy-nippled breasts, flat stomach, round hips, long legs, and brown-tufted mons Veneris glowing with perspiration, coupled with the looming specter of violent death, aroused and stimulated his senses like an intra-venous injection of cocaine.

He leered at her as she slid off the bed and slinked to the chair by the dresser. She slithered into her Victorian outer layer of linen, lace, and silk, slowly and suggestively, while her smoldering eyes fixed on his. Betsy's erotic movements and gestures were a calculated distraction. Thrilled by her performance, Sir Henry failed to notice as she palmed the hidden Derringer from its garter holster, executing this feat with all the deceptive skill of a magician or a Barbary Coast gambler dealing seconds.

As she finished dressing, he walked to the window, intermittently glancing back to keep an eye on her. He peered through the closed pane and the shutter slats. A couple of pinpoints of light glimmered behind the acacias. *They're out there, all right. I've always thought the police were an assortment of unimaginative plodders and dimwitted thugs, but apparently the French have a clever detective.*

He turned toward Betsy and saw her standing with the Derringer aimed at him. She had stealthily advanced a few paces while his back was turned, to close the range and make sure of her shot.

He smiled with admiration. *She is indeed extraordinary. I'll never find another like her.* "Well my dear," he said, "I believe this is what your American dime novels call a standoff."

She replied with a cold, hard edge to her voice. "You're wrong, Henry. A standoff implies equality, and there's nothing equal about our present situation. I'm ready and aimed; at this distance I can't miss. You, on the other hand, have my revolver at your side. I could drop you before you leveled your weapon and got off a shot."

"Ah, but you have one bullet to my five. That little pop-gun might misfire or jam. They often do, you know."

"This is a Remington Double Derringer, two shots instead of one. It's quite reliable and I maintain my firearms in good order. After all, a woman must protect herself from all the predators prowling this wicked planet. You killed Virginie Ménard with an overdose of morphine. I did my best to help you. But now it appears the game's up and the police are after *you*. All the evidence points to you. I made sure of that. Even if Jojo talks, he can't identify me. I made sure of that, too."

He sighed. "You can't be absolutely certain, my dear. I'd say we're in this together, right to the end."

"No Henry, I wouldn't say that. At the very worst they might charge me as an accessory after-the-fact. If that happens, I'll hire the best lawyers and cooperate with the authorities. I can play your victim convincingly. I'm sure the French judges will sympathize with a woman in my position."

Sir Henry laughed bitterly. "I always suspected you gave Virginie the overdose and set me up for the fall, but it may surprise you to learn I don't care. I love you, Betsy. If you come with me, I shan't harm you. I need you to evade the police. When we were walking about town I noticed some boats at a secluded landing. I handle a boat quite well. I rowed at Oxford, you know. Help me escape and we can remain together, or you can leave me at your first opportunity. You may keep the Derringer for insurance."

"You'll never get out of France. I doubt you'll get much further than the front gate, with me or not. At any rate, I'm not going with you. You're on your own. And I'll thank you to leave my revolver on the bed. You might shoot someone, and I won't have that on my conscience."

Henry's eyes narrowed; his tone hardened. "I'll go it alone then, but I'll take your gun. Without it I'd be as defenseless as a creature in the jungle without its fangs and claws."

Betsy's features transformed into an inscrutable mask. "Then you'll be as vulnerable as the women you suckered with your 'treatments'. I don't pity you.We had an amusing fling, Henry, but I never trusted you. Put the revolver on the bed now, or you won't leave this room alive."

He shook his head with resolve. "No, I'm taking the pistol. If you intend to kill me, you'll have to shoot me in the back. Good-bye, my dear. Remember I loved you."

He turned and walked toward the door. As he grasped the brass door-knob, Betsy aimed at the back of his head and squeezed the trigger. The Derringer flashed and popped like a firecracker; black powder from the expended .41 caliber cartridge emerged from the barrel in a plume of grey smoke, filling the small room with its acrid stench. The bullet grazed his left temple and spent itself on the oak door.

Sir Henry wiped the wound with his left hand, glared at the blood, spun round and leveled the revolver at Betsy. "You bloody bitch!"

She did not hesitate. Betsy aimed and fired the second barrel. The bullet punched a gaping hole in Sir Henry's forehead, lodging itself deep within his brain. He squeezed the Smith & Wesson's trigger in a reflex action, firing a shot that struck her chest and entered the heart. Bulging eyes staring into the void, blood streaming down his once handsome face, he staggered two steps, slumped to his knees, and fell forward unconscious at her feet. Betsy collapsed and lay prone by his side.

Two *brigadiers* with drawn revolvers burst into the room, followed by Achille and Féraud. The dark room blazed with light from the policemen's lanterns. Betsy and Sir Henry sprawled together on the floor, unconscious and dying in a pool of commingled blood.

Achille examined the bodies and frowned. He felt cheated, somehow. Their last willful actions had thwarted his fine sense of justice. *I wanted to bring them in for questioning. Now, the missing pieces to this puzzle will remain lost.* He glanced up at Féraud. "They're both mortally wounded. We should call a surgeon, though nothing short of a miracle could save them. I guess he'll just go through the formalities, pronounce them dead and sign the certificates."

Chief Féraud shrugged, lit a cigar, and took a couple of puffs before saying, "Case closed, Achille. At least they spared us the trouble and expense of a trial."

17

AFTERMATH

Anima ejus, et ánimæ ómnium fidélium defunctórum, per misericórdiam Dei requiéscant in pace.
Amen.

Following Jojo's instructions, the police discovered Virginie Ménard's arms and legs buried in the abandoned windmill. Her remains were gathered together at the Morgue and then transported to Montmartre, where Toulouse-Lautrec had anonymously arranged for a modest funeral service and internment in the cemetery. Arthur and Marcia cabled their condolences from England.

Virginie's grave was located in a shady, crowded corner beneath the iron latticework viaduct over which the busy Rue Caulaincourt passes.

Poets, artists, writers, actors, and musicians kept her company, their final resting place within walking distance of the Moulin Rouge. On this particularly bright blue autumn afternoon, a brisk wind stirred chestnuts and poplars, scattering leaves over the tombs and paved walkways.

A small group of mourners attended the graveside ceremony. Among them were Virginie's aunt and uncle from Rouen. They wore black, stood apart from the others, looked sad, spoke to no one except the priest, and put on airs as though they had paid for the funeral. Achille and Adele were there, along with Chief Inspector Féraud, Le Boudin, Marie, Delphine, the Gunzberg brothers, and the painters Lautrec and Bernard. Following the service they all sprinkled dirt on the casket and took a flower from a small display as a memento. The Merciers then made a hasty departure, as though fleeing from their unfortunate niece's ghost.

Le Boudin and his small entourage approached Achille, Adele, and Féraud. The tough old one-handed legionnaire wiped tears on his sleeve. He coughed into his hand and cleared his throat. Then, his voice still half-choked with emotion, he addressed Achille formally as though he were speaking to a superior officer. "Inspector Lefebvre, I, my family and friends owe you a debt of honor that can never be fully repaid. You pursued justice in an unjust world, you defended the rights of those who are rejected by society, outcasts who—" Le Boudin stopped and took a deep breath. Then: "I'm sorry, Monsieur. I prepared a fine speech for the occasion, but it makes me sound like a politician. What I really want to say is this. You're a damn good man, and France could use more like you. If you ever need my help in future, you know where to find me. And I speak for the *chiffoniers* and most of the folks in the Zone."

Achille smiled and shook hands. "I ought to thank *you*, Monsieur. Without your help, and the assistance of Mlle Lacroix and the Gunzberg boys I couldn't have cracked this case." Then he turned to Delphine. He wanted to say something personal, but under the circumstances and considering the nature of the women's relationship he had to choose his words carefully. He spoke gently, but appropriately. "I grieve for the loss of your friend, Mademoiselle. At least there was some justice for her; may she rest in peace."

Delphine nodded silently, turned and walked away; Le Boudin, Marie, and the Gunzbergs bowed politely and followed her.

Émile Bernard seemed overcome with emotion; he did not linger. He returned to his studio where he had begun and rubbed out many sketches of Virginie, all drawn from an imperfect memory. Lautrec remained to pay his respects to Achille and Féraud. Achille introduced the artist to Adele.

"Adele, this is M. de Toulouse-Lautrec, a fine artist. His studio's not far from here."

Lautrec doffed his bowler, looked up at the handsome young woman and smiled. "I'm very pleased to meet you, Mme. Lefebvre. I'm indebted to your husband. If it were not for his detective skills and dedication to the cause of justice I might now be languishing in prison. If there's anything you want of me, I'm at your service."

Adele's eyes lit up at the offer. "Oh Monsieur, we have a charming little daughter. Her fifth birthday's not far off, and I'd so much like a portrait of her."

Achille frowned and half-whispered to Adele: "Really, my dear, you ask for too much."

Lautrec laughed. "Nonsense, Inspector; I'd be pleased to paint the child's portrait. You may call upon me at my studio or contact me through Joyant's gallery. We'll set up an appointment for a sitting at your convenience. Now I must be off. Madame, I'm delighted to have made your acquaintance. *Au revoir*, Messrs." The sometimes cynical and acerbic artist left them with a sunny smile and another polite tip of his hat.

The other mourners having gone, Féraud turned his attention to Adele. He addressed her with a friendly tone and a fatherly grin. "Well, Madame, it seems your husband has become something of a celebrity. The newspapers are gushing praises for our brilliant young detective. Some have suggested that if Achille had been working for Scotland Yard they would have nabbed Jack the Ripper. There has even been speculation as to whether or not Collingwood *was* the Ripper."

Achille frowned. "Please, Chief," he muttered, "the newspapers are full of rubbish. The Yard has nothing linking Collingwood to the Ripper murders or their unsolved torso killings. As for our case, we'll never know if Collingwood and Mlle Endicott acted together in the murder, or if one killed Virginie and the other conspired afterwards with the murderer to cover up the crime. I wanted to bring them in alive for questioning; I wanted to know the truth."

Féraud put his hand on Achille's shoulder. "What is truth? This is all we know; they were both guilty of a crime, they executed each other, our justice is satisfied and the case is closed. The rest can be left to God. At any rate, from my perspective, things worked out all right. You're entitled to bask in the glory of the moment. When he was considering a young officer for promotion, the Emperor Napoleon said, 'Yes, I know he's brilliant, but is he lucky?' In my opinion, you are both brilliant and lucky, and, as you well know, I'm stingy with compliments." Then to Adele: "Madame, I believe you and your husband are due for a nice holiday. Please give it some thought." With that, the Chief bid them good-day.

Achille and Adele took a cab back to their apartment. On the way he remarked, "I'm glad you've smoothed things over with your mother."

Adele sighed and looked down at her hands. "After our harsh words, I doubt we'll ever be fully reconciled. Formal mutual apologies are one thing, true forgiveness is something else. At least we can remain together as a family, although I still worry that her prejudices might infect our daughter." She turned to Achille with sad eyes. "The spirit of the Exposition was so hopeful, so forward looking. We've made such remarkable progress in science and industry, but I wonder if we'll ever change for the better as human beings? Do you remember that day at the Fair when we heard the choir singing Gounod: *Lovely appear over the mountains: The feet of them that preach, and bring good news of peace.* . . . Will such a time of peace and love come in our lifetime, or Jeanne's?"

Achille shook his head. "I'm afraid not. We can't overcome human nature. People prefer self-serving lies to unflattering truths and blame others for their own faults. We'll have technological progress all right. The times change, but people will remain the same." Noticing the sadness in her eyes and thinking the conversation had turned too gloomy, he smiled, put his arm around her, and whispered in her ear: "Besides, Mme. Lefebvre, in a perfect world I'd be out of a job."

Adele pulled away from him. "Don't be cynical, Achille. It doesn't suit you."

Realizing that his attempt to lighten their dialogue had fallen flat, he asked, "What would you have me say?"

She smiled, gently stroked his cheek and noticed an unaccustomed roughness. "Didn't you shave this morning?"

He rubbed his chin. "No, I've decided to grow a beard. Now that I've become Chief Féraud's heir apparent I thought it would make me look older and more suited to the position." Then he took her hand in his and kissed it. "So, Madame, I'll repeat my question: What would you have me say?"

She gazed at him fondly for a moment. Then: "Simply this, my love. Even though we know it won't come in our lifetime, or the next generation, or the one after that, we should hope for an era of love and peace, we should strive for it."

"Of course, Adele, but until that time I'll settle for just laws and honest, capable, and compassionate people to enforce them."

"Honest, capable, and compassionate; that's you my dear. That's why I love you so." She kissed him and rested in his arms.

Horse hooves clip-clopped, coach wheels rumbled over the cobblestones. After awhile Achille said, "Your mother was right about one thing. We ought to give Jeanne a little brother or sister."

"I agree, darling. Féraud said we're due for a holiday. There'll be plenty of time for. . . ."

She didn't finish the sentence. His mouth covered her lips.

⌐∞⌐

A crisp autumn breeze rustled the branches of tall elms and oaks; sudden gusts rattled yews, pines, and stout shrubbery. Gold, brown, and russet leaves stirred on the garden path, took to the air, and drifted for a time before falling back to earth. Some of the scattered leaves floated on the surface of a small, mirror-like pond crossed by a weathered footbridge.

Wrapped in a warm, brown cloak, a broad-brimmed straw hat pinned securely to her thickly coiled auburn hair, Marcia Brownlow sat on a camp stool on the edge of the path near the footbridge. A pochade box rested on her lap as she captured the scene in watercolor. With an unerring eye and deft hand she carefully limned the garden view; washes of autumnal earth tones, bright pastels covered over with a shimmering haze that hovered over the reflecting pond, glimmering highlights and subtle shading, all materialized in recognizable forms and shapes on white sized paper. Marcia was so engrossed in her work that she failed to notice the sound of boots crunching on the leaf-strewn pathway.

"It's a bit brisk out here. I think you'd better come inside."

She set down her brush on the portable easel, turned her head and looked up. "Oh Arthur; you startled me."

He smiled and rested his hand lightly on her shoulder. "I'm sorry, my dear. I was watching you from my study window and I was worried. The wind's kicking up and the barometer's dropped. There may be a storm coming in from the sea."

"Perhaps you're right. At any rate, I'm almost finished; I can add the final touches in my studio."

"May I see it?"

"Of course you may, but please be careful. It's still damp."

Arthur bent over her shoulder and studied the watercolor. His eyes widened with admiration. There wasn't the least hint of decline in her work; if anything it had improved. If only she could have more time. He had consulted with doctors; they recommended taking her to Italy before the cold, heavy rains of late autumn and the first snows of winter.

"This is extraordinary," he remarked. Then: "What's this?" He took out his pince-nez, adjusted the spectacles on his nose, and examined the watercolor more closely. On the opposite bank, the figure of a woman in white emerged from the mist beneath a stand of trees. "You've put someone in the picture. Was it for effect?"

Marcia smiled enigmatically. "Perhaps it was for effect. She just seemed to insinuate herself into the composition like one of the ghosts in your story."

Arthur frowned and scratched his beard. Was the woman Virginie Ménard? That was a morbid thought. Or perhaps it was Betsy. That was more than morbid; it was downright sinister. To sound Marcia out on the subject, he decided to make an inquiry about her late companion. "You had a letter from Betsy Endicott's lawyers recently. I don't mean to pry, but was it of any importance?" After a tense moment in which she did not reply, and fearing he might have upset her, he added considerately: "Of course, if it's something you'd rather not discuss, I apologize for asking. I won't mention it again."

Marcia finished packing away her watercolors and brushes before answering. "Will you please help with my paraphernalia and the camp stool? I'll tell you about the letter on the way back to the house."

"Of course," he replied. He folded the camp stool, took it in one hand, and carried the pochade box in the other with the portfolio tucked under his arm. They strolled up the leaf-strewn path toward the garden gate.

Marcia spoke without looking at Arthur. "I was waiting for the right time to tell you, but I suppose now is as good a time as any. Betsy left me her entire fortune."

Arthur stopped dead in his tracks. He turned to her with a wide-eyed look that was so comical it made her laugh. "Good Lord, "he sputtered, "she's made you immensely rich."

"Yes she has, Arthur," she replied calmly after getting over her little fit of laughter. "And I intend to do the same for you. You shall have half the fortune, and the rest shall go to charity, a shelter for indigent and abused girls and women. I think Betsy would have approved."

For once in his life, Arthur Wolcott was speechless. He continued staring at Marcia in stunned silence.

She took his hand in hers and smiled. "I owe it to you, Arthur. You were the first to recognize my art and make it known to the world. You've cared for me and supported me in my time of need." She paused a moment before adding with a mischievous twinkle in her eye, "I certainly fooled you back when I was Mark."

Arthur did not need the money, but he was profoundly touched by her gesture. They walked along the path, Marcia clearly pleased with herself. Once he got over the shock, he was happy to see a change in her mood, and he decided to play along. "Yes, I certainly was fooled, and that was very naughty of you. Mark was a clever fellow all right, but I much prefer you as you really are. Now let's put away all gloomy thoughts, and think of sunny Italy and seeing old friends again. As for the fortune, my main object in life will be to use it to make you happy. We'll drink to it when we get back to the house, though you mustn't have more than one."

Marcia smiled; she reached up and stroked his beard. "Arthur, I've never told you this, but I do love you."

Arthur coughed; his lips trembled. He sniffed a couple of times, put down the pochade box, removed his pince-nez, and wiped his eyes with a handkerchief. After awhile, he picked up the box and started walking again. "Blasted wind," he muttered. "It must have blown dust in my eyes."

Marcia took him by the arm and walked on. "Yes darling, it is awfully brisk out here," she replied.

END

ACKNOWLEDGMENTS

My thanks to friends and fellow authors who read early drafts of this novel. I am grateful to Donald P. Webb, Dana M. Paramskas, Bill Bowler, and Marina Julia Neary. Their insightful comments and suggestions were most helpful in developing a raw manuscript into an almost finished book.

Many thanks to my agent, Philip Spitzer, for his courtesy, unerring judgment, persistence and expert representation, and to his associates Lukas Ortiz and Luc Hunt for their efficiency and kind assistance.

Finally, my thanks to Claiborne Hancock and his staff at Pegasus, most particularly my editor Maia Larson for her patience, understanding and professional expertise.